In the epic tradition of Stephen King, Dean Koontz, and Jonathan Maberry, the terrifying second novel in the Haunted Hollow Chronicles.

GRIM HARVEST

Still reeling from last year's Pumpkin Parade disaster, the people of Ember Hollow are unprepared for the horrors yet to come, as Halloween returns to their shaken farm community.

A brutal biker gang, armed with a spell that turns people into werewolves, is roaring into town with plans to resurrect a sadistic mass murderess in the body of an unsuspecting local. Teens Deshaun and Stuart, best friends and death metal fans, must protect their friend Candace from her own psychotic brother—dubbed The Trick or Treat Terror by the press and who Candace is certain will rise from the dead just in time for Halloween. And Minister Abe McGlazer is acting like a man possessed after a secret passage is discovered beneath his ancient church . . .

With the aid of a pair of punk rockers, Deputy Hudson Lott will have to work overtime to help his friends and family confront a host of horrors before this year's pumpkin crop unleashes a wave of evil too hideous to imagine . . .

Books by Patrick C. Greene

The Haunted Hallow Chronicles
Red Harvest
Grim Harvest

Published by Kensington Publishing Corporation

Grim Harvest

The Haunted Hollow Chronicles

Patrick C. Greene

LYRICAL PRESS
Kensington Publishing Corp.
www.kensingtonbooks.com

First Electronic Edition: September 2019
ISBN-13: 978-1-5161-0831-2 (ebook)
ISBN-10: 1-5161-0831-0 (ebook)

First Print Edition: September 2019
ISBN-13: 978-1-5161-0834-3
ISBN-10: 1-5161-0834-5

Printed in the United States of America

Author's Note

The classic rock and roll action flick "Streets of Fire" begins with a simple note: "Another time, another place."
So it is with Ember Hollow. This is American heartland; modern, more or less, minus the safety and convenience of mobile phones and the internet.
The people of this community depend on and care for one another.

Chapter 1

Werewolves on Wheels

If not for the nature of his crimes, Nico Rizzoli might not have been in the van, on his way to Hutchinson Correctional in Kansas, where his reputation and influence would theoretically carry less weight than the Craven County prison system of North Carolina, where he had become a superstar.

Upon learning that an associate had ratted out his Mid-Atlantic Fireheads motorcycle club for their growing meth business, Nico had chosen not to flee, but rather to play the long game. He'd meticulously selected, measured, cut and taped a length of steel pipe. He'd tracked down the rat and smashed his ribs to jelly in full view of the poor bastard's girlfriend and mother. Ruined ribs, he had reasoned, would lead to a long and agonizing healing process, whereas mere head trauma potentially offered merciful blackouts and memory loss.

It was as much a calculated measure, a warning for future business partners, as it was revenge. Nico had correctly surmised that the women would sob about that shit to every square in sight for years to come.

He had kept at it until the cops came—in full force knowing they were facing Nico—then fought all the way to lockup, bellowing curses at the boys in blue for not letting him finish. He'd been having such a good time that he'd decided to gelatinize the man's *legs* as well. Cops had rushed to the scene.

Now on a fortified transport shuttle van amongst a bunch of morons doing time for possession, robbery and other small fry garbage, Nico wasn't thinking about the past. He was more interested in the immediate future.

It was well after midnight. They had been on the road for nearly ten hours. A glance at their faces, sagging and bleary in the dash lights, made Nico crack the thinnest of smiles. The extradition agents were like fruit, ripe to be plucked.

"Yo! You gon' stop at Boogie Burger, or *what!?*" inmate Georgie "The Juice" DeWitt harangued Extradition Agent Higgins, stretching the shackles on his wrist and seat armrest to their full extent to yell through the steel mesh partition. "I'm 'bout to *starve!*"

Neither Higgins nor his partner Dutton responded. They had been instructed to have minimal communication with DeWitt, as he was notoriously short-tempered and easily riled.

"*Huh!?*" DeWitt persisted. "I need ta *eat!*"

"Shut the hell up," Nico said.

DeWitt spun with an expression of early stage rage, which vanished when he saw it was Nico talking. DeWitt took his seat and proceeded to shut the hell up.

Normally Nico didn't bother talking to lesser cons for any reason, but he needed distracting noise kept to a minimum, so he could hear the familiar roar of beefed-up Harleys.

Intensely focused, purposeful, cold-blooded as a viper, Nico was not beyond feeling something that could pass for love. His old lady Ruth, easily the most passionately devoted chick he had ever banged, undoubtedly owned his heart—even in death. Not just because of the way she'd dug canyons in his back with her nails when they screwed, or the way she'd bitten him even harder than he wanted her to when he came, but because of how she'd spoken to him like there was a future, given him even more than she'd *taken.*

That bitch had walked the goddamn walk.

Now she was dead.

On Halloween night, while just trying to make the world a better place, to do God's work. Ridiculous as the idea of "God" was to Nico, bottom line was that something that belonged to him had been taken away, and that would not stand. Nico would find every son of a bitch who had played even the least significant role in steering her toward her demise at the hands of the costumed freak Everett Geelens. To drive his point home, he would wipe this little jerkwater town called Ember Hollow right off the map, along with that big deputy Hudson Lott, who had assisted in his arrest.

Nobody takes what belongs to Nico Rizzoli. Not any God, and *damn* sure not any man, sane or psycho.

Nico rubbed his rock-solid stomach and chest, and the fresh tattoo he'd just gotten the day before. He liked the way it itched and stung. The inker—some lifer had named him "Mozart" because they'd thought the composer was a painter, owing to the "art" in his name—had referred to a picture of a ragdoll Nico had ripped from an encyclopedia in the prison library. "Mozart" didn't blink an eye when Nico had told him what he wanted: the doll, crucified like Jesus. The completed work stretched from throat to groin.

Ruth had loved rag dolls for some reason. Had kept one from when she was a girl that she wouldn't let him toss. She'd talked to the damn thing, even brought it with her when she came to see him and grumbled at the guards for searching the doll. "Molesting" it.

He wanted to slap the tattoo, just to amp up the sting a bit. But that was for later.

Or maybe sooner.

The beautiful sound of a six-speed 1690 cc engine—*his* bike—reached his ears, a rising whisper, the confident growl of a waking lion. Nico gripped the armrests, bracing himself, and smiled at the poor doomed sap next to him, who cluelessly yawned and settled back to doze.

The roar of two other bikes joined that of the Fatboy. *Perfect.*

Agent Higgins glimpsed at the side mirror, but he wouldn't see the bikers yet. They were riding dark.

"Funny," Higgins said in his Georgia drawl. "Thought I heard hogs."

"What, you mean pigs?" asked his partner, Agent Dutton, a Detroit-born city boy.

"No, you big dummy," Higgins said. "Harleys, man."

Higgins rubbed his eyes, as he and Dutton sank into complacency.

Then came the sound of the bikers gunning it. In less than a second, they had flanked the van.

A couple of inmates stirred in their seats, muttering with unease. Nico nodded down at his brother Rhino coming up just outside on the Fatboy, the only one riding solo. Rhino roared far ahead.

The first bike zoomed in place next to the van's driver side, while the second bike eased up parallel to Nico.

Nico almost wished one of the sleepy cons would glance out and witness the impossible vision of madness: both machines carried huge, hair-covered passengers riding behind the smaller drivers. They rose to crouch on the seats with the agility of trapeze artists.

Higgins frowned as he heard the Harleys growl. "Hey, what are these assho—?"

The two hirsute passengers pounced in unison, their claws attaching them like magnets to the side of the van.

Agent Higgins swerved the wheel as his window exploded in on him. A huge hairy hand found his throat like a guided missile and tore it out in an explosion of scarlet. Higgins's scream became a weak gurgle.

The van careened off the road and into a scrabbly patch of wasteland, where it flipped onto its passenger side with a grinding groan. Dutton's sidearm was lost in the chaos.

Inmate DeWitt, showing amazing lung power, bellowed like an opera singer.

Nico, pulled downward to his right by gravity, held onto his armrests, chuckling at the sound of steel mesh tearing away from his window. The glass broke, and a slavering snout was in his face, growling and snapping.

"Yeah, yeah." Nico pulled at the chain that fastened him to the seat. The wolf, Aura by name, bit it in two, rubbing her hairy breasts across Nico's face. She gave him a lick, nipped at his eyebrow just hard enough to draw blood, then clambered in to go to work on the passengers.

Nico slid out of his seat and landed feet first on the left side of a skinny first timer he knew as Mousy. The boy cried at Nico for help, but Nico booted him in the face instead.

Blood splashed across Nico and everything else, as Aura went about sloppily wasting the other prisoners. She was showing off for him.

Finishing up on the extradition agents, the other lupine Firehead, Pipsqueak, tore through the front partition and slashed into the still-shrieking DeWitt, wasting a lot of meat as he worked his way to the man's heart, only to spit it out upon finding it brown and stinking from cigarettes.

Aura dropped a brawny arm at Nico's feet. The gang leader kicked it away. Pipsqueak went after it and so did Aura. They scuffled over it, massive hindleg claws digging into what was left of the inmates.

"Knock it *off!*" Nico called. "Let's roll."

Pipsqueak had something to show him first. Dropping to all fours, the lean red wolf went toward the front. Nico followed, flinging his long, blood-soaked hair out of his face.

Pipsqueak growled as he bit Higgins to draw a cry of pain, then climbed out the driver window, getting out of Nico's way. Pip smiled down at him with tongue hanging out like a playful bulldog.

Nico regarded Higgins. "Damn boy," he said. "You ain't gonna make it."

Hanging at a sharp angle, Higgins spilled blood by the pint onto the squashed corpse of Dutton. Deep claw marks separated the driver's face and throat into sections. His left arm was half torn away, tendons and cartilage still holding where muscle and skin had given way.

With heaving and hitching breath, Higgins felt around for his sidearm as he beheld Nico sneering down at him. He found the gun. Though Nico didn't react, Aura muscled past him and clamped her jaws shut on the guard's head, bursting it like a grape. Eyeballs arced from the pink mess. Nico squashed both with his state-issued pull-on sneakers. "Can't wait to do this with my goddamn boots on."

Aura rolled onto her back and smiled a predator's smile at Nico, clearly expecting a rub on her fuzzy belly—or perhaps her exquisite, very human breasts.

"Never gonna happen, girl," Nico said, as he unbuckled Higgins. Aura rolled out of the way as the messy bag of meat fell. Nico stepped up on Higgins's messy torso and climbed out, followed by Aura.

The panting wolves hopped on the bikes and sat like gargoyles while Jiggy and Rhino draped them with oversized tarps.

Nico, anticipating the fresh taste of high-speed freedom, hopped on his Fatboy for the first time in months. Rhino climbed on behind him, and the machine roared to rival the wolves.

* * * *

Before consciousness came shame.

Stuart jerked up and jumped out of bed by reflex, knowing before his feet hit the carpet that he had done it again.

Pissed the bed.

"God *damn!*" he whispered.

This profanity, long considered the ultimate "cuss word" all across the South, was still fairly new to him. In fact, he had only started using it around the same time his bladder had begun betraying him in his sleep, just less than a year ago. No exclamation seemed even remotely more appropriate.

He patted himself to see how bad it was. God damn bad.

Top sheet too, but that was all. Having trained himself to always sleep on his back to minimize the spread was one of several hacks he had tried since the problem had started. Multiple pairs of shorts—up to four, at one point, and that was *July*—rubberbanding a Ziploc over his unit, placing garbage bags under and on top of himself—nothing worked.

Stifling his self-loathing rage, he jerked the top sheet off and crept to his bedroom door, which he kept cracked at night, the hinges always well-oiled, and eased it open.

Good thing Ma always left the living room table lamp on so Dennis wouldn't brain himself stumbling in from—or still *on*—his latest bender. *He can't keep from soaking it up these days,* Stuart thought. *And I can't keep from leaking it out.* Dennis's issue might have been selfish, dangerous and destructive, but at least it was more socially acceptable.

Just four steps across the hall and to the bathroom door—he couldn't hide the sheets forever but better to deal with that in the daylight.

Unfortunately, Ma didn't sleep very heavily anymore; not since her two baby boys had nearly died alongside dozens of parade goers, and especially not since Dennis had taken up the bottle again, just weeks later. It was a fifty-fifty shot she would wake up and come out, but he had to take it.

Her door squeaked minutely, like a mouse mocking a fat cat. "Stuart?"

Stuart rushed into the bathroom and slammed the door, no longer caring about stealth or common courtesy.

He regarded his shadow-soaked reflection, leaving the light off. His own dark reflection used to scare him, and not even in a fun way. Now it just seemed like an annoying playground tattletale.

Ma knocked, a sound even lighter than the mute squeak of her door. "Stuart?"

He didn't answer, though he was already resigned to having this conversation again, hoping he wouldn't blow his stack like other times. "Just…go back to bed, Ma."

"Honey, I'm going to call a doctor tomorrow."

"No, *Ma!*" Stuart smacked a little basket of fragrant soaps to the floor. He was losing it. "Leave me *alone!*"

He flipped the light switch, then spun and slapped the shower curtain open. He started the water, turning it up as hot as it would go, to—what? Scald himself? As punishment?

Ma was still standing there at the door. He could *feel* her, feel the worry and layers of long-suffering coming off her in waves. She bore it with grace, sure. But this was *his* problem.

"Go away, Ma."

"It's okay, Stuart," she said over the sound of the water. "You just need someone to talk to. After everythi—"

"I *got* it," he interrupted. "Now leave me alone."

He fixed on the rising steam and flashed back to the dense smoke rising from the many fires that had raged along Main Street a few months before. And he felt like a real heel.

"Ma?" he called, opening to the door to try and catch her before she retreated to the bedroom where she had slept alone for years. She was halfway there, clutching the pockets of her maroon bathrobe in little trembling fists. "I'm sorry. I'm really sorry, Ma."

She trod back to him and put an arm on his shoulder. "Can I call somebody?"

"I'll get past it, Ma." Had he heard Dennis say this to her about his drinking? "Reverend McGlazer is doing better. You could…"

"Ma. Please." Her expression reminded him of his father's funeral. *Hey, is there anything besides downers rattling around up there?* he asked his own brain. "I can't."

* * * *

For the first hour of his shift, Security Officer Bartholomew Cheek always stood in the breezeway of the rest stop's vending building.

Rowed with soda, snack and sandwich dispensers along either wall, the corrugated hut was a good lookout onto the exit from the highway to see vehicles pulling into the rest stop. An ex-Military Policeman, Cheek found his post-retirement gig made him feel almost important, or at least justified in settling in at his desk for hours at a time to toss occasional glances at the stack of six monitors displaying the lots, the lobby and this very building. He glanced up at the camera and almost winked, as if he might rewind and watch it later, just for chuckles.

A handful of big rigs idled in the far lot, and maybe an average of seven cars at a time dotted the lot in front of the restrooms. Farther out, isolated spots hosted catnapping motorists.

His expression was vigilant, but his mind was already slowing for his (early) mid-shift nap.

A few folks would no doubt slink in for semi-discreet sexual *rendezvous,* and Cheek didn't see any need to disrupt them. He had engaged in the same a few times himself back in the day.

Motorcycles, though—that might be a different matter.

He heard them half a mile away and raised one of the few prayers he ever did that they would pass on by.

They roared right in though; three of them. A couple of the Harleys bore passengers bundled up in rain slickers or something. Big fellows.

The bikes made a beeline to a dark spot at the edge of the lawn, next to a little patch of forest behind the wooden sign that clearly read:

'RESTRICTED AREA

NO VISITORS ALLOWED'

Then the bikes fell silent.

Bikers parking in the distant dark of a rest stop meant one thing only: doping.

* * * *

Nico closed his eyes to inhale the scents of leather, perspiration, and autumnal woods behind them while the wolves shook off their tarps and dropped to all fours to prowl around the trees, their roving instincts uncorked after sitting still for too long.

Rhino extended a tiny brass telescope—acquired during a horrific home invasion—and gazed over the parking lot. "Rent-a-pig coming."

Indeed, an overweight security officer was ambling across the lot, hand on sidearm.

"I got it," Nico said. "Been too long anyway."

Hobie, the sixth Firehead, tossed Nico his leather jacket to cover up the prison coveralls.

Nico walked to the edge of the shadows to meet the guard, casual as Sunday afternoon. "Hey brother," he said. "A friend had a wreck." He gestured to the blood spatters on his face and neck. "A coupla my crew are changing clothes. Need privacy."

Officer Cheek gave Nico a once-over, half unable to see the prison garb in the darkness, half unwilling to, out of complacency. "Still trespassing, buddy," said Cheek. "Your pals can use the john, like everybody else."

Nico smashed the guard's nose with a headbutt, catching his necktie as he fell backward. Nico dragged him into the shadows, issuing a quick whistle.

Officer Cheek came to just in time to see two sets of curved fangs, just ahead of two sets of glowing eyes. The fangs descended on him like pinpoints of consuming starlight. His throat was gone before he could scream, his body torn to pieces in seconds.

While Aura and Pipsqueak feasted, Nico caught a pack of smokes and a lighter tossed to him by Hobie. "What about my Luger?"

Rhino drew the antique Nazi handgun from his jacket and handed it over. "I kept her clean, Chief."

Nico smiled as he checked the magazine and chamber, then stuffed the weapon in the waistband of the prison-issue denims he was soon to replace, as he gestured toward the visitor center and parking lots. "Jiggy, shiv anybody in the crappers. Rhino, nab that Jeep."

He whistled again, and the two skinwalkers rose to acknowledge, blood dripping from their massive muzzles "Save room for the truckers. Then, we find you two a place to change back."

It took less than ten minutes for the wolves to savage the sleeping truckers, the anonymous copulators, and the travelers resting and relieving themselves, while the three human-form Fireheads collected money and valuables for the adventure ahead.

The Fireheads finished by torching one of the big rigs to keep local emergency services busy while they gained distance—*after* slitting the throat of the sleeping driver.

A few miles later, the bikes took an off ramp into the country and went dark, parking behind a hay barn, where Aura and Pipsqueak tore off their tarp covers.

Jiggy took a clay jar from his saddlebag. He and Rhino scooped out double handfuls of the musky, goopy contents and rubbed it on their wolf brother and sister.

Aura snapped at Rhino as he moved to apply the goop to her breasts, eyeing Nico with wild hunger.

"Oh, for Christ's sake." Nico took the ointment and slathered Aura. She responded with a lazy-eyed panting.

Transformation completed, the naked Aura stretched languidly, making lustful eye contact with Nico as he lit another cigarette. "Don't you want a roll in the dirt?" she purred. "You know, to celebrate your freedom?"

Nico didn't hide his head-to-toe study of her taut six-foot frame. "Hot or not, girl, you're pushing it," he told her. "Let me mourn."

With a playful pout, she dug into her backpack and dressed, pulling on leather chaps over panty-cut denim shorts. A black vest to match the pants and a steel chain choker completed the Looks That Kill.

Pipsqueak rolled on the ground, snuffling as his fur and fangs withdrew. "You gotta try it, boss."

"Don't you worry about that, Pips. The Fireheads are all gonna run as wolves together," Nico said.

Chapter 2

Devil's Gateway

Ember Hollow's town Main Street ended at an iron gate that opened into a hilly cemetery leading up to Saint Saturn Unitarian Church. Forty-year-old Stella Riesling had served full time there as Reverend Abe McGlazer's assistant for the best part of a year.

The previous Halloween's parade tragedy had claimed McGlazer's previous assistant, Ruth Treadway, a.k.a. Ragdoll Ruth—after she had logged a good few dozen murders herself.

Trying to stop her, McGlazer had come close to joining the casualties. He still bore deep scars and nagging pain to show for his heroism.

Luckily, Stella had been on hand that night. She was a trained EMT, a job she had since relinquished so she could help McGlazer work and heal.

Today, McGlazer had attended a town council meeting, then lunched with his friend Chief Deputy Hudson Lott. It was a rigorous schedule considering he was still recovering. Upon returning to Saint Saturn, he had retreated to his office where he'd remained for a long time, until Stella felt compelled to check on him. She held off, hoping not to disturb him if he was dozing or praying.

Does he still do that?

She found him awake and pensive at his desk, a letter from Cronus County's Department of Social Services lying open before him. Staring at it, he pried at the deepest of his facial scars, a jagged line from eyebrow to hairline.

"How was the meeting?" Stella asked.

"They're still not sure what to do about this year's parade. Mayor Stuyvesant wants to cancel it."

Stella was careful not to express her opinions, which were mixed.

"And Hudson?"

"Busier than usual, even for this time of year."

She sat and waited for him to talk, troubled by the twitchy blinking habit he had picked up.

Stella pointed to the letter. "What's that?"

McGlazer glanced at it only briefly. "The adoption appears unlikely."

Stella frowned. She wanted to hug him. "I've been thinking." She smiled, hoping he would too. "How would you feel if Bernard and I took a shot at it?"

He blinked several times, rapidly. "Adopt Candace, you mean?"

"We don't have the hurdles you have. She would be here, in town, with us. All of us."

He was speechless—and, clearly, a little hurt.

On that same fateful Halloween night, the little girl's parents were killed by her brother Everett; now world-renowned as "Evil Everett," "The Trick or Treat Terror," the "Halloween Hacker," and any number of variations.

"I know it was important to you to take her in," Stella continued. "I know you love her and want to make up for her hardships. You would see her as much as you wanted, I promise. Between us all, she would have so much love."

McGlazer was silent for several seconds. "What about Bernard?"

"Might be an obstacle," Stella admitted, frowning.

Lately her husband, forever seeking knowledge, was obsessed with learning all he could about the hallucinogenic candy Ragdoll Ruth had inflicted upon the town. At times, Bernard barely seemed to tolerate *her*—much less even the best behaved of children.

"But I think I should try." She reached across the desk to him and took his hand in a tight squeeze. Tears welled but did not spill.

Stella feared she had said too much too soon—she hadn't even considered how to broach it with Bernard yet.

But after all that had happened to her extended Ember Hollow family she understood that what they all needed, more than anything, was each other.

* * * *

The Fireheads roared through the night till they reached the hilly outskirts of Ember Hollow, then onto Crabtree Road, into a vast wilderness that expanded with its miles. They headed toward the camp set up days earlier in an isolated clearing at the end of eight rough miles, not all of which could reasonably be called road.

Nico swung his leg over the Fatboy and looked around as the morning sun unfurled upon the clearing. "Not bad, brothers."

Four tents—Nico always got his own—a row of coolers, a tarp-roofed stump with a police band radio, and a thick poplar to which paper targets were nailed, already pocked with closely-grouped holes left by Rhino, the best shot, when he'd dialed in the sights on Nico's Luger. Looser shot patterns from everyone else scattered out from there.

"What's next, Chief?" asked Pipsqueak. Despite his name—and his size when transformed—he was of average height and build, sporting neck-length straight brown hair. He might have passed for a normie if not for his bushy mutton chops.

"We eat, we smoke, we rest" Nico said, lighting a fresh cigarette. "Then, the boneyard. After that—the mission."

Nico caught a beer tossed by Hobie. "There's a square on the other end of the county, into my pin-stripe kin for about twenty thou. Hobie and Rhino, you'll handle that."

Jiggy lit the campfire as well as a joint, which he gave to Nico as he continued. "Pip, you'll take me to see this nice lady you've told me so much about." Whistling a Jethro Tull medley, he rolled several more.

* * * *

McGlazer propped his feet on his desk, something he had not done since before Ruth Treadwell got saved and had come along to make herself his assistant. Her attention to detail in keeping Saint Saturn Unitarian running smoothly was now long-lost in the lurid sensation of her exploits as mass murderer Ragdoll Ruth.

Hoping to get his mind off the rejection of his application to adopt Candace, he thought of his one and only glance into a possible afterlife.

A year ago, to the very day. A piece of hard candy, lying on his desk had *darted* into his mouth, his esophagus. He'd immediately choked on it. Panicking, he had witnessed a strange white cloud forming from nothingness to glide toward him as he fought to cough out the killer confection, vanishing once he was in the clear.

He would later learn that the candy was planted by Ruth—one of her deadly hallucinogenic treats meant to end Halloween. Could the effect have been retroactive? He'd had a clear image of it *attacking* him.

Yet, given what Stella's chemist husband Bernard had determined, the candy should not have had time to take effect.

Thus, the entity had been…real?

The phantasm had glided toward him, as if to *cloak* him—until he'd vomited the candy out and caught his breath—no small labor.

In the year since, he had heard all the accounts—Stuart, DeShaun, Candace, Stella—describing the ghostly presence that had brought an end to the murderous rampage of Everett Geelens, and then wafted back to the grave like a magician walking off stage.

McGlazer gave thought also to his alcoholism—yet another phantom hovering over his head, marking itself clearly by a border between "before" and "after." As it ever would be.

And what is really the difference? asked nobody. No *body. A drunk is a drunk.*

Burgeoning rock star Dennis Barcroft, whom he sponsored, had fallen.

Off the stage, off the wagon, off the towering pedestal on which so many had placed him. This despite McGlazer's weekly support sessions; his hours of work helping to rehabilitate the young musician.

"Why should you—*I*—be any different?"

McGlazer grasped the hasp of the bottom desk drawer, where he had once kept his stash of Jefferson Select—and later, moonshine. It slid half-open. Maybe McGlazer did it. Or maybe something else.

It held only a half-empty bag of bite-size chocolate bars and some scattered index cards.

McGlazer was ready to push the drawer closed when he spotted a darkness in its far back corner, more substantial than shadow. He pulled the drawer all the way out to see a patch of fuzzy brown mold there.

Tiny black tendrils—like *capillaries*—meandered from the core. Peering closer, McGlazer saw that this fine fuzz surrounded a mushroom sprout about an inch in width, speckled with tiny white dots.

He took a pen from his desk and lowered it toward the mushroom to break off the button. Then he'd get a bottle of disinfectant, and—

On contact, the fuzz puffed a surprisingly thick little cloud. Fascinated, McGlazer leaned closer.

"Where did you come from?" He closed the drawer and knelt to look under his desk, where he found a much larger patch growing on the carpet, its powdery fibers attached to the desk drawer bottom like black cobwebs. A good-sized cluster of bulbous heads squatted amid the threads.

McGlazer took a long-stemmed candle lighter from the upper drawer. When he extended the flame to within a few inches, the mushroom caps shriveled upon themselves like a triggered Venus flytrap. He had never seen anything like it, but that was the least of his concerns.

McGlazer sat up and huffed, annoyed that he would have to get someone to come in and check for mold. The last thing he needed was for the church to be shut down due to a health hazard.

Perhaps it was better to deal with it himself for now, as best he could. He rose from the floor to close the desk drawer and stayed his hand. A sealed bottle of Jefferson Presidential Select now lay on its back like a seductive temptress, just inches from the fungus in the corner. The label and wax stamp were like the comforting cover of an old family bible to him.

McGlazer felt the saliva gather in his mouth, felt his fingers tingle to twist the cap, to hear the snap of the paper seal.

A quick prayer gave him the strength to shut the drawer. But curiosity was stronger. He immediately opened it again, finding himself profoundly disappointed to find the bottle was gone.

No matter. He could always hop down to the spirits store…

…And *what?*

McGlazer closed and reopened the drawer three times before storming out of the room, angry with himself for being angry that the bottle hadn't been real—nevermind the implications of *hallucinating* it.

He decided to do something about the fungus before Stella discovered it and worried *both* of them to death over it.

He went to the closet and collected an old towel, a bottle of cleaner, and an ice scraper. As he set himself to push the desk back, the temptation to check the drawer again came to him like an attack dog; charging for his throat, determined to overpower him. It succeeded.

No Jefferson Select. Instead, the drawer was filled with neat rows of Mason canning jars.

Madison County moonshine.

Well, this was unprecedented. He decided he'd better examine one…

The cold, smooth curve and heft of the full jar were undeniable. He did a shake for quality assurance. The telltale maelstrom of tiny bubbles rose to the surface, eager to please.

McGlazer felt sudden paranoia—and no small amount of guilt. Someone was tormenting him, working some sadistic sleight of hand.

He set the jar on the desk and reached for another. But that jar was empty, and *light,* even so. The glass was a thin illusion made of spun sugar, or less. It disintegrated in his hand; dissolving to flimsy filaments, the lid rusting to dust in a millisecond.

McGlazer panicked that the same fate would befall the other jars. He reached for one, like a man trying to rescue a thousand-dollar bill from a fire. But it collapsed and dissolved on itself, the liquid soaking into the wood of his desk like varnish.

He heard his own strident groan of despair, fighting shame as he inspected the drawer.

Empty except for the candy, the note cards and the mushroom cluster.

"God *dammit!*" he bellowed, heaving the desk over onto its back and sending a mini storm of sharp pains across his half-healed injuries.

Despite the discomfort, he knelt to check under the desk. The fungus on the carpet still held to the bottom of the drawer by a few thin strands stretched to near-breaking. A brown plume rose like a tiny Hiroshima—a very literal mushroom cloud.

McGlazer instinctively covered his nose and mouth and backed away from the puff of spores, reasoning that a good snort of hundred-fifty proof would probably kill anything he had just inhaled. But right now, it had to be cleaned up.

The reverend covered his lower face with a handkerchief, but he knew some of the weird spores had entered him, and he knew he was kind of *glad,* because it somehow promised a return of the precious shine…if he did its bidding. Whatever "it" was.

Rather than getting rid of the mushroom, McGlazer decided to hide it.

He grappled his desk upright and put everything back in order, then opened a hymnal and tented it over the fungus in the drawer, like he was just saving his place.

For the growth under the desk he cut the top and bottom out of a small box and formed it as a shelter. Stella would still eventually find it, but this would buy him time to—what?

Inhale *more* of it?

The ghost of a sweet taste from days of chaos haunted his mouth.

It was there in him; the memory of every precious drop, every second of euphoric escape. That perfect peak before the crash and aftermath. The mushroom would help him find it again.

* * * *

Miss Dietrich whispered into the phone as she walked past the bedroom Candace shared with little Emera. Between kitchen, dining room, and the so-called family room she strode, and then back again, gesticulating less subtly than she spoke.

Fourteen-year-old Candace Geelens, the newest arrival at the group home, just a month behind Emera, knew it would sound paranoid if she ever told anyone she was certain the housemother's whisperings were about her. But it would be a safe bet.

No sooner had Candace arrived home from school that day than little Emera, her hand-me-down Corpse Bride printed dress decorated with juice stains, took her hand and pulled her to their room, excited to have the older girl's help with some coloring.

Both girls lay on the floor filling in a picture in a dog-eared coloring book of an arch-backed cat. Though the caption read "A black cat screeches at the moon!" Candace chose to render it as a vibrant orange tabby. Little Emera, glancing over from the next page, beamed. Barely four years old, Candace's little roommate gravitated to her like a tiny moon. When Emera spoke—which was rare—it was usually to call for Candace in a joyous tone.

Candace pushed the book toward Emera and gave her the orange crayon. The happy child took it reverently and did her very best to retrace Candace's light shades and darker stripes.

There was more sibilance from Mrs. Dietrich as she came to their room and clicked off the phone. "You girls okay?"

"Yes Mrs. Dietrich," Candace said. The formal title had not been insisted upon, yet Candace felt it was only appropriate. Her own deceased Mamalee had not been perfect, but she'd been loving and attentive, and she was the only "mom" Candace would ever have.

"Dinner will be in about forty." Mrs. Dietrich pointed at her watch with the phone's antenna, her smile creasing her face. Late thirties looked more like late forties on the woman, thanks to a stressful lifetime spent caring for troubled children of every age and origin.

Just a few days ago, Candace had found a single gray strand in her own shoulder-length curls and examined her face for similar worry lines. The lines weren't there, but Candace was sure they were coming soon—just as sure as she was that her "dead" brother Everett was.

"You sure you don't want to go outside while you can?" Mrs. Dietrich asked.

Laughter and a high-pitched shout came from the home's other six kids in the back yard. Candace wasn't enticed. She found it strange that the house mother even made the suggestion, given Candace's recent history with the others. "No ma'am. I'm fine with Emera."

"Okay." Mrs. Dietrich left. Emera hopped up and peeked down the hall for any other kids that might have straggled inside. Satisfied to see no one, she went back to the orange tabby and gave it a name. "Canniss!"

Chapter 3

The Children

The ragged putter of Pedro Fuentes's Honda Civic assailed the ears of Stuart and DeShaun through the open garage door, as they pushed several garbage bags full of infant clothes under Hudson's work table.

"Pedwo!" said Wanda, splashing her chubby little hands in Bravo's water bowl. The big mastiff, presently closed into DeShaun's room, was living with the Lotts while the adoption system buffeted his owner Candace.

"Yep," responded Wanda's big brother DeShaun. "Unca Pedro."

"Well, that's one," noted Stuart.

"We can't make 'em show up, dude," DeShaun said.

A minute later, Pedro entered, dressed in cargo shorts and a long sleeve Cannibal Corpse T-shirt, carrying a guitar case. "Yeah, this could work."

"You're welcome," DeShaun said, as he and Stuart lifted the lawnmower and set it against the wall.

"Not hatin' man," Pedro said. "Just don't expect Dennis or Jill to show."

"Great," grumbled Stuart. "All this work for nothing."

Bravo barked excitedly from the backyard, more than ready for his afternoon walk.

"Just a second, Brav!" Stuart answered. "Gotta get Pedro started."

Wanda toddled over to Pedro. He set down the guitar case and picked her up to rock her. "Maybe you losers could start filling in and I could get some real practice."

"Yeah right," DeShaun huffed. "You want me to sing?"

"Maybe, if your nuts ever finish dropping."

Stuart laughed out loud, while DeShaun, ever the good sport, beamed. His changing voice had been the source of much recent ribbing.

"You think they're gonna break up?" Stuart asked.

"Dude, I'm no couples counselor," Pedro answered. "Last time me and Dennis talked it was at an alarming volume. If those two pull through, it won't be because of me."

They cast uncertain frowns at each other, until Wanda pointed at Pedro's guitar case and proclaimed "Aah, *eh*."

"All right lady," Pedro said. "You want it, you got it."

DeShaun went out to get Pedro's amp, while Stuart opened the case and checked tuning on the beat-up bass.

* * * *

Candace sat beside little Emera in the TV room, on the couch that bore overlaid smells of the home's staple snacks and drinks. The little girl was engrossed in an episode of *The Funky Phantom* she'd already seen at least seventeen times that Candace had counted.

With the other kids now in the basement to play ping pong and board games, Candace slipped off to her room and sat down to write Stuart, as she often did in her rare spare time, whenever Emera was occupied.

She took her notebook from its hiding place in a desk cubby under Ana's stack of coloring books and closed her eyes to see the faces of her friends from Ember Hollow, especially Stuart Barcroft's sidewise smile and squinty laugh expression. Writing to him was release, confession, venting and personal assessment.

Mr. Dietrich knocked lightly on the open door, careful not to startle, and stuck his head in. "Getting groceries," he gently whispered. "Any requests?"

"A pumpkin pie, if it's not too much trouble?" It had been a perennial favorite, back when she had a family.

He left, and Candace opened the notebook and switched on the desk lamp.

Dear Stuart,

Not much has changed since last time. Emera still follows me around like a puppy. She's so cute, but sometimes I get tired. Not really making friends with the other kids. Maybe it's me. It's so hard to be around people I don't know right now. Sometimes, I think about Everett.

He's still out there. Somewhere. But I can't talk about it to anyone. I know better now.

Sometimes though I wonder if what I feel is not really him.

I wonder if maybe I ...

Emera cried out a little bit, from the family room. Candace thought the girl must have noticed she was gone. "I'm in here, Emenemema!" The little one always liked it when Candace called her that.

The little girl did not respond. Candace expected her to come running in, grab her hand and drag her back to the TV.

She gave the letter a read-through, wondering how she had meant to finish that last sentence. But for her handwriting, it seemed foreign to her, like someone else had written it.

Emera remained quiet.

Candace got up and went to check. When she entered the family room, she didn't see Emera. The other children stood in a circle, holding their hands over their mouths for some reason. To muffle their giggling. To keep Candace from hearing.

"What are you guys doing?" she asked, pushing through the circle.

Emera was on her back, held by Rebecca. "Oh look." The hulking girl had Emera pinned with one hand and covered the little girl's mouth with the other. "It's the bitch from the crazy family."

The other kids, no longer needing to be discreet, burst out in laughter.

Beside Rebecca stood Radley, leaning over Emera, drooling a rope of spittle toward her terrified face.

Candace spun toward the hall, certain that Mrs. Dietrich would be standing there, righteous fury on her face. No such luck.

"Leave her alone, you *asshole!*" Candace lunged, shoving Radley away just as the saliva rope broke loose. It missed Emera and pooled beside her head.

She glared down at Radley sprawled with his back against the television, spit strung across his chin. She was not prepared for the hard shove from behind that sent her face-first nearly into the TV screen beside him. She caught herself with her hands but was helpless to prevent the double kick to the ribs from the prone Radley that sent her crashing on her side.

"Go to *hell* you crazy bitch!" yelled Radley.

Rebecca kept her foot on Emera's little arm, daring Candace with her cruel eyes to try to defend the squalling girl.

Candace was not afraid. But the feeling wasn't bravery either.

She got up and stormed past Rebecca and out of the room, no longer conscious of Mrs. Dietrich and her negligent absence. Navigating through a haze of scarlet, she went to the kitchen. Bypassing a rolling pin and a frying pan, she went straight to the butcher block beside the sink that sprouted a gorgeous bouquet of steel flowers.

She drew an eight-inch boning knife that was beautiful and perfect.

She stormed back to the living room where hostile faces waited. Rebecca still had Emera pinned. Radley loomed over the little one, sneering, set to punish the child for having a friend. Then the faces changed, and the circle cleared when they saw the knife—and Candace's eyes.

Screams erupted from gap-toothed mouths. Young bodies contorted into panicked poses as the kids sacrificed one another to escape razor wrath.

Rebecca muscled past the others and bolted for the front door, but Radley didn't get the chance. Candace stormed toward him with the knife raised.

"No, please!"

"Candace!" came a shriek that froze her, and suddenly Mrs. Dietrich had her in a crushing hug. Radley issued a sob, darkly satisfying, as he scrambled to run away.

"It's *me*, Candace," Mrs. Dietrich said breathlessly. "Calm down!"

Candace's mind reeled. She replayed the last few seconds in her mind. It felt like she had only been a spectator.

"Put the knife down," Mrs. Dietrich ordered softly.

Candace dropped it and eyed Emera. The toddler was like a shell-shocked soldier.

* * * *

"Aaaagh, dude it's like trying to walk an effing triceratops!" Stuart complained, as he and DeShaun struggled to keep hold of Bravo's leash.

"How does an eighty-pound mutt out-muscle two teenagers?" DeShaun asked breathlessly.

"Bravo!" Stuart called, *"Heel!"* The dog *did* stop, regarding the boys patiently as he caught a few quick pants. They plopped onto the curb at the edge of someone's lawn and caught their breath, all hands on the leash.

"He just wants to get home," DeShaun noted.

"You think he thinks Candace is at their old house?" asked Stuart.

"I think he knows *exactly* where she is," DeShaun noted. "Remember how he found her last year after the parade?"

"What a smart dog."

Bravo turned to regard the boys, as if appreciating the compliment, but then his ears pricked, his nose went to work, and he peered off toward the horizon again.

"I hate keeping him chained up all the time," DeShaun said. "But if we let him get loose, we might never catch him."

Still gripping the leash vigilantly, the boys lay back on the grass and examined the yellow sky and the leaves spiraling across it.

"Too bad we can't take him to visit her with us," DeShaun continued.

"Been meaning to talk to you about that," Stuart said.

"What's up?"

"Her letters. She thinks her brother is coming back."

"Damn..." DeShaun shook his head slowly.

"And the other kids at the home pick on her about...him."

The boys furrowed their brows at each other. "That's not cool," DeShaun said.

"It's worse," Stuart said. "The grown-ups are really weir—"

They were hoisted to their feet. Bravo was pointing like a setter, straining at the leash, even as he rasped from constriction.

"He's ready to go, I think," DeShaun said, stumbling to catch up.

"I think he knows, man!" Stuart said. "He senses something wrong and he wants to protect her."

Bravo just trudged, one foot after the other, dragging the boys relentlessly. Panting and panting, ears perked up, he ignored other dogs that barked at him and pedestrians who wanted to pet him, ever focused on going forward.

"When he gets tired again, we gotta try to get him turned around," DeShaun said. "Or one of the Mas will come searching for us again."

Chapter 4

Season of the Witch

The sunset, a crimson comet plummeting behind the emptying trees, did not comfort her as usual.

Matilda Saxon stood at the edge of her porch, scratching the scalps of her goats Argyle and Amos, watching the shimmering orb meet the treetops. The nightly ritual always connected her to nature and refilled her reserves. It brought peace and balance. She used to rock in her old chair, petting and baby-talking her goats. Now she stood rigid with dread.

The evening ritual had changed the day that first letter came from the penitentiary, the one that all but screamed to be burned and forgotten.

Matilda's profession was witchcraft, as it had been her mother's, and uncounted generations of Saxon women before. At forty-two, healthy and youthful, Matilda was well-versed in her craft.

Her specialty? The black arts.

She had seen her mother and grandmother work baneful magic on occasion. When a no-good philanderer had made threats of harm, and then made good on them. When an arsonist had left an immigrant family homeless and went untouched by the law.

The matrons had agonized and fought each other over these decisions. They had banished themselves, accepting a lifelong self-imposed isolation in the aftermath. They warned Matilda, *begged* her, made her *promise* never to do as they did.

Matilda, once grown and on her own, had carried on the magical traditions of her bloodline, content to keep her promise for many years. But for Matilda, as for everyone, life became ever less simple. Black and white became gray, money matters got mean. Matilda knew that human nature leans toward quick fixes to stupid problems. Wisdom is just hindsight coupled with wishful thinking.

She had inherited an ancient house in need of upkeep, surrounded by daunting forest, on a scrubby tract connected to unused fields, far up in the hills of Cronus County. Her mindset and value system made her too *odd* to marry. It was a formula for bitterness, a rationale for cynical self-service.

On occasions that a client's desperation aligned with Matilda's, she accepted money for raising petty blights and banes—to cool a love affair, delay a destiny, plant a seed of illness—feeling less remorse with each commission. Those who can afford to feel spite can afford—or will *gain*—the means to see it satisfied, and the demand for baneful spell-work far exceeded that for the benevolent kind. Over time, Matilda had gained a clientele of shady types, and soon after that, outright criminals. She no longer found herself approached for such matters as blessing crops, influencing love, or ensuring job promotions.

As her craft had gotten blacker, she'd found herself drawn to the Greek wilderness deity Pan, focusing and calling upon him most often. Why, Matilda could not say for sure. Rumor had it that town founder Wilcott Bennington had favored Saturn, a.k.a. Cronus. Perhaps there was something about Ember Hollow's endless fields of pumpkins and corn and hay, the breadth of its plunge into the essence of autumn that attracted fertility and agriculture spirits.

Whatever the connection to Pan and/or Saturn, Matilda harbored no illusions. Her work changed lives for the worse. But her clients were adults with free will. She was only an intermediary, bearing no responsibility for how her services were used.

Then the letter had arrived.

It lay in her mailbox atop bills, junk mail and a gardening magazine. She had felt only a second of innocent curiosity before the sender's name jabbed into her mind like a poison-tipped needle. The deceptively childish script had said Nico Rizzoli, but her mind's eye flashed the catchier moniker assigned by the newspapers: Nico The Knife.

The Sampson Correctional Institution return address was below, in the same innocuous script. It could have been a child's valentine.

Like Matilda, the Mid-Atlantic Fireheads Motorcycle Club understood well the way of doing things in a less than widely-accepted manner to reap quick benefit. And they paid well for it.

In retrospect, she wished she had written *incorrect address*—better yet *deceased*—and put the envelope back, or just burned it without responding.

But her curiosity was strong—not to mention the scent of money. She had begun a correspondence with the biker, ignoring all the warning signals. Soon she was recommending, and then *sending* books to Rizzoli, always surprised that the Department of Corrections, in its ignorance, would allow a dangerous criminal access to such powerful information. It was a matter of religious freedom, after all, and to them, a silly recreation. Hence, Rizzoli had been able to hide his scheme in plain sight, until it was time to entrust it to his man on the outside, Pipsqueak.

Then it had all snowballed far beyond Matilda's ability to reconcile—or control.

The sun was gone. The moon, only a sliver.

* * * *

Just before bed time was best for arguments.

Stella felt some guilt for making use of this stratagem. It seemed manipulative. But this was crucial, and she needed to use every advantage she could.

There he stood at the sink, in his striped flannel pajamas, brushing his teeth and gargling, tired from a long day at work and hours in the basement with his chemistry set. At least he seemed satisfied with the lasagna she had made him.

"I want to talk about something," said she.

"Yuh?" He spat, then brushed some more.

"It doesn't look good for Abe to adopt Candace."

"Crap. That's a shame." At least his concern was genuine.

"I think we should consider it." She wished she had skipped the "I think" part. It seemed indecisive.

Bernard turned his whole body to face her. He seemed less like a head of household than a great big twelve-year-old in his pajamas with toothpaste at the corner of his mouth. "I don't see how we could swing that. No."

His "no" was a strong counterweight to the pajamas.

"We could manage it easily, Bernard. Abe is getting better and I'll be able to return to work with the county." She took a hand towel and wiped his mouth, a mother tending to a child. Mothers knew best. "She's old enough she wouldn't be any trouble."

"No trouble? *No trouble!?*" Bernard took the towel away and dropped it on the sink. "She grew up in a family of weirdos. Whom…her brother… *killed*. I'm sorry to be insensitive, but that's a lifetime of 'trouble.'"

He had a good point.

"We could do it, Bernard. And it would be *so rewarding!*"

She realized how paltry this sounded when he returned to his brushing with a scoff.

"If we're ever going to be parents, we'll have to start soon, you know. And this way, all the diapering and late feeding is already over!"

"I thought you said you were okay with not having children."

"When I thought we never *could*. Under these circumstances, I think we would be favored to—"

"Everett Geelens." Bernard interrupted. "The Trick or Treat Terror. Estimated lifetime body count of over *one hundred* men, women and children. Conjecture is, his environment contributed heavily to him becoming a serial killer." Bernard spat in the sink, rinsed and took a drink of water. "His environment. The same as—"

"I know, Bernard. I know. But this environment would be diff—"

"No." He held up his hand in her face. "Period." He bumped past her and went directly to bed without his usual twenty-five minutes of reading.

* * * *

When Burt Darnell, manager of Darnell Hunt and Tackle, left work after 6 p.m.—midnight dark this time of year—his attention was drawn to the far end of his lot by a deep rumbling rhythm that made him uneasy. He and his evening stocker Jordie were further spooked by the portentous sight of an antique hearse parked beyond the streetlights emitting doomy music.

Then Jordie recognized it as the Haunted Hollow Hearse, official vehicle of local punk rock outfit The Chalk Outlines—currently disbanded—and better known these days for their aborted show atop the theatre marquee during the infamous Pumpkin Parade massacre, when Dennis had taken an unintended stage dive off the marquee roof after a flying whiskey bottle had conked him a good one.

Knowing who it was mostly reassured Burt, except that he couldn't think of any good reason for the hearse to be parked at his store in the darkest sector of the lot. Add the notoriety of typical musician behavior, the stigma of the tragedy, and well…one could see where he might get the urge to call the sheriff.

En route to the station to sign out and head home for dinner, Chief Deputy Hudson Lott heard the call and answered before anyone else could. "I'm about a block away," he white lied. "I'll take it."

Friendship and duty know no set schedule. This was both.

As Hudson pulled into the otherwise deserted lot, he swallowed the permanent knot of dread that grew from a perpetual fear that Dennis would one day follow his father Jerome on a shortcut into the Great Wide Open. He recalled the sight of Dennis in a pool of his own blood after the fall from the stage; recalled how empty and sick he felt, thinking the tragedy of the young man's life had finally come to a climax, as inevitable as it always seemed.

If he were to find Dennis *dead* now, in another pool of blood—or vomit—it would change his life, his career, his *everything,* forever. But it would be best for *him* to bear that burden. It was an albatross he would wear dutifully.

He did not flash the lights or hit the siren, as he eased up nose to nose with the modified '70 Caddy hearse. He hoped he could determine Dennis's state in increments, rather than in widescreen 3D at the driver side window.

Hudson got out and walked to the hearse. From the hearse's speakers, Black Sabbath's "Falling Off the Edge Of The World" faded away and restarted. Hudson recognized it from the Outlines' rehearsals. Something about its emotional spectrum always got Dennis's juices flowing.

The front was empty.

A clutter of dark clothes and pale tattooed skin filled the back seat. It was Dennis all right. His black sneakers, his black jeans, his naked torso curled in fetal position. Hudson watched his ribs for movement and was relieved to see a slight rise and fall.

He tapped the window once with the flashlight, but he'd roused enough drunks to know that wouldn't do it.

The door was unlocked, as he'd expected it would be, in keeping with Dennis's self-destructive tendencies. On some level, the rocker would welcome a murderous prowler.

Hudson took Dennis's wrist and pulled him up, careful to protect his head. As the empty Diamante bottle—same brand as the one that KO'd him a year ago—clinked onto the concrete, Dennis stirred. Hudson took him in a hug, as he had many times after the elder Barcroft's passing, and lifted him to stand, alarmed at how light and thin he was.

"Come on, son," Hudson patted his cheek. "Wake up now."

Dennis fluttered his eyes to half-mast and propped himself against the hearse, dim recognition coming to his reddened eyes. "Hey man ..."

"Glad you're not driving," Hudson said. "Thanks for that."

Dennis gave a sloppy salute.

"I'll take you home. Have someone bring you your car in the morning."

"Dude," Dennis clamped his eyes shut and exhaled a noisy breath. "I can't go home."

"Why not?"

"I can't let Ma and Stuart see me like this."

"Then why'd you *get* like this?"

Dennis didn't answer, and he didn't need to. He had some damn good reasons.

"How about we go get some coffee then?"

"Coffee then..." Dennis agreed.

Hudson helped his friend to the patrol car and called in to have dispatch phone his wife Leticia and ask her to prepare an extra dinner plate.

Chapter 5

Frailty

Candace had been distantly aware of little Emera coming to her side and gently shaking her, patting her cheek, whispering that it was "time to giddup" throughout an epoch of slumber. She was grateful for these rest stops on the winding miles of nightmare road she trod like a death march, during which Everett had come and gone in her head as he pleased.

Her ballooning bladder, desert-dry tongue and a vague sense of urgency forced her to sit up. She vaguely remembered the ordeal of the sleeping pills, of the Dietrichs insisting she take them, then checking her mouth to make sure she'd swallowed them.

Emera wasn't around now, and that raised a sludgy, helpless panic somewhere beyond the sedative's reach. If only the rest of her could shake it off.

A weak call for the little girl found its way out of her. Before Candace could make herself fall out of bed the Dietrichs were there.

"There we are," said the Mrs. "Bet you're thirsty." She held the glass to Candace's lips and carefully tipped it.

"So glad you got some rest," said Mr. Dietrich, patting her on the shoulder. Their familiar smiles did not waver. At the window, the sun-dotted shadows of the big maple in the backyard told Candace it was at least noon.

Mrs. Dietrich stroked her hair and answered the question Candace struggled to ask. "Emera is fine. She's in our room while we tend to you."

Candace gulped more water and received more praise for it. "Don't worry. You'll be back to normal in half an hour or so," said Mr. Dietrich.

"We should talk about what happened in the TV room," Mrs. Dietrich said. Her husband shut his eyes and set his jaw in a caricature of concern.

"Okay," Candace managed. She remembered too well, having swum amid nightmare versions of the incident over the last few hours.

"We know you want to be near Emera. And she needs you, no doubt about that," Mrs. Dietrich said. "We're just afraid your case worker won't understand if she hears that you went after Radley with a knife."

Not to mention Emera being picked on by Radley and Rebecca, while you two were off doing who-knows-what, Candace thought. *Right?*

Mr. Dietrich put his big hand on Candace's. "We just want our little family to stay together and get along. Emera's making progress coming out of her shell, thanks to *you*. We wouldn't want her falling behind again. Understand?"

"Whud 'bout Radley and Rebecca?" Candace slurred.

"Don't worry, Sweetie." Mrs. Dietrich said. "They are being dealt with."

"The main thing is, we want everyone to get along," Mr. Dietrich finished. "And we need you to try."

"Oh...kay." Candace yearned to go find Emera and make sure she was all right. Because she wasn't about to trust these two half-present adults.

When they left, Candace shuffled to the bathroom. She splashed cold water on her face and then went to her journal and ongoing letter to Stuart.

"They were supposed to be giving me one sleep pill every night! But they didn't give me ANY till last night after the fight with Radley and Rebecca! And then they gave me TWO! But I saw the bottle, Stuart. It was almost empty!"

* * * *

Afterwards, the Dietrichs called all the kids together to the scene of the incident for a catch-all reprimand and some customized punishments.

"No Saturday phone calls for a while," Mrs. Dietrich told Candace. "You can use the free time to reflect on how to get along with ..."

Candace didn't need to hear the rest. Instead she focused on her surreal recall of the incident, of just being along for the ride when her legs tromped to the kitchen and her hand took the boning knife. She never wanted to feel that way again; out of control and fated to draw blood.

But the terror on their faces, when they all saw the knife...

"I'm sorry everyone," she said, as Mrs. Dietrich wound down her lecture. The Dietrichs never forced apologies, but Candace *was* sorry and *did* need to express it. "I hope I didn't scare you guys too much."

She furtively made eye contact with her housemates. Their expressions ranged from confusion to...nothing. Remorse and personal responsibility were already long lost for most of them.

Then she glanced at Radley and found him smirking. Beside him, Rebecca pointed and expelled a *"Ha!"*

"Rebecca, *dammit!*" Mr. Dietrich grabbed her elbow and hauled her off to her room.

Candace had wanted to mend the rift, but she was alone.

She wondered, was this why God made killers, like her brother?

She chased away the black thought and waited to be dismissed.

* * * *

"Okay, Bernard." Hudson nodded vigorously, perhaps believing he was convincing the man on the other end of the call that he was deeply interested in what he had to say. "Hopefully, I'll get a minute to drop by and see what you've come up with th—"

DeShaun tittered, Leticia shook her head, and Dennis mouthed *"W-T-F?"* as Bernard's interrupting voice needled out around Hudson's ear.

They watched Hudson peer into his mashed potatoes.

It took Leticia's unwavering eye contact to motivate Hudson to cut off the garrulous scientist. "Listen Bernard, we've got dinner ready here and a guest. Call you tomorrow, bud!"

He clicked off without allowing Bernard his customary ten minutes of wind-down conversation. "That man is damn near obsessed."

Little Wanda had recently graduated from her high chair to migrating across various laps throughout the course of dinner, sampling from plates along the way. Enchanted by the novelty of a beloved dinner guest, she currently occupied Dennis's.

"How'd he get on this kick anyway?" Dennis asked.

"I gave him a couple samples of Ruth's poison treats because he was curious about what was in them. Wanted to do tests."

"Wanda!" The toddler had just begun to roll her finger in Dennis's mashed potatoes when Leticia called her down. "Now that is *rude!*"

Wanda raised the finger to Dennis' face, perhaps hoping to convince her mother that her intentions had been good.

"Thank you, Wanda." Dennis scraped his finger across Wanda's and transferred the mash to his mouth. "He a chemist or something?"

"Chemist, engineer—that dude has more degrees than a thermometer," DeShaun said.

Hudson offered his son an approving fist bump.

"You don't have to do that," Leticia said, as Dennis accepted another finger of potatoes from the baby.

"I want her to stay for a minute." Dennis gave Wanda a kiss on the head.

"Feeling any better?" Hudson asked.

Dennis made an "iffy" gesture. "Thanks for collecting me. Feeding me."

"What are we gonna do next?" Hudson asked.

Dennis just looked at his plate.

"You need to think about your mama," Leticia said, bringing a reproachful expression from Hudson. "Well, he *does!*"

"I know, yeah," Dennis agreed.

In the living room, Bravo pawed at the door and whined, as he did every night.

"He wants to go find Candace," DeShaun explained.

"I need to see if we can bring him when we go visit," Hudson said.

Taken in by the Lotts after the parade disaster, Bravo had been given all that he never had in his past.

Patriarch Aloysius Geelens had wanted a big dog to intimidate his increasingly unpredictable son Everett, or even *attack* the boy, if worse came. But like everyone else, Bravo was made uneasy by Everett. The dog had only ever truly bonded with Candace.

Here at the Lotts, he had a big garage and the foot of DeShaun's bed to sleep in, a backyard to roam and the best dog food money could buy. DeShaun and Stuart walked him every day. He often wagged and rubbed against his new housemates to show his love and gratitude. But there was no denying his heart and thoughts were with Candace.

"I want to talk about that," DeShaun said quietly, spinning his fork in his gravy.

"Talk about what?" asked Leticia.

"Well, we're worried, Stuart and me." He glanced at Bravo. "Stuart says her letters make it sound like it's...just weird over there. Something seems really wrong."

He chose not to mention Candace's obsessive certainty that Everett would somehow return.

Dennis knocked back the last half of his coffee in one smooth motion. Leticia had the pot up to refill before Dennis had even lowered his cup.

"The adoption system is crap," Dennis said. "Pedro tells horror stories. Or did, anyway, when we were speaking."

Wanda waved her chubby hand at the steam rising from Dennis's coffee.

"We're worried about her," DeShaun said.

"Because you're a good friend, baby," said Leticia.

"I better get home and check in," Dennis said, rising to hand off Wanda and don his jacket.

Bravo perked up, wagging in anticipation, ever hopeful he was about to go find His Little Girl.

* * * *

"It's just for a while," Mrs. Dietrich explained. "Who knows if you might walk in your sleep given your state? I know you don't want to be all drugged up every night." She pulled the Velcro straps reasonably tight, binding Candace to her bed. "And all you've been through."

Emera sat up in her bed, confusion on her face. Candace smiled at the little girl.

"Hi Candace." Mr. Dietrich entered and placed a white plastic audio baby monitor transmitter on the dresser between the girls. "This is just something we have to do. Just in case. Okay?"

Just in case *what,* Candace couldn't understand. She was already restrained. "Do you know when my caseworker is coming?"

Mrs. Dietrich cleared her throat to fill the silence as she constructed her lie. "I called today and asked. They're terribly backed up, sweetie."

Mr. Dietrich, his sparse brown hair beaded with sweat, gave Candace an earnest, even *kind* expression, and said, "You weren't the only one who lost their parents in the parade, you know."

Candace lay there, strapped to her bed, trapped with her confusion as Mrs. Dietrich sang a rote lullaby to Emera. The little one didn't seem to grow any sleepier, only more confused.

The house parents said good night and left the room, leaving the scarred Casper the Friendly Ghost night light burning and the door half-open.

Candace turned her head to see Emera staring at her. "Are you okay Emenememema?"

Emera shook her head.

"Don't worry about this," Candace held up the restraints. "I won't ever hurt you."

Even after Candace's rage episode, Emera seemed to know this. The little girl's worry was for Candace, not herself.

Candace closed her eyes and tried to relax, or at least to convince Emera she had fallen asleep, so the little girl would do the same. In her mind, she went over the family room drama, wishing to go back in time and make everything different.

Through a blood red haze of fury, she watched the brisk trip down the hall, relived her gaze sweeping across the counter and landing on the butcher's block. She saw the knife slide from its slot and gleam under the overhead light. She saw it swim like a shark back to the family room. She saw the panic in all the young eyes.

And when she tried to shoo the incident away, she saw a flash of her brother Everett; grinning and soaked in blood from the twisted bodies of her stiffening housemates.

Chapter 6

Dark Echoes

The long morning spent going over the visions of whiskey in his desk drawer made his sobriety seem like a brief interruption until the whiskey inevitably regained control.

All that crawling around under his desk, tossing it, righting it had worn him out. Left him thirsty.

When Stella left, it seemed like a good time to get outside and walk the church grounds a bit to take in some fresh air.

The second he stepped out a strange thought came to him; everything had radically changed since he'd last set eyes on it.

A good many graves had been added after the parade calamity, but that was a year past. It seemed like the additions numbered in the hundreds.

The trees dotting the landscape seemed out of place. The parking lot was like some uncharted desert island.

It was as if he was seeing his familiar place of work and worship for the first time in years.

...Centuries...

His feet took him around the rear, past the gymnasium and to the far side of the sanctuary's exterior. They stopped him at a wooden enclosure that had been installed to house a lawnmower and other equipment for landscaping, which was done by local contractor Guillermo Trujillo these days.

McGlazer knew that the little plywood structure predated him. But he couldn't shake the weird feeling it was *new*.

He found the key on his ring and opened the lightless shed. There was no lawn equipment these days; Guillermo brought his own. Mostly just a pile of mementos left by mourners. Stuffed animals, plastic flowers, etc. Not many; every few weeks, Guillermo took them for recycling.

On the wall hung some tools—hedge clippers, shovels, a mattock.

A crowbar.

McGlazer thought he was standing still and trying to figure out why he had this sudden interest in the shed, unaware that he was gathering up the discarded mementos to get them out of the way. The iron of the crowbar was just cold enough to make him realize what he was doing. He hesitated. "Why would I need *this*?" he asked aloud.

"*Put it to use,*" said a voice. "*Against the floor timbers.*"

...Floor timbers? Who called them *that*?

He blinked, and when he opened his eyes, the crowbar in his hand was a bottle of Jefferson Select; sparkling with the reflected rays of a spring sun.

McGlazer beheld the bottle and then the floor, which he now somehow understood was covering a massive stock of the golden elixir. He needed to get to it, to *see* it. And, maybe, keep one or two around. As props. For when he told the story of this weird day. That's all.

He licked his lips and resolved to pulling up those "floor timbers" so he could get to the treasure waiting beneath. He stabbed the blade into a joint, forced it deep and started prying. The corners soon popped loose. The nail hit the wall with a mute *ping.* A familiar scent wafted from the blackness; a warm, pleasant, *enticing* scent.

McGlazer pried loose more nails along the crosspiece. With the first slab removed, he could easily enter. Just a few steps, and crate upon crate would lay open before him, liquid riches made to electrify and satisfy his craving.

He tossed the crowbar against the shed wall with an angry roar. "I'm not doing this again!"

Still, the thirst.

McGlazer dropped to his knees and threw his head back, stretching his clasped hands so high his shoulders burned. "God give me strength! Temptation is upon me like locusts, O Lord!" Even his words of prayer seemed chosen by someone else.

Before he could continue there came a reply. "*You* keep His holy name *out* of your filthy drunkard *mouth!*"

McGlazer shuddered at the familiar voice. Undercurrents of serpentine hiss and grave dirt musk lay over its tiny hint of humanity.

It was the voice of Ruth Treadwell.

Ragdoll Ruth.

But it was also the voice of a giant. It came from *everywhere*—except the just-opened cellar.

His gaze was drawn to the nearest grave, less than a couple of yards away. The grassy earth violently pulsed, as if preparing to vomit up its rotting contents.

A bass-filled impact shook the earth, like a ten-ton boulder falling somewhere just out of sight. Then *another,* the footsteps of a titan.

McGlazer's gaze darted to the high corners of the church. He thought of the Night Mayor; the stilt-legged mascot of the Pumpkin Parade, whose oversized head and cartoon-insane eyes would appear above the roof tops of Main Street, always preceded by the same kind of amplified footfalls that now left his heart hammering, his throat arid and desiccated.

"I will carry you to hell myself...*Reverend!*" The last word dripped with gallons of disdain, like a sickening syrup strained from tumors.

McGlazer trembled, skin crawling—something like the feeling of DTs—at the thought of facing an incarnation of Ragdoll Ruth that held such immense power, the power to see her limitless hate satisfied.

From the blackness of the cellar the scent bloomed, not of decay or earth, but of sweet whiskey. "She won't find you down there," the inner voice told him. "Do as I say, and you'll be safe."

McGlazer knew it wasn't the voice of God, but the next crashing footfall was ten times louder, twenty times closer. "You will burn in *my hell!*" raged the ragdoll colossus.

McGlazer squeaked and skittered into the musky mousehole to escape the hulking harpy.

* * * *

Frowning, Deputy Yoshida handed Hudson a cup of coffee before the chief deputy was barely through the station door. "...What?" Hudson asked. "Did you spit in it?"

"No." Yoshida handed him a bulletin from the state patrol.

"Ah, hell."

The memo contained frustratingly sparse details about the crashed prison transport that had carried Nico Rizzoli—now missing.

"Yep," agreed Yoshida. "Took 'em a while to sort through all the body parts. But Rizzoli's gone. He expressed a pretty extreme hatred for you on his way to the pen, I recall."

"Me and every other black man, cop, and law-abiding citizen on planet Earth." Hudson focused on the key words. "'Wild animal attack'? 'Torn to pieces'?"

"They're saying Rizzoli was probably dragged away and eaten." Yoshida jabbed the bulletin with his finger. "You believe that?"

"*Hell* no."

"Me neither. Which means he's out there somewhere."

"Yeah, but—Mother of *God.* What is all this animal attack business?"

"Right. And they're pretty sure."

"Which means...*both* could be right."

Yoshida held out his arms. "This never happened in L.A."

"If you're planning on moving back, you damn well better wait till after Halloween."

* * * *

Not far behind Hudson was Deputy Sean Shavers.

The nine-year veteran thought of a time when he'd relished the morning drive in his El Camino to the station during autumn, through wispy fog, brisk air, leaves rolling across the road like colorful waves.

The highlight of the journey had always been radio deejay Dee Mentia. With a husky Mae West affectation, she spouted PG-rated innuendoes and played fun Halloween music ranging from classic horror movie soundtrack cues to psychobilly songs to cornball-spooky parody numbers.

The radio station's management, having shrewdly acquired the call letters WICH, milked the hell out of the Halloween season. The station was located at the far end of Cronus County. Barely within Ember Hollow listening range, they nonetheless vaunted themselves as Ember Hollow's hometown favorite, tying in to the annual Halloween Pumpkin Parade at every opportunity.

With the arrival of autumn, WICH always amped up the holiday spirit, with deejays assuming (i.e. becoming "possessed by") different personae, bringing a campy vibe to the broadcast, like a cable access television show with a hammy horror host.

There was "murdererologist" Voodoo Vinnie, who always took credit for *causing* the weather, whatever it was.

Abel the Weird, who took the afternoon shift, was as straight edge as they come but played up a burned-out stoner, issuing incoherent philosophical anecdotes and non sequiturs.

Just as Ember Hollow itself became "Haunted Hollow" for the fall season, the station took to re-naming local businesses and folks by Cryptkeeper-style pun names—anything related to spooks and scares.

Shavers didn't pay much attention to these on-air personalities throughout the year, leaving the radio volume down unless something by Fleetwood Mac or Lynyrd Skynyrd came on. But when green leaves changed to yellow and DeDe Kenner became Dee Mentia—well, that was something special.

Dee took on her character full-bore, just like Elvira, firing off harmless innuendo meant to fly right over the heads of pre-teens and make its way unfailingly to the groaniest part of the grown-up funny bone.

Shavers often told the boys at the station that her characterization hit him in a *different* bone; just as groany. He always raised the volume and laughed aloud when she spoke, be it to deliver traffic reports or kooky spooky voiceover for whatever local farm supply outlet had ponied up for her endorsement.

Shavers wasn't attracted to the real DeDe Kenner at all, and he was decidedly not into goth or alt girls. But he was wildly and lustfully *smitten* with Dee Mentia.

Through the year, he would sometimes see DeDe at public appearances and give her a wave, then move on. But come late August, when she donned full Dee Mentia regalia...

A purple Medusa wig sprouting ruby-eyed rubber snakes from curly tresses.

Matching purple glitter eye shadow surrounding Meg Foster-blue eyes.

Form-fitted black leather vest over a generously-stuffed spiderweb lace corset.

Fishnet stockings under a studded pleather mini-skirt.

...*That* was a different story.

Shavers occasionally worked security at farm equipment fairs or store openings for extra cash, especially if he knew Dee would be there doing promotions. He would sidle up to her and initiate some flirty fun, fishing for personalized silly sexy banter to take home with him. She was all too happy to oblige.

What was the harm? Great God of Earth and Altar, couldn't a single virile man have himself a corny, tawdry little fantasy here and there? Of *course* he could!

Except, he couldn't anymore.

On duty at the fated pumpkin parade, Shavers had been right in the middle of town when Ragdoll Ruth's killing candy had kicked in, sending everyone who'd consumed it into fits of horrific self-mutilation or cannibalistic murder.

He had witnessed what could only be the very end of the world happening all around him. He had been helpless to do anything about it.

In his terror and despair, he had heard himself sobbing like an infant violently seized from its mother. To shut off the cries, he'd raised his service revolver to his head and cocked the hammer.

It was one of the afflicted who had saved him.

The woman, dressed like a "sexy cop" coincidentally enough, had seized his gun hand to claim the weapon for her *own* maddened purposes. There could be no doubt—if she'd gotten a hold of it, she would've immediately killed him. Strangely, that flipped a switch.

Though she was freakishly strong, Shavers had kept control of the pistol and shoved the woman to the ground. Fully aware of what he was doing, he'd shot and killed his would-be killer. No one had seen.

As the smoke had cleared, Shavers understood he would never find the "himself" that had existed before the shooting. The crisp mornings, languid mist, scary songs—even Dee Mentia—would always be tainted for him.

In DeDe's appearances and on-air demeanor, she seemed to feel the same.

Shavers had to give the WICH on-air personalities a lot of credit for keeping up the spirit their home office required of them, the formula that had succeeded for years. Like Shavers, the deejays, engineers and programmers would do their duties. But no one could make them—or Shavers—*feel* it.

The secret followed him everywhere. And he could never tell anyone. Bad enough he would lose his job. Chances were he'd wind up in prison as well, alongside criminals he had busted, or who just hated cops.

Sometime around mid-autumn, Shavers had experienced a moment of clarity. He'd decided to just get through this first anniversary of the tragedy. Then he would figure out how to exorcise the hidden demon, if possible. But as Halloween grew closer, the pressure worsened, the beat of his personal tell-tale heart growing louder.

Shavers feared that, soon, he would rip up the boards that hid the secret heart—give himself away somehow—with only despair and expanding isolation to mark the rest of his days.

Chapter 7

Beyond The Door

Mayor Stuyvesant placed her hands behind her back like a soldier, twisting her knit cap into a tight cylinder. All the signs of stress that had carried her through her privileged childhood—huffing, shaking her head, rolling her eyes—had been trained out of her when she'd begun her political career. Even her assistant Hollis was only rarely privy to expressions of discontent.

Whisking from car to office after the latest headache-inducing town council meeting, the mayor was half-relieved to see none of the town paper's cub reporters waiting to grill her about the status of the Pumpkin Parade. Yet she also felt a little let down. The back-and-forth with inexperienced journalists was invigorating.

"Call Bruner," she ordered Hollis. "I want a breakdown of who is still staging floats there and who is waffling." She sipped gingerly from her espresso like a person with no worries. The Bruner Company, second largest farming equipment manufacturer in the nation and the Pumpkin Parade's biggest sponsor, owned a massive hangar off the highway which they had donated for participants to store their float displays and general parade setup needs.

"Will do," answered her assistant. "But my friend at the paper tells me they had another three ads for the parade supplement pullout this morning."

She shot a warning glance at Hollis. No one was there to see the poor optics, and he was used to it anyway. "You could've mentioned that."

"You specifically told me not to bother you with bad news today."

"Then why did you?"

"I...don't..."

"I'm sorry Hollis." She placed a hand on his arm, and found it tense. "You understand. Between the parade, the election, and..."

"Your brother Kerwin," Hollis acknowledged. "I know. It's a lot."

"I'll have to go see him at the rehab center soon," she lamented. "Or I might appear negligent."

"Yet, he's an...unattractive reminder of the parade."

"Yes. Not that that's the only reason to go."

"I'll have flowers sent."

"That's becoming a cliché I'm afraid."

"Well, any kind of edible arrangement is out of the question."

She shot him a glance. His expression didn't indicate a cruel joke.

Her dear brother Kerwin, in one of his grandiose get-rich(er)-quick schemes, had finagled his way into managing the town's local band The Chalk Outlines, arranging for a record company rep to come see them play atop The Grand Illusion as the parade centerpiece. Then Everett Geelens had shown up, murdered the suit, and inflicted an even *worse* fate upon Kerwin, tearing the gabby con man's lower jaw off with the hook of a claw hammer.

Early on, Mayor Stuyvesant had scheduled visits to her convalescing sibling on Saturdays and Sundays. The optics were good; many constituents would be visiting their loved ones as well. She did not consider the timing opportunistic, just practical. Regardless, many of these loved ones were also victims of the parade—burned, stampeded or worse when it had all gone to hell. These people had questions, and resentments, and frustrations. Weekend visits became more troublesome than helpful. The staff asked her to aim for quieter times to visit Kerwin, helpfully offering a suggested schedule.

Defying their wishes was yet another minefield best avoided as public opinion and local press soured by the day.

Meanwhile, Buncombe County's planners had no qualms about taking advantage of Cronus County's bad luck to bolster their own burgeoning Thanksgiving-Christmas hullabaloo. Sponsors and participants were defecting to the new deal in droves, leaving less mobile parade route businesses in the lurch.

It wasn't Mayor Stuyvesant's fault, of course. But it was her responsibility. Now that it no longer took care of itself, her amusing foray into local politics as a supplement to the family's vast local realty holdings had become one monstrous headache. And while it was tempting to cast blame elsewhere as she had seen colleagues do, that was less accepted among Saint Saturn's pragmatic blue-collar folk than on a state or national level.

In simple terms, if she didn't salvage the Pumpkin Parade, her chances of re-election were as dead as the leaves on the ground outside her office window.

* * * *

"Oh. Wait," DeShaun said, hopping off his bike before they had even left his driveway.

He left it parked at the edge of the street and ran back into the garage, his gangly legs an inch too long for the jeans purchased new for the school year.

Stuart watched his friend, noting how he had grown at least two and a half inches since the previous October's Pumpkin Parade Disaster, for this was how the passing of time was measured in Ember Hollow now.

DeShaun's voice had started changing as well, sounding more like his father Hudson's booming Jim Brown baritone.

They were both amused by this the first few times. DeShaun would exaggerate his own cracking pitch to draw a laugh from Stuart. This, Stuart knew, was a sign of confidence.

DeShaun trotted back with a bike tool. When he crouched to raise his seat, Stuart noted how bunched-up his body was, all folded in on itself, mostly so he could get to the seat clamp without having to bend over and risk the inevitable derriere punt such a posture rightfully called for.

Stuart had figured his own growth spurt would begin shortly after DeShaun's, as he was a couple of months older. However, most of his classmates had soon passed him by. Compared to most boys his age, Stuart appeared a grade younger. The girls' changes left him feeling like a small child. He feared he would soon find himself outside the dating pool. Specifically, he feared he would fall outside of Candace Geelens's league, and that was the greatest tragedy he could imagine this side of his father's death.

There was something else Stuart had told no one, not even DeShaun, not even when they decompressed about the Terrible Pumpkin Parade Calamity and its aftermath. Hell, his own brother Dennis had only found out by accident.

Only Ma knew intimately of his bedwetting incidents. Patient and loving as she was, Stuart was never less than embarrassed that she knew why he was darting into the bathroom to shower at 3 a.m.

And, oh Holy God in his Cotton Candy Heaven—what if Candace *somehow found out!?*

He both anticipated and dreaded her eventual visit to Ember Hollow. The thought of Candace looking more and more like a woman while he remained a twerp of a kid terrified him. He feared being the ugly little duckling to her, in the shadow of confident and manly DeShaun.

Stuart, the third wheel. The little boy with the dirty shameful secret.

He imagined tagging along behind the two attractive tweens who seemed like they might make "such a cute couple! Especially given all they've been through together..."

Already, girls were asking Stuart about DeShaun's relationship status. So maybe there was that. With Candace in a foster home several school districts away, maybe DeShaun would get a girlfriend before she could come and fall helplessly smitten at his ever-growing feet.

But then, that would mean losing *DeShaun,* wouldn't it?

Growing up often seemed like a losing game. Stuart's position on the gameboard had him feeling more like The Incredible Shrinking Man, day by day.

"You're gonna have to get a new bike," he told DeShaun, as the other boy finished raising the seat. Then they took off to go nowhere particular; just to goof off, like any other time.

Stuart glanced at his friend and saw him make a very mature expression as the wind caught his face. He knew it would be a car or motorcycle DeShaun would be driving soon. The bigger boy would zoom by on his way to pick up a girl for a date, leaving Stuart to meander along aimlessly on his kiddie bike.

DeShaun would at least spare him a cool nod, though. And if he was lucky, Candace would give him an adoring head pat at church, between conversations with *real* young men—if Reverend McGlazer succeeded in adopting her, that is.

Adolescence is a crap shoot, a far from reliable predictor of adulthood. His brother Dennis had been so skinny, other rocker kids had called him "Ocasek." These days, Dennis wasn't a beefcake like Pedro, but he filled his blacks nicely enough, or so said Jill—back when she was still his squeeze.

The terrors of the Pumpkin Parade Calamity had at least given him a sense of perspective. Right now, he was grateful for long days with DeShaun and for the weirdly wonderful longing he felt for Candace. A year after nearly dying in horrifically spectacular fashion, Stuart knew he had a hell of a lot. And he wasn't going to waste his time whining like some soap opera square. Not right now.

The blast of autumn air in his face brought the same old exhilaration as always. Stuart rode up beside his best friend and fellow massacre survivor and tried to be okay with still being a kid.

* * * *

Stella arrived at Saint Saturn's early as usual, surprised to find McGlazer's car already in the lot—he was usually at least a half hour behind her. Perhaps the stress of the adoption matter had made him restless.

Inside, other things were different too. She recalled the early signs of the previous October's "haunting," manifested as cold spots, errant piano notes and a general feeling of unease. As a sensitive, Stella often picked up on changes in the *feel* of a given place, seemingly more so since that Halloween night.

She made her rounds, switching on lights and unlocking public doors, expecting to find McGlazer in his office. Instead, he was in one of the daycare rooms, contemplating a print of Nathan Greene's *The Rescue*. The painting depicted a Caucasian Jesus with shepherd's staff, stooping to reach for a dark-coated lamb as it struggles to clamber over the roots of a fallen tree on a steep incline.

Stella remembered how McGlazer had furrowed his brow upon receiving the print from a parishioner. He found it to be a simplistic depiction of the messiah and His compassion, but it *was* for the children after all, so...

He greeted her with his usual "Morning, morning, *morning!*" but in something like an odd lilt, as if he were imitating the Lucky Charms leprechaun. Then he ogled her from head to toe with an expression of smug approval. He had never been one to treat women as eye candy. But that was how his gaze made her feel now. Like McGlazer had assumed an antiquated, even disdainful view of women somehow during the night.

When she saw the state of his hair and eyes, she realized he must have spent the night there.

"You seem lively," she offered, wondering if he had fallen off the wagon.

"I'm a different person today!"

Something about Abe's voice was disconcerting. The accent was gone, mostly, but an undercurrent of elvish mischief remained.

"Anything I should know?" she asked.

"Only that you're as fetching a lass as there ever was!"

She blinked at him.

He rubbed the bridge of his nose. "I'm sorry Stella. Please forgive me. That was rude."

She relaxed. It was his frustration with the adoption matter. He had understandably lashed out, belittling her as *he* had surely felt belittled when she'd offered to take over a commitment for which he had been deemed unfit, unworthy. She stepped closer and touched his shoulder. "Do you need an ear?"

"I think what I need, is some rest."

"Can I drive you home?"

"If you'll just call and postpone my appointments, we can both take the rest of the day off."

"Of course."

"I just want to sit and meditate for a bit first." He squeezed her hand. "Please forgive me, Stella." Where the salacious leer had been icky, the squeeze was appealing. Something was in it besides gratitude.

Chapter 8

Dog Soldiers

The quartet of Fireheads waited in their stolen jeep a few dozen yards from the gates of Cronus County Municipal Memorial Grounds, smoking various substances and laughing at WICH's goofy deejays to pass the time. After the caretaker left for lunch, they hopped the fence.

The clumsily-named cemetery served as the default resting place for the county's dead who had no estate or family to pay for a funeral.

Nico, Jiggy and Aura followed Pipsqueak to a remote corner of the sprawling grounds. Unlike Saint Saturn, this newer graveyard was mostly flat, with clearly marked plots.

Pipsqueak poked at a map he had printed off in the Ember Hollow library, then to a pair of tin markers in the ground. "Here we go, Chief."

The remains of infamous mass murderess "Ragdoll Ruth" reposed here, alongside those of Everett Geelens—her contemporary and, ironically, her killer. Side by side they lay, in a remote corner of the park, under the limbs of a diseased walnut tree that had recently rained its ugly black fruit all around the two block-letter tin plates, like eggs hurled by Devil's Night tricksters at the mean old woman who kept any basketballs that rolled into her yard.

Nico and his disciples formed a somber crescent around the two markers, as even the wind seemed to respectfully quiet down.

Nico's breathing grew less steady, his tattooed shoulders rising just a millimeter higher with each exhale. Everyone knew not to speak again until he did.

"Bastards tossed her out like garbage," Nico said through gritted teeth. "Right beside that dickhead retard that ganked her." Nico pointed to Everett's grave but only stared at Ruth's.

He fell to his knees and rubbed his hand across the marker stamped with her name, stroking it, tracing all the letters and lines. "I'm so sorry, babe." His voice cracked. The other bikers lowered their heads and closed their eyes, refusing to behold their leader in his weakness.

"I wish I coulda been there. Coulda showed you how to do it *right.*" He hunkered over and covered the tin plate with his body, shivering as a wail of agony escaped him. Jiggy doffed his leather cap and held it over his heart.

"I wish I coulda screwed you right in the blood of all those assholes," Nico sobbed, rocking in his child pose, tearing grass away from around the plate, as he trembled. "But I'm gonna make it up to you, Ruthie."

Aura had to walk away, overwhelmed with sympathy.

"*Aaaaagghh!* Wait till you see what I got in mind, Ruthie!" Nico fell to his side, hugging himself. "It'll be all right, Babydoll," he murmured. "You'll see."

Pipsqueak, Jiggy and Aura waited in silence for ten, fifteen minutes, no coughing or throat-clearing, no shifting of feet, no scratching of ears or rubbing of eyes, until Nico had finished.

Nico rose and dusted himself off, accepting a proffered bandana to wipe his eyes and nose. He tossed it to the side, took a deep breath and said, "Get the shovels."

* * * *

Deep in trance, Matilda danced and muttered to Pan. She waved her athame at the monstrous pumpkin before which she cavorted in Ned Winchell's pasture just a dozen yards from her barn, across a barbed wire fence laced with scrubby vine.

This particular super squash, nearly ready for harvest and transport to the Thanksgiving Festival in Buncombe County, had reached more than six feet in circumference.

The festival was a long-standing attempt by the Buncombe folk to compete with Cronus County's Pumpkin Parade, and with the status of the parade unsettled at this late hour, the Buncombe planners hoped to accomplish exactly that. Regardless, the pumpkin promised a nice payday for both Matilda and Winchell. He had promised to give her half the grand prize if she produced a winner—ten thousand dollars.

Growing massive pumpkins was serious business for Winchell. He had an endorsement deal with a seed distributor and regularly contributed articles with growing tips to agriculture journals. He had won growing contests around the south, but as his fame grew so had his competition. He needed an edge.

When he approached Matilda with his proposition, she never hesitated. She'd done far worse than rigging pumpkin contests after all, and five grand could go far for a witch trying to lead a simple life. If only the other entrants and the agriculture journals and the seed folk knew about Farmer Winchell's *real* secret, known only to Winchell, Matilda and her good old black magic.

Well…black*ish*.

The prize pumpkin itself was grown from a seed that Stella and Winchell had selected from a jar, which Winchell had filled with the plumpest spores he could find in the guts of previous winners. The two of them spread out the seeds and examined them the way they would rare coins or stamps, on a black cloth, under a bare one-hundred-watt bulb. Winchell, armed with a magnifying glass and a spritzer, gingerly aligned his tiny ovoid troops. Matilda peered into the heart of each one, rocking as she whispered to Pan (Winchell did not ask) until she felt the right vibrations rising to meet her hovering palm.

Matilda put her pinky finger on The One and slid it to the side. "There."

Winchell nodded solemnly, convinced by her confidence. She placed it on a square of linen she had already blessed, then held it to her heart as he drove her around in his F-150. Despite being a work vehicle, it was kept showroom immaculate, as were Winchell's fields, equipment and home.

Spotting her own barn near the fence, she pointed to a spot as much out of convenience as divine guidance, which could sometimes be the same thing after all.

The pumpkin had become a child to her, like her goats. She tended it every day and caressed its leaves and fattening girth, chasing away beetles with a mere whispered threat.

That had been mid-August.

Now, immersed in the flow of pure intention, she did not hear the Jeep driving up until after the goats had reacted by perking their heads up high and flicking their ears at the distant rumble. Whoever was driving—likely the one called Pipsqueak—treated the vehicle like it was disposable, attacking more than negotiating the rutted driveway to her two-story ranch house. Nugent burst from its cheap speakers.

"Dammit!" She scrambled to the fence line and climbed through, grateful for the line of scrubby growth of blackberry bushes that blocked view of the giant pumpkin, and the hulk of her big barn that hid her panicked clambering. "Make us *move*, Great Pan!"

The bikers likely had no interest in mundane agricultural projects, but their impulsive nature—something any follower of the impetuous Pan knew to expect—had her on guard nonetheless.

She stuffed the athame in the pocket of her long gray sweater and held the barbed wire apart for Argyle and Amos, for if she were to gain eight or so feet on them, the goats would go apoplectic, bleating like infants and likely shredding themselves to ribbons to get to her.

She waved as the Jeep parked, recognizing its occupants by their energy. There was a *new* feel though—one that deepened her unease.

Pipsqueak stepped from the driver side, essaying a broad wave that somehow carried the same sarcasm as his speech and gait.

The new one lit a cigarette with a shiny zippo as he came around from the passenger side. Leather vest over taut tattooed muscles, flowing brown beard and hair—he didn't come off that different from any other biker. But Matilda knew that even for bikers, the Fireheads were hardly average. She knew *exactly* who this newcomer was, in fact.

"Yo, Tilda May!" called Pipsqueak, spreading his arms like some denim-jacketed smart-ass Christ. "I brought somebody to meetcha!"

The gang had already set the table, making the newcomer sound like a rock star or Hollywood actor. Matilda pulled her sweater closed around her neck, as the man named Nico Rizzoli regarded her through cigarette haze and mirrored sunglasses.

"Chief, this is our new old pal Matilda, wicked witch of the south!"

Matilda hated that Pipsqueak's smarmy description of her was so true.

"I'm Nico," said the gang leader, with an expulsion of fragrant tobacco. "Thanks for all your good work."

Matilda acknowledged to herself that nothing she did for these people would ever be considered "good," but it was too late. She had done their bidding. Yet seeing and *feeling* Nico Rizzoli in the flesh, was like seeing the torn bodies in his wake.

Despite his outward icy demeanor, this was undoubtedly a man of fierce passions, violence chief among them.

She greeted him, trying to stand still against the goats jostling against her from behind, begging for shelter from the two-legged predators.

"Hey li'l fellas!" called Aura, squatting and extending her hand to the recoiling goats.

Jiggy, apparently the designated lookout, stood near the jeep and kept constant watch of the grounds and treeline.

"Got a little bonus for you," said Rizzoli, as he extracted an inch-thick slab of cash from his inner vest pocket. He riffled the paper brick and handed it to her, showing clenched teeth in a way that could almost be a smile.

Matilda took it, faster than she was proud of, her eyes wider than she wished. "Well...thank you." At least she was able to keep the excitement out of her voice. Argyle stuck her head around long enough to snuffle at the cash, while Amos nibbled her calf muscle, scolding.

"So," Nico segued, surveying her property, "we still need you. And we have plenty to pay."

Matilda swatted at her familiars, the proverbial shoulder angels, her need and greed muscling past atrophied morality. "What do you need?"

Nico, entranced with the rural beauty and lulling bugsong from which he had been walled away for so long, left Pipsqueak to take over.

"To start with, wolf hides and ointment for everybody you see here," said the mutton-chopped marauder. "Plus two."

* * * *

Candace rolled a ball to Emera—the cheap, simple inflated kind from a tall basket in some department store. The little one giggled and collapsed on it to roll around in the grass and leaves like an armadillo, then rolled it back. Candace loved the music of her laughter.

The other kids played stickball or lobbed pinecones at one another, breaking into their usual cliques. As always, the fun was draining away by increments as troubled young egos fought to rise.

The rising roar of two Harleys bulled between their exchanges and brought a halt to their games. The children stood and watched the neighborhood entrance, waiting to see if the bikes would pass close—all except for Emera. As she squealed and covered her ears Candace calmed her with hugs and pats.

The bikes appeared, raising awed leaps and head turns, especially from Radley. One of the riders wore a helmet fitted with a menacing curved horn just like a real live jungle animal, which it was—a relic from one of the last of the dying species. Rhino had gotten it from a black marketer as a bonus in a gun purchase.

Fireheads Rhino and Hobie parked in front of the yard's chain link fence gate, revved a few times—which made Emera tremble—and shut off their engines. Radley bolted inside to summon the Dietrichs.

When the helmets came off, Rhino's chrome dome and heavy facial hair had the children murmuring, backing away from the fence. He swung his two-hundred-eighty-pound frame off the Harley and walked to the gate, carrying his helmet by its polished horn, his bootsteps on the sidewalk like the footfall of a city-smashing monster to the orphans. Two other kids ran inside.

Candace was not so scared. She held Emera in a relaxed hug, instinctively knowing not to tense.

Rhino left the gate open for Hobie, who remained on his bike, rolling a cigarette. Rhino approached the children, smiling. "Hello there, kiddies!"

"Hi," Rebecca murmured. The cruelest of Candace's housemates was also the bravest with strangers.

"Well, there's just an assload of you little midgets, ain't there?"

"We ain't midgets," Rebecca said, taking a step back.

Rhino knelt on one leg and placed the scary helmet on his knee. "Nah, you sure ain't." He eyed each child. "What, all of ya live here?"

"Yes," Rebecca said. "With Mister and Missus Dietrich."

"We got the right place, Hobe!" Rhino called.

Hobie, nearly as big as Rhino, was like a Viking with his long braided blond ponytail and Fu Manchu mustache. He stood astride his Harley, stretched and lit a cigarette.

Rhino's gaze found Candace and Emera. "Howdy, ladies."

Candace saw the knife handle jutting from his boot. Rhino caught the look and drew the knife. He stood, flipping the weapon over and catching it like he had done countless times—often just before using it—and walked over to Candace.

Emera shrunk away from him but stayed with Candace, as Rhino held it out. "Wanna see it?"

Candace took the knife with no hesitation and regarded her reflection in it.

Hobie shut the gate behind him, hard and loud. "You folks running a daycare here?"

The Dietrichs had come out, and now stood at the bottom of the porch steps. Their faces showed no recognition of the rough-hewn visitors.

"Can I help you?" asked the house mother.

"Hey!" Rhino said, spreading his arms like an old friend expecting a hug. "We're here to help *you!*"

The Dietrichs wore matching looks of veiled alarm.

Hobie walked up to them and exhaled unfiltered smoke well within their personal space. "We run with a fellow name o' Nico. Nico's family is *Family*." Realization and then veiled terror dawned on their faces.

"Nico got word about your debt. Sent us here to help you folks out."

Rhino walked toward the Dietrichs, leaving his knife with Candace. She fought to focus on the uncomfortable situation unfolding but found herself charmed by the shining blade.

"We picked up the bill for ya. Nice, aint we?" Rhino said. "Now you can just pay us! And we won't tack on no more interest." Rhino took a few steps before adding. "*If*...you can take care of this. Right...*now*."

* * * *

Stella always made sure Reverend McGlazer had a hot nutritious dinner every night, rotating between a handful of restaurants. Recalling that Elaine Barcroft had offered to provide a meal anytime, Stella decided to take her up on the offer.

She arrived while Elaine was still cooking, well aware that the widow and mother of troubled sons could use an ear. Elaine always had plenty of worries, but no shortage of good cheer to share.

Stella lamented to Elaine that the adoption services were snubbing McGlazer but didn't mention her desire to adopt the girl herself, or the growing chasm between her and Bernard.

"Poor Candace," Elaine lamented, as she topped off Stella's tea. "She wrote Stuart that Everett is coming back from the dead. It was very strange. Worrying."

"Oh my God." Stella's heart sank with the weight of worry for the girl. More than ever, she felt the urgent need to save her, to do *something*.

"Hudson is planning to finagle some reason to go check on her."

Stella felt like she had failed the girl, that she was selfish for not pursuing the adoption sooner and more tenaciously. She had planned to wait for Stuart to come home—she had a job for him—but she couldn't sit still any longer. Something had to be done about Candace before the girl succumbed to the doom that seemed to follow her throughout her short life.

"I should be getting this food to Abe," was her excuse. "He's probably very hungry by now."

Elaine saw her out, considerate to keep the goodbyes short, sensing that Stella was preoccupied.

En route back to the church, Stella had to keep making herself slow down. She would make sure McGlazer had dinner, and then, home.

There was an argument, surely loud and bitter, to be had with Bernard.

Chapter 9

The Violent Kind

Mr. Dietrich led his wife toward the door. "Let me just talk to them, Miriam. I can work this out."

She pulled away. "No, you can't, Henry."

She went to Hobie. "We don't have it right now. But we will. Soon."

Candace saw Mrs. Dietrich shoot a glance in her direction. Whatever this was about was a big deal all right. The housemother didn't even seem to notice that Candace had the knife.

"Well Miss Lady Woman," Rhino asked. "What makes you so goddamn sure?"

The Dietrichs were silent.

"Let's step around the side of the house, could we?" asked Mr. Dietrich.

"Better idea," Hobie said. "Let's step inside! You can offer us refreshments."

"Okay." The house parents forced smiles to rise beneath their alarmed eyes. "Sure."

Hobie pushed Mr. Dietrich, not terribly hard, but enough to make him pick up the pace.

Rhino essayed a baby wave at Candace and Emera.

* * * *

It was difficult for Matilda to focus on her mental inventory with all the warning voices shouting in her skull. Salivations at the prospect of another fat stack flooded to the fore. "The rub is no problem," she said. "But I think I'm down to four skins."

"*Ha!*" Pipsqueak's quick cackle made her jump. "Foreskins."

"Knock it off, Pip," ordered Nico. "You're making our friend nervous."

Though she couldn't see his eyes through the sunglasses, Matilda felt Nico's gaze on her trembling hands. Sure enough, the fugitive drew *another* stack, though it was smaller by half than the previous. "I dig it. Pelts don't grow on trees. Probably cost you a good bit to get what you got."

"Yes," Matilda said, as she held out her hand.

But Nico did not fill it. "Goods before cash this time."

Matilda turned toward the barn. She didn't start walking, but realized it was too late anyway. In just glancing, she had shown the bikers where she kept her craft stock. She had always known when to expect them before and had their orders ready to go. In the presence of Nico Rizzoli, her poise was melted like a snowball in an atomic blast.

It's not like they wouldn't find it, said her greed, setting her forward. Entwined in dread and regret, she almost fell over the goats as they crowded in front of her.

Argyle and Amos usually loved making the trip to the barn, where Matilda kept treats to occupy them when she worked. *Isn't it telling,* wondered her survival instinct, *that they're so reticent now?*

She twisted the old black key in the rusty padlock and opened the barn's double doors. "Give me a sec."

She entered, leaving the light switch off. But this only raised the curiosity of the gang members, who crowded at the entrance. "Wow!" Aura said. "This is so goddamn *cute!*"

The goats remained outside for once, well clear of the bikers. Matilda went across from the doors to an old unplugged freezer where she stored dry goods, tossing a nervous glance toward a cedar wardrobe at the far wall to her left. On a shelf near it was a sealed clay jar. She had a terrible wish that it was closer—yet the *last* thing she wanted was for the Fireheads to get their hands on it.

Matilda opened the old freezer, took out the hides and draped them over her arm.

The transforming ointment was on a shelf beside the freezer, with other prepared concoctions. She knew where it was; could find it easily without light. But when she reached for it, a pale, demonically grinning face, somehow *familiar*, appeared, its features barely limned in the dimness.

She withdrew her hand, stifling a yelp.

The lights came on, courtesy of Pipsqueak. "You okay back there, Tilly?" There was no real concern in his voice.

"Yes, I just..." There were only the shelves and the sealed clay jars, in all their fifty-watt banality.

She took down two jars, one of which she had engraved with the letters "LUP" using her athame before the clay had hardened, and a second containing the reversing balm. She went to the door, handing Jiggy the hides and Nico the clay jars. He opened one and sniffed. "Smelly stuff." He tossed them to Pipsqueak, who barely caught them, making Matilda wince.

"It's not easy to put that together," she said. "Please don't spill or misuse it." She envisioned the jars falling and breaking, her goats then licking even a *tiny* amount of it—and she shivered.

Nico laughed. "Got it under control."

Matilda switched off the light and dropped the key back in her pocket beside her athame. She decided it would be best to keep her hand in that pocket for now, as she tried to goad the bikers out of the barn.

Aura flipped the light back on and stepped further in, giggling like a little girl as she beheld the roots and stems hanging from the rafters, the open shelves lined with green and black and orange liquids, the vials of powder and mineral.

Amos bleated complaint from a few feet beyond the door. "Come in here, little goatie!" Aura called to him, and Matilda hoped he wouldn't, ever. Matilda stepped just outside the double doors and cleared her throat. The goats came and crowded her legs like snakes seeking heat. They would not cross the threshold.

Nico raised his face to the sun and inhaled another deep breath of free man's air. "Say." He took out the cash again but didn't immediately hand it over. "There's one more thing, and I'm guessing it's a pretty goddamn big deal." He withdrew yet *another* block of green, and pressed it into the other, the bills between his hands in prayer pose against the blasphemous tattoo on his chest.

Matilda had no choice but to hear him out, while trying to keep an eye on Aura's wanderings.

"My girl. You may have heard of her." Nico stuffed the cash into his front jeans pocket, so its top half could flop around in full sight. "Ruth Treadwell." He lit a cigarette and patted the tattoo on his chest, then placed hand on heart. "Ruthie."

Matilda's spine went cold. "Ragdoll Ruth." She took a step back from him.

Pipsqueak raised a hand of warning. "He hasn't decided whether he digs that particular nickname or not."

"Wh…what about her?" Matilda asked.

"Just kicking some ideas around," Nico began. "Does the skinwalker spell work on corpses?"

Matilda grabbed the bustling goats by an ear in each hand to steady them. "What are you asking?"

"I just had this idea," Nico knelt to pet Amos, making the kid tug and squirm that much more vigorously. "Maybe I could throw somebody's skin over poor Ruth's bones," he motioned toward the van, and Matilda realized with a nauseous spasm that the killer zealot's remains were in there. "And bring her back."

* * * *

Rhino closed the front door behind as Hobie roughly nudged the Dietrichs through the family room, past the hallway and into the kitchen. "We don't want the kiddies seein'," explained Hobie. "'Case there's an accident or something," Mr. Dietrich wore the countenance that Hobie loved seeing in debtors and victims, the one of pure dread.

Rhino stood at the door into the kitchen, while Hobie hovered near the rear kitchen door that opened outside. "Prih-tee nice digs you got here," Hobie said. "Must take a lot of work keeping it up what with all those kids."

"We're stretched to our limits," said Mrs. Dietrich. "Between the children, and—"

"So, y'all get a check from the guv," said Hobie, reaching into the refrigerator and helping himself to a beer. "Rhino?"

"I'll take one o' them juice boxes," he answered. "Grape, please."

Hobie tossed it and Rhino caught it in his helmet.

"The check barely covers our basic needs!" Mrs. Dietrich explained. "It's like pulling teeth to get—"

"Pulling teeth," Hobie interrupted. "Ouch."

"I guess somebody needs to get a goddamn job," noted Rhino.

"We both work overtime, every week," said Mr. Dietrich.

"That ain't what I mean," Rhino elaborated after a long pull from his juice box. Hobie grabbed Mrs. Dietrich and pushed her up against the counter. Her cry was muzzled by Hobie's big gloved hand.

Mr. Dietrich reflexively moved to help her and found himself breathless and pained. He collapsed, his face inches from Rhino's scuffed boot.

"Nico ain't gonna like hearing you blew us off," Hobie said evenly. Then he ripped Mrs. Dietrich's top, exposing her bra. Her squeal stopped at his iron hand.

Mr. Dietrich tried, despite his pain, to stand. Rhino kick-shoved him onto his back against the counters.

"He'll wanna know we got at least *something* outta you goddamn moochers." Hobie's face was almost against Mrs. Dietrich's.

"Don't hurt her!" Henry Dietrich's plea came out like a mere whisper; the air needed for speech unavailable.

Rhino put his size thirteen on Mr. Dietrich's chest. "Why not?"

Mr. Dietrich pointed at his throat. Rhino hefted him and walked him to the sink, shoving his head under the spigot. "It ain't oxygen, but it'll help."

Hobie ran his finger down between Mrs. Dietrich's breasts and tugged at her waistband.

Rhino pulled Henry Dietrich away from the spigot.

"We have a plan," Henry puffed. "It's gonna make us *rich*. And we're gonna pay everything off." He looked at Hobie and then his wife. "*Double* if you like."

"That sounds like one hell of a plan," Rhino said.

"Some real Frank Sinatra-Ocean's Eleven type shit, I'd say," Hobie contributed through gritted teeth.

"No, *really!*" Dietrich gulped and sputtered. "It's foolproof. I *promise.*"

Both Fireheads chuckled. "Promise, do ya? How 'bout a pinkie swear?"

Dietrich held up a hand. "One of these kids…is our ticket."

"Ticket to what?"

"Book deal, TV, everything."

"You got the next goddamn Hannah Montana here?"

"Better. She's the sister of that slasher from the parade disaster over in Ember Hollow last year."

Hobie released Mrs. Dietrich and turned to Rhino. "Keep talking."

"Everett Geelens's sister. That's her out there with the littlest."

"I'll be a sumbitch," said Rhino. "How do you figure to cash in?"

Mr. Dietrich checked around to make sure none of the kids had found a way in. "She's crazy like her brother," he said in a low tone, "She's gonna…*break* at some point. And we're helping her along, you could say."

Rhino and Hobie laughed, long and hearty. "*Damn,* brother! You are one sick son of a bitch! How long?"

Mr. Dietrich went to Mrs. Dietrich and held her, wiping her tears. "Not long! She's already had a dangerous episode."

"You get three days to make her pull some kinda serious goddamn Lizzy Borden-level action." Rhino said. "And it better be splattered all over every newspaper and TV station from here to goddamn Timbuk-the-hell-tu."

"What!? We can't—"

"We ain't sticking around forever, boy," said Hobie. "Get it done." He yanked Mrs. Dietrich away from her husband roughly. "Or *she* gets done."

He shoved her back to him and followed Rhino back to the front door.

* * * *

Nico rose, giving up on trying to make friends with Matilda's skittish goats, and perhaps on any niceties.

"I mean, in all those books you sent, I ain't seen nothing says it can't be done."

Matilda was speechless. She released the goats in her distraction, and they pranced a few steps from her, whining their unease in eerily human patterns.

"You want to…to *skin* someone, and…then…"

"Some kind soul would donate their birthday suit, see." said Nico nonchalantly. "Then she'd come back, inside of said suit."

Matilda regarded each Firehead. "Such a thing…there would be no redemption for *any* of us," she whispered. "*Ever.*"

"But it *can* be done." Pipsqueak came and put his arm around her shoulders, like a condescending brother who didn't really love her. "Right, Tilly?"

"I…" she waved her hands across each other. "I can't do that. It's…" she met Pipsqueak's contemptuous gaze with utter sincerity, even though she knew she was about to lie. "No. It's not even possible."

Nico beheld all the fields surrounding Matilda's farm. He blew a slow stream of smoke. "I read a lot, back in lockup," he said. "Lot of books, lot of faces."

Giggling as though giddy with anticipation, Aura ran at the two goats yet again, just to watch them scatter.

"The books told me magic is damn near limitless, long as you're willing to pay the price," Nico continued. "The faces, they told me that *lies* are a kind of magic. Did you know that?"

Smiling, Pipsqueak maintained his faux-friendly side hug, as Nico finished. "But a stronger magic is *fear.*"

Giving up on the goats, Aura twisted a batch of thistle hanging from the barn's crossbeam and let it spin back the other way.

"I'm willing to pay the price. And I'm willing to pay it to you." Nico's calm and even tone felt like a knife to her throat.

Knife—she fingered the athame in her pocket.

"But if you won't accept, then *you* can pay the price." He faced away from her. "Ain't it weird how that works, Jiggy?"

"Weird, man." The fourth of the bikers had followed at a distance and now stood a few yards from the barn doors, watching her.

"Now, I've been good to you." Nico motioned his cigarette at her sweater pocket, the cash there. "Hell, I already talked you up around the pen; sent you some business, probably. And all I want is to bring back my baby. Is that really so goddamn evil?" he asked.

"It's not just about you or...*any* of us." Matilda felt like her voice was coming through a tiny radio speaker. "It's about consequences that could last...*forever.*"

Nico laughed, and then everybody else did too. "Told you, lady. That's on me."

"It's *not!*" Matilda made herself loud and clear this time. "You *don't know* what you're asking!"

Nico blew a breath through gritted teeth and drew the Luger from the back of his waistband. As he brought it to her head. Pipsqueak released his embrace and side-stepped away quickly.

"I'm betting you *will,*" Nico said, still utterly calm.

Matilda realized that the path she had chosen, the dark gray path, was nearing its end, and she would soon pay her penance. She wasn't ready for that, but magic *this* black...it was for the remorseless, the *amoral* practitioner. "Please, you need to study more, to learn what magic truly is."

"It is what I *say* it is." Nico thumbed back the hammer. "Now. You gonna do it?"

"Okay!" Matilda said, tears welling.

"Hell, that wasn't so ha—"

Matilda drew the athame as she spun fast, lunging at Jiggy in the same move.

"Whoa Nelly!" Pipsqueak cried, as Jiggy leaned back, almost casually, and caught Matilda's arcing wrist. He crushed it in his big mitt till she dropped the blade. He pulled her toward him with a grunt, then shoved her on her ass. The goats cried out.

Matilda rose quickly and ran toward her house, knowing she wouldn't make it far.

Her best hope was to die as close to her home as possible.

She was struck hard in the back, driven to the ground. In the same instant came the cracking report of Nico's Luger.

An insidious sensation, somewhere between hot and numb, blossomed in her midsection. She smelled earth, grass and gunpowder, soon overpowered by the taste of blood. She thought of her life, her embrace of the craft's easy way, of how she'd seen others on her path fall into massive pits of karma, far earlier in life than her.

Barely even aware of it, she silently uttered an ancient Tibetan verse, unlocked from her subconscious by trauma.

She thought of her goods in the barn, hoping these highway hoodlums would never possess the knowledge and training to make use of them.

She thought of her goats and hoped they had gone to hide somewhere safe and warm until someone could come along and take care of them. Mr. Winchell, perhaps. Then she despaired, as wet noses snuffled frantically against her face.

"Go!" she croaked weakly. "*Ssskit!*" But they only trotted a few feet before stopping to bleat at her, confused. She could not muster the strength to truly startle them.

Matilda closed her eyes and pushed herself up to her knees. She raised her arms high like lightning rods, ready to receive her penalty from the universe. "Kill me. Quickly, please," said her outer voice, while the inner repeated the archaic chant.

Nico and Pipsqueak, now standing on either side of her, burst out laughing.

"Jesus *H*," said Nico. "I thought my Ruthie was a drama queen."

Nico kicked Matilda in the back, smashing her face-first into yellow leaves and brown grass. Consciousness grew fickle, threatened to leave.

The goats came to her again, terror in their calls; then, one of them became shrill and panicked, rising away from her.

"Gotcha!"

No...

"Quick hands, Pip," praised Nico. "Hold onto it."

Matilda rose, only a few inches. "Leave my goats *alone!*" She only wished she had been *more* devoted to the Darkness; enough to call up a rescuing—*avenging!*—demon with a mere venomous syllable.

"Wait!" called Aura. "*I* wanna finish the bitch!"

"Whatever," said Nico. "I ain't wasting no more goddamn bullets on her." He squatted and yanked Matilda's hair, pulling her close to him to show Matilda her own battered face in his mirror lenses; the blood running from the corners of her quivering mouth.

"But I'm done with this here cig," he said, taking the cigarette from his mouth and holding it straight up. He slowly inched it toward her face. The giggling Aura held her hands together in gleeful anticipation, beaming as Nico pushed the ember into Matilda's forehead and ground it. Matilda didn't scream at the searing dot of pain, only because she was too drained.

Pipsqueak and Aura laughed, then Jiggy knelt beside her. "Hey don't forget this!" He showed her the athame just before he poked her cheek with it, just deep enough to draw blood and a squeal.

Sniggering, he jabbed her a few more times.

"Let *me!*" said Aura, motioning for the knife with eager fingers. She tittered like a stoned college girl as she took the athame. "We'll take good care of your little baby goat," mocked the girl. "Tender and *juicy* care." She sunk the blade into Matilda's upper back.

Matilda felt blood draining from the gunshot wound by the ounce. She wanted to let go—but cruel despair for her goats kept her alive.

Aura crouched on all fours to watch the life draining from the witch's face, cocking her head to the side like a curious puppy.

Matilda touched her hand; a slight gesture that Aura initially thought was a weak beseeching. As Matilda withdrew, Aura frowned. It hadn't been that at all.

"Looks like we got ourselves some new digs," Nico said to everyone. "Aura, round up that other billy and let's settle in. Pip, toss this witch bitch in the ditch." He allowed for laughter from his crew. "Better yet, lock her in her gingerbread house. Don't need no coyotes or vultures giving us away. Jig, head back to camp and get the others."

Matilda went black with the image of Aura's confused frown fading in her head. But now she was free of any compassion, and in her last seconds of lucidity, she roared vengeance in her head, infusing it into the inner chant.

* * * *

Rebecca and Radley had snuck to the door to listen. Now they scattered like mice as Hobie and Rhino lumbered out, their faces even harder than before.

Candace had stayed with Emera, holding the knife behind her back. Was she hiding it? There was no way to know if the Dietrichs, in their duress, had registered seeing it, but the motorcycle man would remember.

She was hiding it from herself. From someone inside her.

Rhino walked to her and leaned down, smiling. "Wish I could let you keep it, little lady." He seemed both sincere and threatening. "But it's my good luck charm."

He extended his hand. Candace knew without doubt that she could—and *should*—stab the big man right then and there, and probably save everybody a lot of misery.

But she didn't. She put it in his hand. He flipped it caught it, winked at her and re-sheathed it in his boot. "I bet you can find another one."

It was a few minutes before the Dietrichs came out, seeming twenty years older since the arrival of the leather-and-denim-clad visitors. Mr. Dietrich clapped and issued a weak whistle, ordering the children in a wavering voice to come in for dinner.

Chapter 10

The Hidden

"Three…two…*one!*" Stuart and DeShaun braked, sliding their bikes to a simultaneous stop, a feat they both found endlessly satisfying.

Walking into Home Stock, both drew from their jeans pockets shopping lists from their mothers. These mid-week grocery trips had become a ritual when Dennis had started drinking again back around February and could no longer be counted on to take them for a more comprehensive weekend shopping trip.

"Gates be *opened!*" Stuart pronounced, pretending the automatic doors responded to his magical command and horn-fingered gesture.

"Corny," DeShaun said, taking a shopping basket from the stack.

"I'll get two milks and meet you at the comics rack."

"Right. I got the lunch meats."

"Boys!" It was Miss Stella from the church, pushing a cart loaded with communion supplies: grape juice and matzo crackers.

"Glad I caught you!" She was breathless and haggard; not the poised lady of whom they often found themselves thinking mildly improper thoughts.

"What can we do for you, Miss Stella?"

"I remember you doing grave rubbings on"—she seemed reticent to say the name—"the town founder."

"Yeah, we did a whole unit."

"How would you feel about digging a little deeper into all that?"

DeShaun raised an eyebrow. Stuart frowned.

"I know," she acknowledged. "Who wants extra school work? Thing is, it's really important. And I'll pay you."

"Jeez, really?" DeShaun said. "What's the big deal, if you don't mind me asking?"

"That would take a while. I understand there are some materials at the library." She opened her purse and took out her wallet. "Anything at all you can find on the church, the cemetery..."

"We'll do it for free," Stuart offered. "It'll give me an excuse to go there and check on something anyways."

"One other thing," she lowered her voice. "Please don't mention it around too much. Just for now."

They agreed, and when she thanked them and moved on, DeShaun frowned at Stuart. "What if we're getting ourselves into some crazy soap opera type stuff?"

"When are we *not?*"

* * * *

"Leave that boy *alone!*" McGlazer screamed.

But the scream was only a thought, no matter how hard McGlazer focused it.

In a comfortable corner of his mind, McGlazer had languished in his office with the memory of his highest highs; that tenuous Moment when the alcohol made his head and heart and hands feel good and strong. He graciously *accepted* this buzz, for however long it would last. It wouldn't be long.

He had relished the Moment and even, strangely, prayed gratitude for it. The problem was, the Moment had one drawback, and this was that a shred of his sense of decency lingered outside the party to keep him in check. The Moment could not wander beyond it.

As he unwillingly walked up the hill he slowly, silently, even painfully dropped to his knees to halt, again and again—but only within his head. The possessor used McGlazer's legs to make his way toward the mourner, stretching McGlazer's mouth into a painfully broad crescent.

"Get away, Dennis!" McGlazer projected. *"Run!"*

"Your resistance will cost ye, Reverend Man." The voice was getting clearer as the presence settled into the nooks of McGlazer's mind. "If you won't sit in your cell and take your poison, a visit from the harridan will set ye right."

Then, McGlazer found himself in his office, tugging at the door knob—just before the door smashed in on him as if bashed with a battering ram manned by a dozen templars. He found himself lying on the ground in searing pain, blood filling his vision.

In the doorway was Ragdoll Ruth, her thick pancake makeup splotched and cracked, a giant pistol in her hand. She fingered the cross necklace on her bosom until it glowed with supernatural light. She rose into the air and came down astraddle his groin with a smashing, *raping* impact. "You are a weak and worthless failure! God *hates* you, you wretched liar! He rejects you!"

She lowered her razor-filled mouth toward his face and screeched her demented echoing condemnations. "I will rejoice to behold your hellfire-ravaged body for all of eternity!" She smashed the butt of the massive handgun against his skull, over and over, battering to nothing his efforts at fighting the invader's will.

With each fresh burst of pain, McGlazer felt his will, his righteousness crumble, the spaces filled by the need to drink.

Just as abruptly as she had entered—just like magick—the zealot stood and left, politely easing the restored office door closed behind her.

McGlazer peered up at his desk, knowing what he would see there, and glad for it. He *would* free himself, and he would undo any damage done to those outside. He *would,* damn it all!

But first, he needed to gather his strength, nurse his pain, calm his nerves.

He struggled to a stand, propped himself up comfortably at his desk and lifted the squat glass of amber fluid waiting there beside a fat bottle of the same.

"Which do you prefer?" asked the powerful voice in its archaic accent.

McGlazer pressed his mind's eyelids shut, knowing he could not ever truly hide from the unholy acts in which he was complicit.

* * * *

"Bet you'd be real proud of your biggest boy right now, old man," Dennis slurred, extending his bottle of Diamante toward the gravestone that bore his father's name, as if to offer a swig.

"Of course, I can't exactly bitch and moan, like you're telling me to grow up and get a real job." Dennis set the bottle down in front of the stone, mocking something but not really knowing or caring what. "You were always a real sitcom dad, werentcha, Pop?"

Dennis had not been to the cemetery in many months; not since just after his last visit with his sponsor, Reverend McGlazer, for some good hard heart-to-heart, and mediocre coffee.

"And yet, here I am; this pretend punk rocker, whose only gripe is that his ever-lovin' daddy bought him a car and a guitar, then buzzed off to the Great Beyond."

Dennis laughed and fell back to watch the sky swim.

The Chalk Outlines had been well on their way to a decent level of success a year ago. Record company suit Cordelia Cantor—rest her soul—had come to see them play their set atop the Grand Illusion Cinemas; the centerpiece of the Pumpkin Parade.

Everything was peaches. They were on the money with every sick note. Then the whole crowd had gone violently apeshit, not because of the devil's music they played, but thanks to that demented bitch Ragdoll Ruth and her pocketful of poison potion.

One flying bottle to the head later, and Dennis was taking the most hellacious stagedive this side of Eddie Vedder. So much for that Big Break.

"Ma hid my keys, by the by," he told his father's grave. "Didn't know I had an extra set hidden. I just wanted you to know she's trying, bless her soul."

He sat up and took the bottle. "Oh yeah. I keep forgetting. Souls are not a real thing. You'd know that better than anybody though, huh?"

Dennis downed a few ounces and hissed though the burn. "Except there is…just *one* thing that I…just can't seem to slap together, Dad."

He considered his next sentence carefully, as if he *believed* he was speaking to a reasoning sentient being. "See, our town founder," Dennis pointed the bottle at Bennington's towering memorial obelisk some sixty yards away, "*he* managed to put in an appearance last year, or so say a handful of witnesses—including Stewie."

"I gotta ask myself, ya know?" Dennis leaned way forward, like an interrogating detective. "Why can *that* long-dead dude pop up to do his thing, and yet…you're a no show. Can you help me out on that?"

The stone marker could not.

"Didn't think so." Dennis stood. "Well, I'm off to drink and drive, so, might see you soon anyway. Except…I won't. Right?"

Dennis stumbled away. "Right."

"Hello Dennis," came McGlazer's voice, from just to his right.

Dennis spun so fast, his head pounded like Jill's most brutal drum beat.

McGlazer wore an unsettling smile, like an exaggerated mask of himself. "Indulging in a bit of necromancy?"

It was unlike McGlazer to be so flip. Dennis wondered if he was hallucinating the minister.

The silence between them was as heavy as the surrounding stones, until McGlazer spoke again. "I haven't seen you in quite a while."

"Yeah." Dennis produced a pack of cigarettes, offering one to McGlazer, who declined. "You were…pretty messed up, last time we talked."

"Oh yes." McGlazer lilted, as if pleasantly reminiscing over his difficult healing process. "I suffered."

Dennis tilted his head. "What's with the brogue?"

"Brogue?"

"Nevermind." Dennis raised the bottle. "Not gonna insult you by offering you some of this."

"How considerate."

Another awkward staredown.

"I'm not ready to pray this away right now," Dennis said. "This drunk. This…*hate.*"

"I suspect not." Still, the Cheshire Cat smirk. "Well then. Don't let me spoil your plans."

Dennis didn't bother with a goodbye. The honest part of him would have said it was a little hurtful, not being rebuked or counseled by McGlazer—his *sponsor*, for Christ's sake.

Nothing a fresh bottle of Diamante couldn't wash away, though.

* * * *

Mrs. Dietrich paced in the hallway, chewing her left pinky nail while Mr. Dietrich, hands jittering and twitching like a rabbit's nose, prepared two family-sized microwave lasagna dinners. As the meals cooked, he poured himself a tall glass of tea, though he never cared for his wife's too-sweet mix, and carried it around with him. The constant faint clinking of the cubes further gave away his nervous state.

He set the big disposable dish on the counter to cool and—goodness! clumsy fellow—dropped his glass.

He leaned toward the dinner tables with his darting eyes and lips stretched weirdly across his teeth. "Candace, would you please sweep that up for me?"

It was odd how quickly he had chosen her, and odder still that he made a point of facing away from her, yet strained to watch over his shoulder as she whisked the sharp pieces into the dustpan, then the trash can.

After doling out the lasagna, Dietrich took the lid off the trashcan and pretended to rearrange the contents to make room for the meal cartons. But Candace knew he was inspecting the shards she had deposited. Dinner was served. Seeming to have shaken off her nervous immobility, Mrs. Dietrich distributed the plates. She usually served the youngest first, but tonight saved Candace and Emera for last, setting plates with much smaller portions before them.

The servings were too small to satisfy, barely three or so bites. "You young ladies have made things difficult for everyone around here," she said coldly, petting Radley's shoulder for added effect. He seemed as puzzled as anyone by this. "You can make do with less and go directly to bed after dinner for the next few weeks."

Mr. Dietrich supportively came to stand beside his wife, essaying a resolute frown.

It all seemed forced, artificial, awkwardly *theatrical.* Even Emera was more baffled than upset. The children finished their meals in silence, as the Dietrichs went off to their bedroom to trade urgent whispers.

* * * *

Wearing a scarf and hat taken from Matilda's bedroom closet, Aura chased Amos around the house. The goat cried out in terror and confusion as he slid about on his hooves, giving Aura frequent excuses to fall across Nico on the old velveteen-covered couch in the living room.

He ignored her, focused on the thick old book the witch had compiled over her lifetime. It was written in a hodgepodge of languages ranging from Old English to Latin to Druidic runes, to elaborate scripts he didn't recognize.

"Anything good in there, babe?" asked Aura, as she plopped down beside him.

"Plenty. Pips'll have to make another trip or two to the library."

Pipsqueak, thanks to study discipline he'd gained in college, was adept at gathering information, such as the location of Ruth's grave.

While Nico was in prison it had been Pipsqueak who'd tracked down and sent him the first few books on witchcraft, and then located Matilda, the most famous witch of any branch in several counties. Pip had paid her well for the wolf transformation spell and supplies, and to influence Nico's transfer, then planned the assault on the bus for months.

Now, with Matilda's books and gear in hand, Nico reasoned he was better off having eliminated the middle man, so to speak, and doing what had to be done himself—including the resurrection of Ragdoll Ruth. There would be a learning curve, but that was how Nico always played it. Learning to ride, hitting a gas station, forming a gang—all done on the fly, just the way he liked it.

"Yessir," Nico said, turning a heavy brown page. "I'd say we hit the goddamn motherlode."

"They're back!" Aura announced. Her senses still heightened after her transformation, she heard Hobie and Rhino's bikes several miles away.

Chapter 11

What Lies Beneath

Jill was glad she showed up early for work. She would need a while to finish up her crying fit and reapply makeup.

On the way, some kids in a ragtop Monza Spyder had pulled up beside her Indian and called to her using her stage name. "Thrill Kill Jill!" they chanted, the kid in the back mimicking a drum solo. She gave a friendly wave.

Parked behind the library, she quickly doffed the helmet and let it out; the tears, the snot, the sounds of an aching heart.

Dressed borderline normie these days, with her hair dyed back to something approaching its natural strawberry blonde, she wasn't recognized as often as she once had been, but for fans, the Indian was always a giveaway, not to mention her custom helmet with the curvy corpse chalk-outline on both sides.

With her tough bitch persona essentially gone dormant, Jill was a regular girl again, with all that entailed. Mrs. Washburn had been happy to give her a job at the library. She was there enough anyway, being a bookworm. Once the head librarian saw Jill was not only settling down, but was very much in need of distraction in the wake of leaving both the band and her boyfriend, it had been a done deal.

But now she bordered on being late—again. Which she reasoned was marginally better than coming off like some overwrought TV evangelist drama queen mid-tithings pitch. Again.

"Better get it together, girl," she told herself, and wiped her eyelashes again, deciding to forego makeup till she could take a break. She locked up the Indian and carried herself in, hoping for a numbingly busy shift.

Jill entered the library with her head down exactly at shift start time. She clocked in and went directly to the re-shelf cart, trying to avoid contact with customers and co-workers as long as possible.

Turning into the YA section, she spotted two familiar figures huddled together over a Neil Gaiman graphic novel. The nearest bore a profile that sent her heart into a tailspin.

"Stuart?"

The boy looked up, then he and DeShaun rose, regarding Jill with pity and discomfort. "H...hiya Jill," Stuart said. DeShaun gave a tentative wave.

Jill smiled, triggering her own tears.

"Aw jeez. I'm sorry," Stuart said. DeShaun scratched a non-existent itch on the back of his head.

"No, no. It's not your fault, babe." Jill had a little flapper style chain purse, studded with the legend "Dead Girl" in rhinestones. She had started wearing it everywhere because it was perfect for carrying the tissues she needed so often these days. Now, for instance. She opened it—and cursed its emptiness.

"Hey, I'll go get some tissues." DeShaun eased past her.

"Thank you, sweetie," called Jill with a wavering voice.

Stuart put his hand on her shoulder, and she pulled him into a hug.

"Really sorry. I didn't mean to come in and get you all upset," said Stuart. "It's just, we got a project..."

"Oh stop," Jill said. "If it wasn't you, it'd be something else."

"I hope you're gonna be okay."

Jill took a step back. "You know I'm gonna ask."

"Dennis is...not any better. Ma's really worried."

"God *dammit*." Jill wiped her eyes with her hands. "Does he just not *care?*"

Stuart found himself once again in the position of explaining and covering for his older brother. "I know he cares. He just doesn't handle stuff all that well sometimes."

They glanced toward the ends of the aisle to be sure no one was eavesdropping on their family business.

"I know how much you loved helping with the band," Jill said. "I'm sorry I broke us up."

"It's okay." Stuart didn't know what else to say; how to keep her from feeling guilty about protecting herself without feeling like he was betraying his brother.

"Listen, I better get to work."

"Yeah..."

"Oh... You guys need help with something?"

"Well, yeah. Stuff on the town founders."

"Yeah." Jill narrowed her gaze as she recalled something, making an irresistible quizzical expression. Stuart wondered how his big brother could ever choose a bottle over that face, that soul.

"Didn't you guys cover that last year?"

"It's not for school." He peeked around the corner and found DeShaun standing a few feet away from the aisle, sheepishly holding a handful of tissues. "Come on dude," Stuart called. "She's gonna help us."

DeShaun came to them and sheepishly handed Jill the tissues. "We're supposed to keep it shushed. Something weird going on."

"Weird?" she asked.

"We can't say too much."

"Sure, no prob."

She parked the returns cart by a seasonal spinner filled with children's Halloween books, then led the boys across the library. Stuart caught sight of a man entering—someone he didn't know but felt he should; someone who might show up at a Chalk Outlines show.

Carrying a road-scarred helmet, his tanned face adorned with bushy mutton chops, the guy was clearly a biker.

"Wait here." Jill went behind the employee counter and worked her way through a maze of desks, carts, shelves and Halloween display projects.

Stuart shared a look with Deshaun that said *this is all too heavy.*

"Screw this grown-up garbage," DeShaun said. "Let's just stay little kids."

Stuart was more relieved to hear his friend make this wisecrack than he could express. It wiped away, for a few minutes maybe, his insecurities about being small, about having a messed-up family, about wetting the bed.

Jill returned, looking mischievous, with a pair of keys cupped in her hand.

"C'mon," she whispered. Some rule was about to be broken.

On the way back to a closed door beyond the reference stacks, she bent over to put back some fallen paperbacks at the foot of a spinner. Barely a second had passed before she heard, "*Woooo* mercy! I'd like to check *that* out overnight, pretty please!"

Jill rose angrily, eager to take her frustrations out on some deserving douchebag. "What the hell did you just say?"

Pipsqueak raised his hands in mock surrender. "Easy, little lady." He reached past her to take a book of crossword puzzles from just behind her on the spinner. "I was talking about this here puzzle book. My pals and I could use something to do around the ol' campfire."

Jill was off her bitch game, unsure how harshly to respond to the smarmy highway hood.

He pretended to find genuine interest in the pages. "Say," he began, eyeing her lithe form with no subtlety. "Maybe *you'd* like to come play some games. At our camp."

She had seen him in once or twice recently. He hadn't been so fresh then. "Nope."

Undaunted, he extended a fingerless-gloved hand. "My crew calls me Pipsqueak. And we have ourselves some goddamn good times, lemme tell ya."

"Don't give a goddamn."

Pipsqueak laughed, and she shushed him.

"Right. Don't disturb the squares. I got it." He hooked his thumb in his belt loop. "We're up in the hills. Just a handful of us. One other chick. She's cool."

Jill just glared.

"We party like mothers, babe. You're gonna want to see."

"Nope."

Pipsqueak was at a loss for words. But his eye strip routine continued until he found his forked tongue again. "C'mon babe. We ain't gonna make you do nothing you d—"

"Leave her alone," Stuart said, with tombstone eyes.

"Whoa!" mocked Pipsqueak. "Who're these li'l cats? Your dads?"

"I'm her *boyfriend's brother*, douchebag." Stuart's voice cracked here, at this worst possible time.

"Okay, shrimp. I was just being friendly." Pipsqueak gave Jill a wink, then started to walk, but not before fake-jumping at the boys. They fell for it, dropping back a step. With a mocking salute, Pipsqueak walked away.

"Thanks boys," Jill said. "You both okay?"

"Yeah." Stuart took a deep breath. "I didn't know what else to say." He was still stinging from being called "shrimp."

"It's okay. I needed a reason to be angry. Maybe we all did."

Pipsqueak made a detour into the reference section to steal something, then slipped out.

* * * *

"I'll be god damned," Nico said, stroking his beard. "She was right there when my Ruthie got sliced up, huh?"

"Unless that whitebread was lying to us," Hobie said. "And I don't think he's that dumb."

Nico knocked back the bottle of tequila he had been nursing, finishing the last half. He set the bottle beside the fire pit and rubbed his hands together, thinking. "New plan, then."

The Fireheads circled close.

"Hell with the money. We need a sacrifice to bring back Ruthie," Nico said evenly, pointing at the grimoire. "We'll use the little sister."

"Oh, that is *beautiful!*" Aura said, charmed by Nico's sense of poetry.

"You sure?" Hobie asked. "I'm thinking the Dietrichs might get jittery and call the cops."

"That's why a couple of us are going full skin," Nico said.

* * * *

"Can't *believe* that assclown," muttered Jill, as she flicked the switch on the unpainted cinderblock wall at the head of an enclosed concrete stairway. The fluorescent tube above was a jolting contrast to the main floor's subdued light.

The thick old door eased closed behind them with a muffled thump. At the foot of the stairs they stepped off to their right, into a room that was familiar to the boys in some vague way, like a place from childhood.

"It's going to be an art room, if the funding comes through for remodeling," Jill explained, taking the key ring over to a tall metal cabinet in a corner next to a wall of windows covered by dusty tin blinders.

"And all this town history stuff will probably wind up in a permanent display here, if…" She rubbed her fingers together, again referencing a wispy hope for funding. She opened the cabinet and the boys beheld neatly stored metal lockboxes, brown documents and old photographs encased in glass. On the cabinet's bottom section lay a stack of thick tomes, more recent.

"Wow," exclaimed DeShaun.

"I can probably make copies of some of this stuff, if it's in decent enough shape, so just leave me a note." She took a mock-stern pose. "I don't have to tell you guys what happens if you get so much as an eyelash on any of this stuff."

"Lady," Stuart yanked a thumb at DeShaun. "This dude has comic books sealed inside plastic that's sealed inside plastic that's sealed inside plastic."

"Nowhere near as valuable as this stuff, I bet," DeShaun said with awe.

"Swell," Jill handed the key to Stuart. "Just the same…" she thrust a box of rubber gloves at them. "Back like you found it. And if one of the staff finds you…"

"We'll make up something good," DeShaun reassured her.

"Damn right you will." She took two steps and stopped. "Thanks."

"For what?" Stuart asked.

"For…defending my honor. And distracting me. And just for caring."

"Yeah, okay." Stuart flipped her the finger and a funny sneer. She returned both gestures and left.

"Jeez, where do we start?"

DeShaun snapped on a glove. "How 'bout with your prostrate, Mr. Barcroft?"

They immediately engaged in one of their frequent wrestling matches. Even though they were careful regarding their surroundings Stuart realized that DeShaun was holding back. He surely knew he was stronger than Stuart, but for whatever reason, didn't want or need to prove it—like he didn't even *want* to be bigger and stronger than Stuart. Like he wanted them to always be the same size, strength, everything.

Stuart recalled his friend's throwaway comment: "Screw this grown-up stuff."

Maybe, Stuart thought, *he's not any readier for all this than I am.*

Chapter 12

Haunted Window

Less than half an hour after dinner, Candace and Emera found themselves in their beds.

Strapped in the useless Velcro fetters, Candace listened to Emera shift in her sheets as the others, gathered in the family room, watched a sitcom, up louder than usual. Their laughter mocked the girls.

Candace understood that it was all meant to hurt more than punish her, she just couldn't guess why. But her young mind was on something else.

The motorcycle man's knife.

She still remembered its weight and shine singing promises of freedom and power to her in the whispered erratic voice of her dead brother Everett.

He too had been restrained once, by a pair of deviant priests. Under the pretense of exorcising the boy, they had unwittingly made him a demon.

An hour later, the home went dark and quiet, and the Dietrichs moved from room to room as always, Candace and Ana's being the exception this time.

Ostracized and forgotten. Candace knew well when evil was afoot.

In the shadowy sepia of the faded Casper nightlight, Candace thought of her rough introduction to the Dietrich home.

Less than twenty-four hours after Candace had watched her brother die, Cronus County social services had shown up in Ember Hollow. As they'd comforted one another in the sanctuary, Reverend McGlazer asked Candace how she would feel if he adopted her. It was the one truly fatherly gesture she had experienced since she was very small. She'd requested, even *begged* of the county officials, to be placed with him, rejoicing as much as her broken heart would allow that she could have a family and be close to her only friends.

But those particular DSS agents, sleepy-eyed and slurry-speeched volunteers roused from post-party beds, had only been there to collect her. Placement was not their job.

A hearing was held a few days later. McGlazer, battered and broken, could barely stand, but he had been there, with help from Stella.

She would be right in the heart of the very town where her family had literally been torn apart, the judge had determined, and McGlazer could not even care for himself at the time. The judge, feeling that Candace needed distance from the town and tragedy, had ordered her transported to another county.

The Dietrichs had stepped in like haggard angels, strangely eager to volunteer their already maxed out household. Candace was emergency placed with them until hearings and more hearings, and meetings and pontifications—most yet to come—could place her where she would fit.

The first few days had been no less challenging than now. She'd done her best to keep to herself, despite encouragement by the Dietrichs to make friends with her new housemates. It had been clear by the expressions on the other young faces that they knew at least *some* of her story.

While the kids had played in the front yard that cold sunny November day, Radley had broken away to approach her, followed by a sneering Rebecca. "Did you ever see your brother kill anybody?"

Candace had just looked down.

"You better leave her alone." Rebecca, tall and strong as a linebacker at eleven years old, was as bold as she was spiteful, once she'd seen Candace's reaction. "She might be a psycho too."

"I ain't scared," Radley had asserted, simultaneously flipping off Candace and sticking out his tongue, even knowing that Mrs. Dietrich was coming over.

"Radley, you get inside right now, mister, and Rebecca you can go too!"

"I didn't do it!" Rebecca had protested, giving Candace a vengeful scowl over her shoulder.

Radley had hidden his hand behind his back and flipped her off again, but the housemother had been too savvy for that. She'd grabbed his elbow and yanked his arm straight, firing off a blistering litany of rebuke that would have withered Candace. Radley had seemed to just take it in stride.

Watching them go, Candace had realized what she had to do, and it was not personal or vindictive. It was simply a very important task she had to complete, for there was something missing from her environment, and more than anything, Candace needed to correct this. She'd gazed all around and felt great disappointment; that there was no Halloween here, no blood, and no death. Yet she knew without doubt she could change this.

These children did not seem to appreciate these wonderful and beautiful things, and so they would have to be changed, transformed, into—what else? Halloween, blood, death.

"*Can—diss!*" called a strange and familiar voice through the barrier of chain link fence that separated the Dietrich's property from the neighbors and the thick, high shrubbery just next to it.

Though the sky was darkening from a fast-moving cloud cover, a glint on the ground beckoned Candace. She knelt to see the mirror sliver of a thin steak knife.

She could just grip the point between fingertip and thumb, if she squeezed them together really hard, enough to draw a little globe of blood.

The figure who slid her the knife was just a vague shape behind the shrubs. But his weird movement was unmistakable.

Candace wanted to whisper to him but the back door slammed, drawing her attention. It was Mrs. Dietrich, stern-faced and righteous, marching her tormentors toward her. Radley and Rebecca walked side by side, annoyance on the boy's face, but possibly sincerity on the girl's.

"Sorry for what I said," offered Radley, rote and meaningless.

Rebecca stepped forward. "That was mean of me. I'm sorry and I'll try not be mean anymore." Candace was surprised by the sincerity. The girl was large for her age—for *any* age—and totally fearless from a brief lifetime of subhuman treatment.

But it wasn't about what they said to Candace anymore. It was about Halloween.

Candace reached into her waistband, drew the knife and stabbed Rebecca in the throat.

Her eyes bulged like gum bubbles. Everyone screamed.

Candace yanked the knife out. The sound of splashes against her jacket as the blood spurted in pulsing bursts didn't sound like Candace expected. It sounded like the ticking of a clock.

She sat up in bed, violently wiping the blood from her chest.

Then she realized that her memory of that first day had seamlessly become a dream. She tried to determine where they had separated, praying she hadn't actually st—

The ticking came again, and now Candace realized it was a timebomb.

Someone had planted it while she was sleeping, and it was counting down. In her mind she saw the dynamite sticks taped together with a coiled wire running to an alarm clock, but made more destructive, more *sadistic,* by the addition of knives, forks, icepicks and hammerheads, tightly taped all around the outside.

There were no numbers on the clock; only letters. There was no discernible order to them, but she knew they were the letters of her name, and of her brother's.

The ticking stopped, for a second, then began anew. Its rhythm was odd; three at a time, every few seconds.

Candace knew the bomb would blow soon. And when it did it, it would destroy the world.

Candace's eyes snapped open. She was sure she was in her brother Everett's bed in his shed out behind the house where she'd lived with her parents, on the outskirts of Ember Hollow.

No. It was not strands of orange Halloween lights casting sharp shadows across Everett's childish drawings and construction paper masks, but the Casper nightlight in the room she shared with tiny Emera, in a group home far from home—*any* home.

Yet the ticking continued.

It was coming from the window, emanating some dark and familiar urgency. Candace checked on Emera. The little one remained asleep. The ticking was subtle enough that the Dietrichs hadn't heard it on the baby monitor.

Freeing herself from the useless bonds, she padded to the window, waiting until she heard the ticking again to draw the curtains, in case it had just been dream residue.

But there it was again—three soft clicks, meant for only her to hear.

Candace stayed back from the curtain, leaning as far as she could to reach the edge, in case she needed to run from whatever was there.

She yanked it open, but did not, *could* not, run.

Big brother Everett stood just inches away, separated only by brittle glass and flimsy wood.

He wore one of his construction paper masks, meant to be a frog. Under Everett's hands, it was a mutant, fitted with jagged teeth, smiling like Everett himself had on October 30th.

He waved at her, his knife tucked between thumb and palm.

Candace blinked, then closed her eyes longer; maybe a second.

When she opened them, her brother was still there, still waving the knife.

She didn't panic or despair. She waved back, happy to see him again.

Everett put his hand on the glass, and she did the same, against his. They blinked at one another.

Then Everett stepped back and placed the knife on the outside windowsill. He waved goodbye and backed into the dark to disappear.

Candace waited, catching her breath. When she was sure he was gone, she opened the window and took the knife.

* * * *

Jill motored home on her Indian, ignorant of the Harley riding dark far behind her. She cut the engine and coasted down the driveway to her basement apartment entrance, careful not to wake her early-bed landlords in the upper house. Mr. Topper had worked first shift his whole life and wasn't about to adjust to godawful late comings and goings, such as Jill's 10:30 arrival time.

She went inside and flipped on the outside light, as she always had when she was still dating Dennis, in case he came by for late snuggles.

Pipsqueak parked his bike a hundred yards away and quietly skulked to the house, making mental notes of landmarks, hiding spots, etcetera. He peeked in the upper level windows of the Topper home, assessing the occupants by their décor and furnishings, then headed back to his bike.

Chapter 13

Identity

Candace went back to bed and refastened her pointless restraints.

She lay wondering how much of the night she had dreamed, whether dreams were real, whether she was insane.

The eight-inch meat knife Everett had brought her, that she clutched against her chest like a deadly steel doll, was real enough, wasn't it? If she used it, would her victim—most likely either Radley or Rebecca—regard her with bewilderment while she repeatedly arced an empty useless fistful of nothing at them?

Why was she thinking of such things?

A fear grew in her that she had lost touch with reality, like Everett. Perhaps she really was soon to follow in his footsteps. *What if,* she wondered, *there really is no difference between us?*

She found herself wishing the Velcro straps weren't useless; that she was securely restrained. She could not imagine herself hurting anyone, but, oh God—had Everett ever *known* that *he* was really killing?

She needed help. She had to do something soon. Before she hurt someone, God forbid Emera.

Candace got up and put the knife in the elastic waistband of her pajama bottoms.

...*Why* though?

Everett.

If he was real, she couldn't take any chances, right?

She had just stepped outside the bedroom when she was startled by grabbing hands—on her legs.

Little Emera clung to Candace like a baby possum, her imploring sleepy eyes leaving Candace helpless to do anything but let her tag along. Candace peered down the long shadowed hallway, trying to ignore her anticipation of a blood-covered Everett emerging from any one of the doors. Emera hugged against her hips, creeping with her into the kitchen.

The cordless telephone sat just a few feet from the familiar butcher's block, which was still in easy reach, oddly enough, blued by moonlight like a violin soloist under a spotlight.

Candace punched Stuart's number into the illuminated keypad, clenching her teeth and holding Emera tight to her side as she listened to the dial tone, certain it was loud enough to wake the Dietrichs.

Stuart's mom Elaine answered on the second ring, sounding harried.

"Mrs. Barcroft?" Candace whispered.

"Candace? Is that you?"

"Yes ma'am. Sorry I have to whisper."

"Is something wrong, Sweetie?"

"There might be," Candace kept her eyes on the dark hall beyond the kitchen doorway. "Could I please speak to Stuart?"

"Certainly," Elaine answered. "But don't get into trouble!"

The line was quiet for a full harrowing minute.

Then: "Candace?"

"Stuart!" Her whisper was too loud. She was so relieved, and *happy* to talk to him, she could barely contain it.

"Hey! What's wrong?" Stuart asked in a groggy voice.

"It's just, I'm not supposed to call, you know. So I'm sneaking."

"Oh. Wow. Glad you did, but—"

"I know, don't get in trouble." She drew a quick deep breath, hoping to get out everything she needed to say. "Listen. I think something's really *wrong* here."

Emera tensed and hid behind Candace's legs.

A shadow in the hallway—someone about to catch her. Candace swung around to hang up the handset but dropped it in her panic.

The overhead light came on and there stood Mr. Dietrich in his wrinkled striped pajamas. "Candace? What in the name of God are you doing out here?" The question was soaked with melodramatic accusation, indignation. "And with *Emera*?"

She didn't answer, but Dietrich saw the phone on the floor. "Who did you call?"

"No one! I was just starting." Candace pushed Emera behind her. "I just wanted to talk to Stuart."

Dietrich scowled at Candace, then lunged to seize her by the shoulders. He jerked her away from the phone so fast it made her dizzy.

Emera screamed to wake the dead.

Perhaps it was the abruptness of Dietrich's movement, along with Emera's scream, that triggered something already hovering close.

As Dietrich held her out at shoulder length to scold her, she snapped her teeth at him, missing his nose by a hair's width.

When Dietrich released her and fell back, Candace reached into her waistband and drew the knife. She saw his terror, and she *liked* it.

She felt her legs coiling for a pounce onto the house father, when Mrs. Dietrich arrived, screaming at Candace. *"Stop!"*

Candace did.

She gazed down at Mr. Dietrich with instant remorse, the knife shaking. Mrs. Dietrich stepped around her husband and took Candace by the shoulders, much quieter and more gently than he had. "Candace. Calm down baby."

Mrs. Dietrich hugged her, as much a restraint as an embrace. "Shhhhh, shh, shh…"

Candace beheld the knife, wanting to drop it as she had the time before, but unable. Mr. Dietrich seemed like he was trying to decide whether to reach for it or not.

Emera came close, wanting to join the hug. Candace motioned her in. Just as Dietrich gained the courage to reach out for the knife, she released it, letting him catch it.

In the embrace, Candace sensed something strange in Mrs. Dietrich, though she could not see her mime the words *I can't do this* to her husband right before she pulled away. "Is everyone okay?"

"…Yes." Candace knew she would cry soon. "I'm very sorry, Mr. Dietrich."

He got to his feet, his gaze darting between Candace and his wife. "It's okay. Everything's okay."

When he cast a glance down the hallway Candace realized the other children stood outside their rooms. All except Rebecca, who peeked around her door nervously.

"I'm going to give you a sleep pill again," said Mrs. Dietrich. "We'll deal with all this in the morning."

As Emera clenched against Candace's hip again, Mr. Dietrich gave his wife a look like she had just signed his death warrant.

* * * *

Shivering, Reverend McGlazer tightly clutched himself, as if he could squeeze out the malignant man whipping his body like a horse into committing awful actions.

"That girl deserves better than to be used again, damn you," Reverend McGlazer told his possessor.

"*What does it say about ye, Man of Yahweh and Yeshua,*" countered the spiteful spirit, "*that you expect me to ravage the girl?*"

"I *feel* what you are," McGlazer said.

"You're but a fading voice," said the voice. "A slave to the demon drink, quickly outgrowing any usefulness to anyone."

Ragdoll Ruth's pistol, covered with his own blood, appeared to McGlazer on the desk of his mind's office. Beside it, the glass and the bottle. The tranquility. Both the opposite and the complement.

McGlazer sobbed, unaware that his hijacker had to plumb considerable reserves of otherworldly power and resolve to keep this sadness from spilling out upon the material world and revealing itself.

* * * *

Stella realized she was on edge when she yelped at a wet maple leaf that stuck to her windshield.

Given the silent sprinkle falling from the sepia sky, she might have dismissed her tension as autumn melancholia. WICH radio personality Abel the Weird had spun a string of moody tracks—Gothminister's "March of The Dead," Bauhaus's "Stigmata Martyr" and Mechanical Moth's "Cathedral"—that only underscored her gloom.

She pulled into Saint Saturn Unitarian's gravel lot and parked beside a Nissan truck she knew belonged to Brianna Holland. The young lady, struggling with suicidal thoughts after her divorce, had a counseling session with McGlazer, which must have gone over the scheduled hour. The reverend was already behind on his sermon for the next day's service, a task he aimed to finish immediately following Brianna's session.

She stopped at the church's rear door, fearing to open it. Retracing her day, Stella searched for some mundane instant of tiny distress so she could see it for what it was and chase it away along with the haze of dread that clung to her like wet clothes.

It didn't help that the corridor lights she had switched on that morning were now dark. She entered and flicked the switch, grimacing at the erratic flicker of two ancient fluorescent tubes she'd been meaning to climb up and change for months.

McGlazer's office door was closed. Stella's heart reached out to poor Brianna, who must surely be in need of—

Giggling filtered through the door, of a kind that Stella recognized as relaxed and easy, like...post-coital banter. She crept to the door, ears pricked, and tried to stifle both her judgment and her—*what the hell?*—jealousy. She leaned against it and listened, certain she was ever closer to a let-down.

Then the door opened, and there Stella was, leaning toward McGlazer. Like a busybody.

"Hi there, Stella." He stood there as if he'd expected to see her, an all-knowing expression on his face.

She had enough poise to act natural. "Abe. I was worried."

Brianna stood behind McGlazer, smiling as she minutely adjusted the collar on her silk top—too dressy for a counseling session.

"Was wondering about you," said the reverend. "Come in. Join us."

"Oh *no*," said Stella. "I just wondered if...you still had company."

"We're quite finished."

Brianna waved at her. Stella couldn't tell if it was a self-conscious gesture.

"I...bought the supplies." Stella felt compelled to raise the bags and show him.

"Good lass," said McGlazer.

Brianna breezed past Stella and made her way out with a "Thank you!" to the reverend.

"Well then. What shall we do now?" McGlazer's glance might have fallen to her breasts—or was it the grocery bags she held too high?

"You...have the sermon to finish."

"Yes indeed." McGlazer stepped back into his office with a jaunty flourish and closed the door.

* * * *

Jill dropped the kickstand, removed her helmet, and slumped in the seat, grateful for a better day than yesterday. She loved seeing Stuart again, yet it was too close an association with Dennis.

She felt selfish. Stuart had become nothing less than *her* own little brother too. She felt like she was spurning him, Ma, even DeShaun.

Stuart needed a good ear for his many blooming insecurities, especially about Candace. Bless her heart, Ma was not prepared for this stage of the boy's life. It was a time when he really needed a father—or a big brother.

It would have been easier if Dennis was a philanderer, but he was far from it. Yet it *did* feel like he was cheating when he went off and got drunk, refusing to let her help him with his problems; instead simply feeding them by trying to drown them.

She couldn't watch him self-destruct. She couldn't stop him. Music was no longer a sufficient outlet for him.

I guess...neither am I. Jill hopped off, thinking of Dennis and how they used to be.

She didn't realize she was smiling at this, not even when a leathery hand slapped over her mouth, and a slick, devious voice said, "Aww, you happy to see me, baby?"

* * * *

"Remind me to take two weeks off next year," Hudson huffed. "Before and *after* Halloween."

"What about now?" Leticia was nothing if not proactive.

"The whole situation is…"

"Delicate," Leticia finished.

"Yeah. I call social services, it might be weeks before they get somebody out there," lamented Hudson. "I go myself, I might make things worse. But I don't like this feeling in my gut, Teesh."

"Your gut's usually right."

"Maybe I can just drive down. Sit and watch for a while, like a stakeout."

"What about the chief?"

"I don't think I should mention it. I don't want to ruin McGlazer's shot at adopting her. But I can't just leave it hanging."

"Take a personal day, baby. I'll call in for you."

Hudson hugged her, inhaled the comforting scent of her hair, and felt better. "I'll go tomorrow."

"You can't go alone, Huds,"

Hudson frowned at her. "Shavers has been…odd, since last year. Yoshida's the only one I can trust. And he's already pulling doubles."

Leticia went to the phone.

"Who're you calling?"

"Who do you think?"

He raised an eyebrow with realization. "Pedro."

Chapter 14

Intruders

Pedro shifted his big frame in the passenger seat of Hudson's Blazer. "Jeez, is police work always this lame?"

"Yeah, well I'd be a 'musician' like you"—Hudson made air quotes—"if only I was as 'talented' and 'handsome' as you are."

Pedro threw his head back and gave a hearty guffaw. During the hour-long drive to the Dietrichs' neighborhood, Hudson and Pedro had caught up on what they called town gossip, though their conversation actually carried a good deal of gravitas, covering McGlazer, the parade aftermath and Dennis. When it all became too gloomy the men slipped into their old habit of bagging on each other, never too far from smiling, no matter how cheap the shot.

With twilight giving way to dark, they became serious again.

"What's worst case scenario, here?" Pedro asked, peering through Hudson's binoculars.

"We just gather intel," Hudson said. "Get as close as we can. Get a read for the place. If it seems dangerous for Candace or any of the other kids…"

"What?"

"Hell if I know. I'll either call it in, or I'll go in, and you'll stay out here and out of trouble."

"Yeah, right," Pedro scoffed.

His window shattered.

A massive clawed hand closed on his throat.

Reflexively, Pedro sunk his chin and flared his trapezius, crushing down on the steel cable fingers, knowing it would only buy him a split second.

Hudson's .44 discharged; thunder and lightning in a tiny space. The monstrous hand withdrew.

Pedro felt blood soaking into his favorite Sex Pistols shirt. He was as pissed as he was startled. "What the—?"

He peered out the window for the assailant, but there was nothing to see. Hudson's shot had dropped it.

Then a low growl vibrated alongside the ringing in Pedro's ears.

Hudson was already outside. "Slide out over here, Petey!"

Pedro had started doing just that when a sudden gravity shift kicked in to assist. Something was flipping Hudson's Blazer on its side like a card table.

* * * *

Every night at bedtime, the Dietrichs went from room to room encouraging progress where needed. Tonight, the ritual smashed to a halt at the sound of the back door violently splintering apart.

A split-second later it was the *front* door shattering, accompanied by an unearthly guttural snarling.

In Rebecca's bedroom, Mrs. Dietrich screamed and backed into the hallway wall, knocking off a painting of a sad-eyed puppy. Mr. Dietrich froze solid at the sight of a musclebound biker armed with a German Luger coming from the family room, and something straight out of hell from the kitchen.

The hirsute horror loped down the hall toward Dietrich—then past him. He was shaken from his state by Mrs. Dietrich's terrified cry coming from Rebecca's room.

Before Mr. Dietrich could respond, Nico shoved the Luger against his temple, kicked his trembling feet out from under him and placed a boot on his chest. "The Geelens girl," Nico said.

Mrs. Dietrich's shrill cries sounded like pleading in a foreign language, but abruptly went quiet.

"Miriam!?" Mr. Dietrich called, presenting to Nico an open mouth, into which the biker jammed the handgun's barrel.

"Now!"

Dietrich heard Miriam sob, and found cold comfort that she was still alive.

* * * *

Sliding toward the driver side, Pedro realized the Blazer would be on its side before he was out. His legs would be crushed. Pedro shut his eyes and prepared to scream. For the second time, a big hand closed on him—his jacket lapel this time—and yanked him hard. He found himself tossed behind Hudson. The chief deputy had just saved his bacon and was already trying to draw a bead across the upended vehicle. His target: a seven-and-a-half-foot man with a wolf's head.

The upended Blazer was coming at them again, the roof bulldozing Hudson toward Pedro, and the big poplar behind them. Pedro grabbed Hudson and spun him away from the crushing juggernaut in a classic wrestling waistlock throw.

The roof of the Blazer bashed in as Pedro and Hudson got to their feet and beheld the beast in its fullness: Muscular legs jointed at the calves, long hairy arms ending in inch-long claws, slavering teeth in a huge snout, glowing eyes burning with hunger and hate.

* * * *

Groggy and disoriented, Candace nonetheless rose and stumbled to Emera, unaware of the useless straps.

She covered the little girl with her body, quickly regaining her senses as the din beyond her door reached her ears. Neither girl was comforted when the hysterical Mrs. Dietrich burst in and fell upon them. "I'm so sorry, Candace!" she sobbed. "I'll do my best—"

A silhouette shaped like a giant standing wolf appeared in the doorway. It ducked its head, tucked its ears and stomped through. The underlit abomination's deep rumbling growl shook Candace's very bones.

Emera screamed. Mrs. Dietrich tightened her embrace, but suddenly flew away from Candace like a startled finch, tossed into the far wall by the furry demon. The little girls were exposed, helpless.

Candace heard the other kids crying. She felt sad for them.

* * * *

Crouching beside Hudson, Pedro pressed his hand against the stinging scratches on his neck.

Hudson fired off three quick shots, hitting the monster full in the chest and abdomen. It stumbled back from the force, but no wounds appeared.

"Aw hell," whispered Hudson, as it regained its balance and advanced on them. As the wolf thing lowered its head and drew back its huge paws to attack, Hudson fought to steady his grip on the handgun.

"What are you *waiting for!?*" Pedro shouted.

Unbelievably, Hudson took a quick step *toward* the thing, then quickly withdrew.

A feint. The monster opened its maw for a snap at the lawman—and Hudson fired.

The beast yelped as its head and body snapped back like a wet towel. It hit the ground and instantly rolled to its feet.

Blood poured from the creature's mouth and pattered on the ground. Though it hacked and coughed, it showed no signs of pain, or real damage.

"Dammit!" Hudson knew he had only one round left, and he knew it wouldn't be enough.

A series of whistles sounded from somewhere near the Dietrich house. The beast pricked its ears toward the sound. It lunged at Hudson and Pedro, shoulder bashing them to the ground before bounding away with unnatural speed.

* * * *

"Sheriff's deputy here!" Hudson called as he and Pedro ran toward the house. "We're coming in!" He stepped over the wrecked door and repeated the declaration.

Hearing sounds of distress, they jogged through the hall to the room from whence the cries emanated and found Mrs. Dietrich lying stiff and breathless, blood pooling around her broken body.

Kneeling beside her was Mr. Dietrich, hysterical and incoherent.

The housefather babbled a litany of apologies and regrets at Hudson. Upon seeing Pedro behind him, Dietrich cried out, assuming the big leather-jacketed Hispanic to be another biker. Hudson holstered his weapon and clasped Dietrich's shoulders, calming him with reassurances.

While Hudson dealt with the housefather, Pedro found a dish towel and applied it to his neck. He lifted a toaster to use as a mirror, relieved to find the puncture wounds superficial, but still pissed about the ruined Sex Pistols shirt.

He went room to room and collected all the kids from hiding places under beds and in closets, corralling them in one room, trying to calm them. They all burbled about a werewolf, swearing they weren't lying. They couldn't know he and Hudson had just done battle with one.

Finding little Emera trembling and balled up on the far corner of her bed he coaxed her to come to him. He cooed to her as he carried her to the kitchen, where he poured milk for all of them in plastic cups, then rolled these to the bedroom on a serving cart.

He saw Hudson keeping Dietrich's hands still, trying to get some sense from his gibberish. "Your wife's gonna be okay," Hudson kept telling him, and Pedro knew he meant it only in the long view; the lady was busted up like a china teapot in a train wreck.

"Drink it slow, you guys." Pedro passed out the milk then placed a call for an ambulance using the same cordless phone Candace had used to call Stuart.

He returned to the kids, who continued to shout about the monster—all except the biggest kid, Rebecca. She just kept saying, "I'm sorry, I'm sorry!"

Pedro managed to shush the others and ask her why.

"Just last night. I…I pranked her!"

"Don't worry about that right n—"

"No, it was really *bad*!" Rebecca sobbed. "I dressed up like her psycho brother and went to the window!"

"What!?" Despite his innate concern for the children, Pedro was enraged. "What the hell's *wrong* with you, kid?"

"I'm so *sorry!*" Rebecca said, barely comprehensible in her terrified state. "Mr. Dietrich said it would help her. But we didn't know this would happen!"

Pedro tried to wrap his head around the revelation. He had only enough calm left to give her a pat on the head. Then he tromped back to the living room. Hudson immediately sensed his fury and stepped in front of him before he could seize Dietrich's scrawny neck.

"Whoa *whoa!*" Hudson had to brace himself to hold back the big bassist. "What the hell, Pedro!?"

They engaged in a brief shoving match, before Pedro relented. "That son of a bitch is pulling some seriously screwed-up shit with these kids, man!"

Hudson saw guilt behind Dietrich's terror. "What did you do?"

"I…had no *choice!*"

Flashing lights filled the air, car doors slammed, radios squawked.

Dietrich remained a jittery mess. If he were ever to learn how close he had come to a beatdown from a bulked-up Mexican punker, he would have surely listed it right alongside the werewolf and biker attack.

Chapter 15

Captivity

"Lucky you can ride, baby," Pipsqueak mocked, as he hopped on his Harley behind Jill. "Careful though. I doubt you ever rode a beast like this."

He kept the muzzle of his .25 pressed into her spine as she maneuvered onto the highway, digging it a little deeper whenever they rode close to other motorists. The ride got rough once they passed the pumpkin and corn fields and headed up into the rocky curves of Cronus County's fabled hills and hollers, where the moonshine industry had once thrived as mightily as the pumpkin crop did in the present day.

Despite the gun in her back, Jill was quick to respond with a middle finger or a "Go to Hell!" at every word or movement from the snarky biker. But her bravado didn't make her feel any better about the many miles piling up behind her, or the thickening forest beside the worsening road.

She knew there were still homes, even sprawling farms up in these hills. But no one she knew, or knew *of*, lived up here. Anyone willing to live this far out usually didn't have much use for malls or bars or even grocery stores—and would just as soon mind their own business as get involved with the doings of an outlaw biker gang.

Eventually, the road opened up some, and a chimney top came into sight, attached to a good-sized farm house.

It didn't bode well that the hoodlum uncomfortably close behind her and his friends were operating out of such an isolated location. Jill felt a terrifying uncertainty rise to join the despair of her broken heart. Yet she eagerly anticipated the prospect of field-goaling some nutsacks, en route to whatever horrors awaited her.

Maneuvering the big Harley into the scrubby yard, she caught sight of the well-kept barn off toward the neighboring field and had a strange feeling she would wind up inside of it.

A striking leather-clad Amazon stepped out from the house and leaned against the porch post, followed by two more bikers; big shaggy men with faces of hate and chaos. They waved to Pipsqueak. She saw him in the mirror, sticking out his tongue, raising his arms to point down at her triumphantly.

"Kill the engine," he said, issuing a wolf-howl whoop, answered by the others. He hopped off and yanked Jill to her feet by the arm.

"Still got the touch, I see," said the tattoo-pated one, whom she would soon learn was called Jiggy.

"Stick it up your ass, dirtbag," Jill said.

This was met with casual chuckles.

"Hey Nico!" called Hobie. "Come see!"

The name Nico meant *something*—and not good.

"I take it this wasn't her first choice of date destinations," Jiggy said.

"I know. Ain't she perfect?"

"What, for all of us?" asked Hobie.

"No," Nico said, as he walked toward them. "For Ruthie." He took out his cigarettes. "To wear."

Nico. Ruthie. Pieces were falling into place.

The leader came close, removed his mirror lenses and met her defiant gaze. "Damn, honey."

Jill responded by spitting in his face.

With a roar, Aura attacked her, swinging a gloved fist. Jill ducked it and countered with a slug that sent the biker bitch to her ass.

Jiggy burst out laughing—then cried out in agony, as Jill arced her boot point into his scrotum.

"Whoa, lil' filly!" said Pipsqueak, as he wrapped his arms around her from behind. Jill smashed the back of her head into Pipsqueak's chin, making him release.

From the ground, Aura lunged to grab Jill's ankle. Jill knelt and rained blows on Aura's uncovered head.

"God...*damn,*" said Nico, as he stepped toward Jill. She swung a blistering right. Nico dodged it, then dropped her with a headbutt.

The others re-oriented themselves, only the uninvolved Hobie laughing. Nico helped Pipsqueak up. "Brother. You done good."

He brushed dirt out of Pip's muttonchops, as Pip rubbed his chin. "Thanks Chief."

"My Ruthie's gonna *love* sporting *this* little hellcat around."

* * * *

Hudson and Pedro recruited a few of the emergency responders to help right the wrecked Blazer. Braking for a bunny rabbit, he'd run off the road and flipped, Hudson told them. It sounded better than the truth. Hudson was glad he had chosen to use his personal vehicle for the outing.

As the civil workers returned to the Dietrich house, Hudson and Pedro took the chance to speak in private.

"What the hell am I gonna write in my report, Petey?"

"Nothing about wolfmen, I bet."

"I can't ask you to lie."

"What are you, my scout master? Anyways, do I even look like the guy you'd want collaborating you on some story about a real-life overgrown Lon Chaney Junior?"

"*Corroborate*," Hudson corrected. "Dietrich seems to feel differently. He's crying wolf to everyone in sight."

"What are you gonna say?" Pedro asked.

"I had my suspicions based on what DeShaun and Stuart said. Reasonable enough, that I would come out unannounced to check on their friend."

"Sure. Then what?"

"We didn't see what happened in the house, because of the wreck."

"So, the truth, more or less, minus major chunks of crucial information."

"There's no other way to play it. Tell the whole truth and I'll be on psychiatric leave for about the next six hundred years. As for Dietrich, anything he says after 'eight-foot dog monster' is gonna fall on very doubtful ears."

"Serves him *right,*" Pedro said. "But I mean…there *is* some evidence. That *The Howling* just got re-enacted here, I mean."

"And probably about a thousand different, scientifically rational explanations that forensics could whip up."

"Okay. So what's next?"

"Dietrich described an actual human being. He sounds familiar. I need to match this up with a report about a prison transport accident. Main thing right now is finding Candace."

* * * *

Whatever they had in mind for her, the Fireheads weren't trying to make Jill suffer in discomfort—yet.

She awoke in a second story bedroom with an adjoining bathroom. Uncarpeted hardwood floors, wallpapered plaster walls.

All the windows had been nailed shut. There was a mattress on the floor; one pillow and a single fitted sheet left for her to put on if she wished. The closet was empty, the hanging rod removed.

A plate with a peanut butter and jelly sandwich and a handful of saltine crackers was left for her on the floor, along with a bottle of beer.

Spite said to ignore the food, but she wanted to stay sharp and strong, in case an opportunity for escape presented itself, or could be created. Though the beer was still capped and didn't seem to have been tampered with, she emptied it down the sink drain and refilled it with water from the spigot.

She went to the window as she wolfed down the sandwich, surveying the grounds to ascertain as much as she could about this place, her captors and their goal.

She heard voices below the window, on or near the front porch. Studying the driveway, she spotted one of the bikers perched in a tree; a denim-feathered vulture keeping watch over the entrance.

She plopped on the mattress and examined the beer bottle, visualizing how she could use it against whoever came to bring her food or check on her.

Then, sounds of heavy boots and low voices came up the stairs.

Six years in a punk rock outfit had made Jill resourceful and quick-witted when it came to brawls. She went to crouch beside the doorway, taking the bottle by the neck and raising it to smash over the first entrant's head.

Then she heard the muffled, distressed, and *familiar* voice of a child. She lowered the bottle and stepped back, still prepared to fight if possible.

The key rattled, the door opened. Three Fireheads gazed in at her, tensed like zookeepers preparing to enter the cage of an uncontrollable silverback. But Jill did not have the luxury of enjoying the healthy respect in their eyes. She didn't even think to return the fierce glower of the female, Aura. Her heart fell at the sight of a beloved friend.

"Candace!" She dropped the bottle and went to the door, where she was met by a kick from Aura that sent her onto her butt. Even this didn't dilute Jill's worried focus on Candace.

Hobie brought the little girl in by the arm. "Well, sounds like you girls already know each other!"

Jill rose and embraced Candace. "Are you okay, sweetie?"

"I don't...know what's going on!"

"Hey that's great!" Aura celebrated. "That means I get to be the one to tell you!"

"Aura," Rhino said in a low tone. "Leave it. We got work."

"Later," Aura threatened. The trio left and locked the door.

Jill walked Candace to the mattress, sat her down, and began rocking the girl and stroking her hair. "Did they come and get you at the home?"

Candace nodded. "But there's something worse." Only now did she seem truly terrified.

"What is it?"

Candace gave Jill a gaze more terrifying than anything she had experienced since nearly a year before. "Everett is coming back."

Jill felt relief for the impossibility of the girl's delusional fear. But she worried that the stress of being abducted had driven Candace over the edge; into the same fevered madness that had driven her brother.

In that sense, perhaps her prophecy *was* true.

Chapter 16

Alone With Her

Sunday Service had been uncomfortable at best. McGlazer's sermon was rife with inappropriate innuendo, long pauses, flippant explanations of scripture and dogma. And had he *winked* at Brianna?

Then he skipped the traditional post-service brunch in the church cafeteria. Seeing him head toward his office, Stella followed. The door was already closed by the time she caught up. She wanted to knock, to check on him. But she didn't. *Couldn't.* When she asked herself why, the answer made her shiver. He creeped her out now.

The sermon *had* triggered a resolution though. She couldn't help McGlazer. But she hoped it wasn't too late to help Candace.

She rushed the brunchers out. Leaving the cleanup for later, she drove home, preparing herself for a showdown with Bernard.

First, to the kitchen. Hoping to catch flies with honey rather than vinegar, she a took glass of milk and a plate of oatmeal raisin cookies to the place where Bernard spent almost all his waking hours these days—the garage.

His chemistry set had grown again. He moved between brand new glass beakers and test tubes, pouring and inspecting with his shiny elbow-length green gloves on; a harmless, paunchy Doctor Jekyll.

On a baking sheet she had been missing lay a piece of Ragdoll Ruth's evil Halloween candy; a fat glossy beetle awaiting dissection.

"Any progress?" she began.

He did not answer for almost a minute, but that was customary. "Traces of Ritalin, of all things. Ecstasy, PCP. All can cause paranoia. Something there I can't really identify though."

Without meeting her gaze, he reached for the plate she held and bit into a cookie as he bent to his microscope.

He swallowed the bite and raised the cookie, saying "Mmm" as his only acknowledgement. She handed him the milk and he took two noisy gulps, the way he always initiated the consumption of any beverage. Stella realized she had begun to find this, and many more of his idiosyncrasies, annoying to the point of distraction.

"What'd you want?" he asked, making it clear he was too busy for her—and unknowingly emboldening her.

"Candace is in trouble."

"What makes you think so?" He showed only the barest interest.

Stella told him what Elaine had told her, realizing the account was now third hand, and thus highly unlikely to impress Bernard in the least.

He still hadn't made eye contact with her. Shuffling from one apparatus to the other, he regarded her like a barely-tolerated pet.

"You know how kids are," he mumbled. "Dramatic."

This sounded so derisive that Stella had to count to ten before continuing. "Something needs to be done."

"That's what the system is for."

"*What* system, Bernard?"

He cleared his throat before tossing out his answer. "The system that oversees orphaned children. They're qualified."

"You were in this system at some point, Bernard?"

"You know I wasn't, Stella. And neither were you."

"Exactly," she countered. "We were both very lucky, and we learned how to be good parents."

Bernard shuffled away from her. He rubbed a pinch of powder into...

"Is that my measuring cup?"

"Non-toxic."

"I want to talk about this."

"Nothing to say," he said. "We can't take in a child right now, and that's that."

He raised the flame on a Bunsen burner, and it might as well have been lit under her temper. He was a child playing with toys, with no thought beyond his own amusement. The center of his own tiny universe.

"Well if *that's that*," she began, hard emphasis on every word, "then you can just have '*that*' to yourself. Along with this house."

She spun to storm away, stopping when she heard him set down the glassware—but only to say, "You're being emotional."

She spun hard, crossing her arms. "Yes I am. And I feel sorry for you that you *can't* be." She was at the door before speaking again. "Candace needs help, and if you won't, then you're in my way. Goodbye."

Much as she was tempted, she did not slam the door. Having already rehearsed this process a few times internally, she had visualized even what clothes she would pack, where she would go—the Blue Moon Inn, a block from Saint Saturn Unitarian—and how she would respond in the unlikely event he argued any of her points or tried to stop her. The only thing that could change her mind was if Bernard changed his *mind*—and heart.

Wiping the few tears that escaped, she finished packing and set off for the Blue Moon within fifteen minutes.

* * * *

Standing to stretch, DeShaun parted the blinds. "Holy cannoli! It sure got dark."

Stuart raised his head from a frustratingly dark photocopy of a handwritten text and smacked the side of his head. "This stuff's starting to bug me out anyways."

"What, the S's that look like F's?"

"No, smart guy. You know what I mean."

"You think that *journal* is weird..." DeShaun held up, delicately, a pair of illustrations that depicted strange symbols interwoven with vaguely organic objects; plants with animalistic properties, and vice versa.

"Sheesh. What the hell was up with these people?" Stuart asked.

"*Your* people," DeShaun noted. "Your lineage is back in there somewhere."

Stuart blinked at the realization. "Okay, let's stow this junk. Just leave the ones you want Jill to copy on top."

* * * *

Stella checked herself in at the Blue Moon, got settled in her room, and sat down to have a good cry. Then she realized she didn't *need* a cry, she needed to get things done.

She called the sheriff station for Hudson, to find some angle toward adopting Candace, but he was out.

She returned to the church and set about cleaning like mad. She made use of the vacuum cleaner's corner attachment and drapes brush, even hitting the underside of the pews to eradicate the most miniscule of unseen cobwebs. She attacked the chancel and choir platform, purifying them to a perfect next-to-godliness.

After more than two hours she shut off the machine, expecting the room's usual heavy silence to take over.

It was the piano's god-forsaken D key though, pinging in micro-seconds; an expectant and simplistic dirge, just as it had the previous year, when she'd been at the church alone.

She spun toward the organ. McGlazer was there. His back was to her, his head raised toward the stained-glass depiction of Jesus in Gethsemane pleading for a mercy His Father would not grant.

McGlazer's arm was extended behind him in a way that had to be uncomfortable, absently and erratically plunking the D key.

"Abe?"

The minister slowly twisted toward her, maintaining his contemplation of the glass mosaic until physiognomy would no longer accommodate. Then he opened his mouth in a smirk so opposite the depicted pensive Jesus that it raised Stella's heartbeat.

"Stella?" Though the name rose on his voice like a query, a mockery, it was impossible that he would not know she was present.

"I just..." Stella felt like this was a near-perfect McGlazer impostor. "Are you all right?"

McGlazer released the D key and strode toward her, smiling, ever-smiling. "You've worried over me for months."

Stella frowned.

"Perhaps even...*years*."

Before she knew it, McGlazer was standing inches from her face, his eyes like twin mesmeric spirals controlling everything within their radius.

He gently cupped her chin. "You're the faithful servant Yahweh doesn't deserve."

She felt light, awkward, enticed; all at once.

"The New Earth will call you goddess, I expect."

Stella didn't feel uncomfortable with this sudden, strange attention, but knew she should pull away; a feat that was not possible. "What...'New Earth?'"

McGlazer wore mock lamentation. "This one cannot sustain itself."

Stella had no argument.

"Your husband. You're like a ghost to him, aren't you?"

McGlazer had always referred to Bernard by name. Now, a degree of separation. Could he know she had left him just a short while ago?

The earnest minister she had known for so long seemed like a masterful, chameleonic actor of the highest order, inhabiting the role of not a character, but some historic figure possessed of exceptional personal drive of imperiousness, conviction of divine purpose, unquestionable destiny. This was far from him. Yet close enough that Stella's suppressed attraction responded to its sunshine and burst from the earth to grow.

She raised a trembling hand to his.

"Let me show you what you are," he said. "Let me show you what he cannot see."

Stella felt blissfully helpless.

He took his hand from her chin and caressed her hair. She needed to make him stop, yet she saw him taking her, in her mind's eye, undressing and ravishing her on a pew with God and the ghosts and the regretful Jesus at Gethsemane watching. She could not even imagine disapproval from the ethereal witnesses; only a regretful sort of understanding. This was too *right*—dogma be damned.

He lowered his hand slowly and took hers. "Come."

He held her gaze as he led her, his insistence holding a sense of destiny. Even thoughts of Bernard and marriage vows, pledged before this very man—some *piece* of him anyway; perhaps a piece that had vaporized itself for this Greater Truth!—did not slow her stride.

He was taking her to a place for lovemaking. She was sure of that. And they could repent later if that was even needed, but for now, what was needed was *this*; this holding of hands and revealing of secret thoughts and desires.

* * * *

"I'm coming to *stop* you, you lying bastard!" McGlazer crashed into the office door like a berserker, unconcerned with pain or injury. "I'll tear you to pieces before I'll let you hurt her!"

He slammed his shoulder, his foot, his fists into the oaken door. "You hear me, Bennington!" He shouted with his next strike, both forearms driven into the barrier like a steroid-fueled defensive lineman.

The thick wood cracked.

As thin filaments of eldritch light broke through, McGlazer grew in confidence and determination, realizing he *could* free himself. With Stella in danger, he no longer had any choice.

McGlazer stepped back to make another running bash and felt his heel kick something. A bottle of course; Jefferson Select. It fell on its flat back with a high-pitched clink and lay there, sparkling and sloshing and calling to him.

"No!" He booted the bottle, sending it spinning into the wall, where it smashed and evaporated in seconds, the glass pieces melting to dust.

He didn't allow the least lament, returning to the door with hammering blows. The crack grew, and the invading light of rescue with it. "I'm coming for you!"

"Be still, ye simple sot! Or I'll make it worse for her! And for *your own ragged hide!*"

McGlazer's righteous rage held firm. He kicked the door, raising dust motes that swirled in the expanding section of light. The brightness beyond gained strength, sucking the door into itself, burning it away. The light was McGlazer's will at work.

Then, something crossed the light, growing to overcome it, to block it out. A giant wooden button came near the crack. Eyes rolled in each of its four thread holes behind the strands holding it to her cracked white face.

"I see *through* you, Abraham McGlazer, ye pretender! Impostor!"

McGlazer wept in mourning for his own quick-bleeding resolve.

"You carry the weight of countless unconfessed sins! You *stink* of its *infection!*"

The light behind the figure weakened, along with McGlazer's will.

"The Lord commandeth me to turn you to a pillar of salt!"

Her voice sounded as though it was being blasted through the maxed-out amps of The Chalk Outlines up on the theatre marquee. The volume threatened to shred him with its force, withered every part of him. McGlazer was The Incredible Melting Man.

"I will cleanse this town of you!" She was either closer or bigger. "Because *you failed it!*"

The crack in the door went obsidian black; so black it oozed in like The Blob, to ingest McGlazer and make him nothing more than a meaningless droplet of all the universe's great despair.

Chapter 17

The Descent

Nico issued a powerful resounding whistle. This had been the signal for assembly long before the gang had even heard of lycanthropy. The humor was not lost on them though. Pipsqueak loped toward the sagging picnic table panting and whining, his tongue hanging out.

"We're ahead of schedule," Nico explained as the bikers all settled in at the table. "Never hurts to be ready for plans to go south though."

"What's the plan now, Chief?" asked Aura.

"On Devil's Night, we pile up some furniture and whatnot. Make a bonfire, just before dark."

Rhino alternately spun his knife on the table and flipped it in his hands.

"Everybody but me and Jiggy goes wolf. Hobie and Rhino will patrol out around the road." Nico pointed toward the area where the trees opened up onto the driveway. "I don't see how anybody could find us, but better safe than stupid."

"But first..." He lit a joint, drew from it, passed it. "We bring back my Ruthie. The ritual calls for 'heightened emotions.' If any of you wanna couple or triple up, whatever, that'll help."

Looking at Aura, Nico made a sweeping gesture, like she could take them all on and he would be fine with that.

"Killing the little girl in front of the big one will bring things to a boil. A little torture beforehand will help. I'll handle that myself."

Aura glimpsed toward the bedroom where Candace and Jill were held and saw the captives watching them. Jill raised both middle fingers.

"Pip, you'll read the spell while I skin the punker bitch. Anybody who's not banging can help me put Ruthie's bones in the fresh flesh. Once she's good to go, the party really starts."

"We wolf out and feast on fat townies!" Pipsqueak clapped once.

"All but me and Jigs." Nico motioned toward the row of motorcycles. "Somebody's gotta drive."

"You ain't gonna go beast, Chief?" Aura asked.

"I'm gonna go beast all right," Nico said. "On Ruthie." He made a thrusting motion with his hips, drawing approving murmurs from the boys. "It'll be reunion night for us. But don't y'all worry. We'll be right there with you, drinking up blood and good times."

* * * *

"It's only for a minute, fella." Stuart scratched Bravo's cheeks and let the dog lick his face.

"Hey, it's your first French!" quipped DeShaun.

"Har...dee...har."

As soon as Stuart rose, the dog strained at the leash, pointing his nose east, whining, imploring the boys with his eyes.

"I hate it when he does that."

"Poor guy," lamented DeShaun. "My mom is talking about trying to get him some doggy sedatives, or something."

"Maybe my brother can spare a gallon or two of his precious whiskey to help him out."

DeShaun patted his friend's shoulder. "Come on."

They went inside and searched for Jill, conscious now of the innocuous door leading down to the town secrets; a portal to another dimension.

"Let's just ask for her."

They went to the window to check on Bravo, found him still yearning and yearning.

"She didn't come in today, boys," Mrs. Washburn told them at the counter. "I tried calling but there's no answer." Mrs. Washburn knitted her brow. "So unlike her."

The boys now felt as anxious as Bravo. "I got a weird feeling," Stuart said.

"Maybe she's just, you know, too upset," offered DeShaun.

"No," Stuart said. "Remember that mutton-chopped douche yesterday?"

DeShaun did, and it worried him.

As they went outside to get Bravo, Stuart walked to the corner of the building, examining the windows outside the storage room where Jill had taken them.

"Dude. Tell me you're not thinking about..." DeShaun clammed up as a couple of ladies walked by and baby-talked Bravo.

"Miss Stella was pretty adamant about us getting that info," Stuart muttered.

"Yeah, but..." DeShaun smacked his forehead. "The son of a sheriff's deputy. Breaking and entering. My butt would literally be reduced to charred hamburger. Why don't we just tell my dad about this? Or Yoshi?"

"Don't you think they've got a lot going on right now?" Stuart reasoned. "And what if Reverend McGlazer fell off the wagon or something, like my stupid brother? If everybody found out, he'd be ruined."

"You're trying to kill me at a young age, aren't you, butthole?" DeShaun deadpanned. Bravo whined and tugged his leash. "You too, Bravo!"

"We'll plan it out and come back tomorrow night," Stuart said.

DeShaun held his hands out in a frame toward the ground. "Here Lies DeShaun Lott. Taken Too Soon. Thanks To a Butthole Named Stuart. See Adjacent Stone."

* * * *

McGlazer pulled Stella to his side, placing a gentle, assured hand on her lower back as he guided her out the church's rear door.

The sky was a white sheet of sun and thin cloud cover. The wind and its smell of crumbling leaves was a familiar cloak of fall Stella accepted upon her shoulders for the first time of the season, as if from her gentleman escort while they awaited a coach for the opera house.

"What's out here?" she asked McGlazer. Instead of answering in words he made a show of closing his eyes and drawing in the autumn scents.

He led her around the corner of the building, where she rarely had cause to venture. The wooden slab flooring of the lawn shed had been pried up and leaned against the church wall. The subterranean rock stairway beneath seemed too black, as if refusing to receive the daylight.

Stella willed herself to see into the dark, but the dark willed differently. Stella knew it was best not to bet against the dark.

"Shall we?" McGlazer said, gently pulling her along. Stella squeezed his hand and stopped. "What's down there? I didn't know..."

"Oh, it's new to me too," he reassured. "Don't worry. There's light."

McGlazer drew a butane lighter from his pocket and sparked it as he led her down the time-polished steps. As he opened the narrow rough-hewn door, all she saw was his teeth.

Stella was alarmed that her first step over the threshold was much deeper than she expected—nearly a foot below. She didn't feel so much beguiled now as dependent on the reverend to keep her safe from bats and spiderwebs. Could she depend on her own good sense to leave if things got *too* off-kilter?

McGlazer lit a dusty oil lantern resting on a crusty sconce on the wall to the side of the door. Wavering light bloomed out onto the room, which Stella found surprisingly larger than it *should* have been.

Stella's attention was drawn not to a sight but to a sound; a shifting and shuffling. As she strained to see, McGlazer closed the door behind her.

Chapter 18

Dead Silence

"Where'd you get *that*?" DeShaun asked in a loud whisper, his eyes wide and bright under the half moon.

Stuart pulled up next to DeShaun and stopped his bike, tugging at the jacket lapel of the full ninja outfit he wore. "It was Dennis's. He was in the Sho Kosugi fan club when he was a kid." He didn't feel like mentioning that Dennis had been a good couple of years younger than Stuart was now when it fit him perfectly.

"Swell." DeShaun smirked down at his own jeans and dark blue hoodie in chagrin. "I look like some loser two-bit burglar from a low budget cop show. All I need is one of those bandit masks."

Stuart was relieved that DeShaun didn't laugh at the ninja outfit. He'd had misgivings about it, wondering if it was a childish choice. Yet it was the darkest clothing he could find that didn't have a band logo on it. And it *did* give him a sense of confidence, as if the cinematic ninja master's badass essence imbued its threads.

It was a short ride to the edge of Bennington Street, where the library stood dark, save for a desk lamp somewhere in its heart.

The boys hid their bikes behind a wall of shrubs and crept toward the back. Stuart took off his backpack.

"You got a grappling hook and smoke bombs in there?" DeShaun asked, the first of many whispered wisecracks to come. "Maybe some throwing stars?"

"No but I might be able to make a gag out of my bandana if you feel like it'll be too hard for you to keep your trap shut all on your own."

The windows were the kind that slid sideways, with the latch screwed into the frame halfway up.

"What are you gonna do? Roundhouse kick the glass out?" DeShaun asked.

Stuart put on a pair of heavy-duty rubber work gloves and pressed his hand against the glass. He shimmied the window back and forth, causing the latch to release millimeter by millimeter. Within seconds, it was unlocked.

"Whoa!" DeShaun whispered, as Stuart eased it open. "Dude. Is there something you wanna tell me about yourself?

"Dennis taught me stuff. He was planning to go pro."

"...Pro ninja?"

"You don't think they do it for free, do ya?"

"What if there's an alarm?"

"I cased it when we were here before. Not in the county budget or whatever, I guess."

DeShaun watched his lithe friend climb in, silent as a ghost. Stuart extended a hand from the dimness to assist.

Once in, Stuart closed the window and drew a battery-powered lantern from his backpack. DeShaun had one of his father's mini Maglites.

"Too bad we can't get those photocopies," lamented Stuart.

DeShaun took a Polaroid camera out of his backpack. "Next best thing."

They donned the latex gloves as Jill had instructed before and made a pile of journals, laminated illustrations, and more recent historian's notes.

"This should be like a good start," DeShaun murmured.

They headed up to the main floor and the reference section for books on Old English terminology and beginner's Latin, ducking when a set of headlights swung past, then returned to the downstairs room and went to work under the light of Stuart's lantern.

* * * *

Bennington Street was practically a ghost town by the time the boys settled into their research.

"I don't think Ember Hollow was exactly the Christmas card community we're been taught," Stuart said as he scribbled notes.

"Yeah, more like a soap opera crapped out by an acid freak," DeShaun added. "On steroids."

"But I can't figure out who were the bad guys and who were the good guys. Every time this Bennington character seems like a douche, he pulls a swerve."

"Anything about mushrooms in your stuff?" DeShaun asked.

"Gateway Blooms keep coming up in this journal." Stuart held up a wrinkled leather-bound volume with the name Corman Sparskind tooled into the bottom edge. "And there's something about some specimens in a...um...cask."

"What's a cask?"

"In that Vincent Price flick, it was like, a barrel with wine in it."

Both boys swung their heads toward the storage case.

A minute later, a dusty little wooden drum sat on the table. The top end had a straight piece nailed across the top that could only be a crude twist top.

"Should we open it?" Stuart asked.

"Yes. And we should also apply live electrical wires to our testicles."

Stuart gripped the mini-tun as if in a headlock under his left arm and tried to crank with his right. DeShaun cupped his palms around the far ends of the crosspiece and torqued. A mute crack had them worried they had broken it apart—but lamplight inspection showed the barrel was fine.

"Been closed a long time."

"Duh."

They put it back on the table and eased off the lid, sitting back to avoid the rising dust. DeShaun beamed his flashlight in.

"Are those dried eyeballs?" Stuart wondered.

"Must be the mushrooms."

"Boring."

"Watch the windows while I snap a coupla pictures, will ya?" DeShaun asked. When this was done, DeShaun took from his backpack two full-size ZingGo bars along with two cans emblazoned with exploding logos reading "DRENAL-ADE!" and handed one to Stuart. "My eyes need a break from all this fancy writing."

"Don't get any on this stuff," Stuart said, popping the top on his. "Jill will de-crap-itate us."

DeShaun grinned at his friend.

Stuart took a long gulp and issued a rattling burp that had DeShaun reaching across to clamp a hand over Stuart's mouth, though he giggled like mad. "We're gonna get caught!"

Stuart pushed his hand away, giggling himself. "Okay, sorry."

The giggle fit died—then DeShaun essayed a burp equal to Stuart's, and it started again.

Stuart gulped a throatful of air and pronounced his new word "de-crap-itate" on the vibrating tide of the Loudest Burp Ever.

DeShaun fell to the floor, pressing both hands against his mouth.

Stuart hunched down like an uncontrollably guffawing gargoyle and buried his mouth in his forearm, grateful to be thinking of Jill as holding up just fine, all things considered, and for his friend to still be childish enough to engage in such goofy gastric hijinks. But he also wondered how many more times like these he could have with his best friend.

The boys rode out the spell and returned to the books.

"Ya ever heard of a guy named Conal O'Herlihy?" Stuart whispered.

"Ain't he the Lucky Charms elf, boyo?"

"Nay! He be one o' the original settlers," Stuart explained. "Had himself a row with ol' Wilcott, 'twould seem!"

"How come we didn't learn about him?" DeShaun said.

"Not too hard to guess," Stuart said. "He was a real butthole."

DeShaun drummed his thumb and pinky on the table, just like his father often did.

"Maybe this is what Miss Stella was wondering about." DeShaun dragged from the pile a yellowed binder the size of a couch cushion, propped it on its spine, and let it ease it open. The crack of pages released from each other after years pressed together, along with the smell of weathered paper, was overpowering; even stronger than the artificial lime scent of their energy drinks.

"Hey." DeShaun traced his Maglite beam along some pattern across the two pages. "This is like a blueprint."

"Of what?"

"I think it's the church."

"Yeah?"

"Main floor..." DeShaun muttered, as he flipped the big page.

"Dude..." DeShaun did not continue till Stuart prompted him. "Did you know the church had a basement?"

Stuart came around to look over DeShaun's shoulder. "Had?"

"*Has*, I guess," DeShaun said.

Stuart had barely asked "Where's the door?" when the big tome slammed shut, sending an acrid blast of air into their eyes and nostrils.

The boys yelped as they sprang back onto the floor. They gawked at the little dust puff that roiled and made ghost faces in the lamplight.

"Oh jeez, look at the time," squeaked DeShaun. "It's go-somewhere-not-scary-o'-clock." He rose and scrambled to the window.

"Wait!"

"Wait, *hell!*" DeShaun clawed at the window latch. "That effing book is *haunted!*"

DeShaun's Maglite rolled to and fro on the floor, making the room appear to undulate. Stuart picked it up and aimed it at the book. It just sat doing nothing. "It's probably some kind of cell memory thing in the binding. Don't let it get to you."

"Too late," DeShaun said, as he struggled with the window latch. "Because now, it's keeping us from leaving."

Stuart went to try the window himself. The latch would not budge, not even when he tried his ninja shimmy trick. DeShaun tried helping, with no result.

"Crap!"

"I don't wanna die down here, man," DeShaun said with a voice that cracked just as it had a few weeks earlier.

A cold wind flew across their faces. The table rose and dropped on its feet repeatedly, violently, tossing the historic materials around.

A chair slid out from under it and hurtled toward them.

The boys cried out, dashing off to either side as the chair bashed into the low wall beneath the windows.

Stuart fell on his back at the base of a tall bookcase, which ejected all its contents onto him in an avalanche of paper bricks.

Lunging to help his friend, DeShaun was tripped by a rolling step stool that rocketed into his shins.

Stuart, his arms and ribs smarting from the falling books, dug himself out of the mound in time to see the step stool rolling back to take another charge at DeShaun. "Watch *out!*"

Still prone, DeShaun raised his head in time to keep the stool from ramming him in the head. It missed altogether, lightly banging into the radiator, where it stopped.

The sudden quiet was as dreadful as the assault of ordinary objects had been terrifying.

DeShaun and Stuart, too breathless to speak, huddled close as the dark crushed in on them.

The door at the top of the stairs clicked open with a foreboding echo. Then came footsteps, like hard leather soles clicking deliberately and coldly into a dungeon where emaciated prisoners hung in chains, praying for death.

Stuart stood to face it, whatever it was. DeShaun rose as well, picking up the chair beside him and holding it poised for attack, like he'd seen professional wrestlers do on television.

Halfway down the steps, the figure, a pure black shadow, passed the stairway's enclosing wall—and stopped.

The only sound was their faltering breath, as they beheld the silhouette of a burly figure in a pilgrim-style hat.

A beam of light blasted into the window behind them—a high-powered flashlight.

They had never been so relieved to get caught.

DeShaun tried the window again, further relieved when it opened easily. He stuck both hands out and called, "Don't shoot!"

"Who's there!?" shouted Deputy Yoshida.

"It's me, DeShaun! Stuart's with me! That's all!"

"Open the damned window, boys. All the way!"

DeShaun made a quick check of the stairway as he complied. The burly shadow man was gone.

Yoshida stepped to the window and checked the room with his flashlight. "Just you boys?"

"Yeah," DeShaun said.

"Get out here."

They did.

"What's this?" Yoshida grabbed the lapel of Stuart's ninja uniform. He was not impressed with this misrepresentation of his nation's history. "You supposed to be a cartoon character or something?"

"No, sir."

"What the hell are you doing, breaking into the library?"

"It's a whole big thing, dude," DeShaun said.

"Yeah, I'll bet." Yoshi was *pissed.* "Start squawking."

"Your dad would bury his boot up to your hipbone," Yoshida told DeShaun. "Then you'd have your mom to deal with."

"I know."

"So what gives?"

The boys explained to Yoshida about Stella's request, Jill's absence, and what they had just experienced.

"Well. The rev *has* seemed a little off-kilter lately," Yoshida agreed.

"Something's up," Stuart said. "Something *weird.*"

Yoshida knew that Stuart meant the Big Picture. Ember Hollow. Its people. Its history. Things no one wanted to admit to themselves.

"As for Jill, it's too late to scare her landlords. Come to the station tomorrow and let's fill your dad in."

"Thanks Yoshi."

"Deputy Yoshida, right now. I just caught you breaking and entering. Remember?"

"Yes sir."

Go home," he ordered. "Don't pull anything like this again. I won't tell your dad, this once."

The boys started walking to their bikes.

"Come to me next time," Yoshida finished.

Chapter 19

Mother of Tears

Though the gates were open, Sergeant Shavers stopped at the drive leading through the cemetery and up to Saint Saturn Unitarian. That was where a good many new graves lay; graves that held deceased friends and acquaintances, victims of the parade tragedy.

His victim.

He couldn't put it off any longer or push it back in his mind any further. The horrors in his head had to come out. If that meant confessing to the shooting, so be it.

The nervous fear he felt was greater than that of the worst calls he had ever gone out on. This simple act of disclosure felt like the beginning of his end. Final. Fatal. Perhaps it was only the culmination of his year-long inner agony he felt coming on. Maybe there was even a chance McGlazer could somehow *cleanse* him.

Like an exorcist.

The thought reminded Shavers of what the press had screamed about Everett Geelens's past. Perverse priests had released some inner demon in him, under the guise of an exorcism.

His sparse optimism scattered like the smoke from burning leaves in a hard gust. But resolve remained. Talking to McGlazer was the only way he knew to start.

Shavers's former favorite radio personality Dee Mentia was on, trying her cute kitsch and sounding embarrassingly forced. He frowned at the realization he no longer brightened when she spoke, never even raised the volume. As she intro'ed The Blackrats' "King of Monsters" Shavers forced himself to tap his fingers to the lively beat. He wound his El Camino up the hill and around the church at a turtle's pace. He hadn't made an appointment because that would seem too…*set in stone*. He'd had to leave himself an exit option, and right now, he almost exercised it.

He parked in the rear lot and sipped from a Drenalade he'd been nursing for two days. He was at the back door about to enter when he heard a scraping sound from around the corner of the building.

Half-hoping he would find McGlazer there in the middle of some project from which he couldn't break away, thus forcing a postponement, Shavers went to the corner and peeked around.

The wooden utility shed built against the side of the church was open. Several dusty, oil-spotted sheets of plywood leaned against the wall—the shed's flooring.

Why had they been pulled up? He could go in and ask McGlazer. Or he could just check for himself.

Was it really that important? Or was he delaying the inevitable confrontation with himself?

Shavers walked to the shed's doorway. Even in daylight, the interior was dark as brine. As his eyes adjusted, he saw a set of stone steps leading down to an ancient wooden door.

Scary, yes. But not as scary as a massive crowd of costumed revelers tearing each other to pieces.

Not as scary as confessing to murder a year after the fact.

Like the shed, the door at the bottom of the steps was left ajar, just less than an inch in its frame.

Whatever else this was, "safety hazard" was the most convenient reason to further investigate.

Someone had sure worked hard to unseal it.

Shavers stepped down the narrow steps, disturbing a quick black rodent into a scurrying fit, like a fuzzy pinball bouncing off walls and bumpers. He drew his sidearm and whipped it to and fro, as if his gun hand could catch the animal's frenetic movement. Uttering a hoarse curse, he shoved his weapon back in the holster.

Coming to the bottom of the stairs, Shavers pushed lightly at the door. Sure enough—the same scraping he had heard a minute earlier.

Shavers opened it a bit further and found only thick swirling dust. Beyond that, black.

"Hello?" he called. "Rev? You in here?" Shavers pushed the door open just enough to squeeze his modest beer belly through, cursing himself for leaving his Maglite in the El Camino.

Before his eyes could adjust, he sneezed three times, dizzy and disoriented in the pressing darkness. Looking behind, he was relieved to see gloomy daylight beyond the half-open door.

Footsteps over his head knocked loose still more dust. He felt more sneezes coming on—and overwhelming disorientation.

Shavers felt his breath coming in struggling wheezes, his sinuses closing up to pinpricks. Dizziness hit him like sudden head trauma.

The door through which he'd barely taken a single step now seemed yards away. Maybe he had waited too long to address his problem and lost his damn mind.

The footsteps seemed to stop just above his position. As if someone up there had sensed him.

Shavers picked through his mind for something from his training or experience to comfort him, help him maintain composure. He was fast becoming reacquainted with the sheer primal terror of witnessing the Pumpkin Parade going to hell all around him. Clearer than any previous episode, he saw the chaos: peaceful townies snarling, attacking one another, attacking *themselves*, some of them *on fire*, for Christ's sake.

The woman in the cop costume, her deranged eyes laser-honed on his sidearm. Seconds from dying.

Shavers focused on the door and reached out to it, hoping it was as close as it was supposed to be. But a new spasm of dazed coughing dulled his senses and reduced his vision to violent neon blossoms, his sense of touch to a mere dull pressure.

By the time he could see again, someone was partially blocking the door. A human? Marginally, perhaps.

He sensed something coming up beside him on his right. His gun hand was seized in an alien-fleshed grip; a bad copy of a hand.

Something clamped over his face, aborting his scream.

* * * *

Stuart and DeShaun, with Bravo sitting between them, watched as a man they knew only as Crabs walked out of a "meeting"—a.k.a. interrogation—room, followed by Hudson.

The denim-clad twenty-something raised a finger at the boys. They recognized him from the audience of Outlines shows.

Hudson dropped his big frame in his rusty swivel seat across from the boys as he tossed a notepad to the side.

"What'd Crabs do?" Stuart asked.

"Nothing. Just asked him to drop by so I could see if he had any info on the Fireheads."

"Well," DeShaun began. "Maybe *we* do, Dad."

They told him about the encounter with Pipsqueak at the library, and Jill's no-show the next day. Hudson leaned toward them on his elbows. "You never saw this guy before?'

"I'd remember this dude," said Stuart. "Had a big mouth."

"...And didn't mind using it," added DeShaun.

Hudson closed his eyes tightly, an idiosyncrasy DeShaun knew was a sign of concentration. His dad was putting together pieces of a very troubling puzzle. DeShaun took the opportunity to glance at Yoshida, who nodded.

"Will you get somebody to go by her place?"

Hudson drummed his thumb and pinky as he thought. Yoshida was already up from his desk and pulling on his jacket. "Let me take it. You boys can come along."

* * * *

Crows exchanged urgent calls, piercing the roiling fog cloaking Matilda's mind.

She raised her head—a labor. When she opened her eyes, she thought she was blind.

An angry stinging on her forehead, a throbbing numbness in her back, an insidious intrusion just above her left shoulder blade. She was messed up. It didn't take long to remember how she got that way.

Beyond a thin barrier, the crows fussed.

Most mornings, they gathered in nearby trees to await the peanuts or corn she tossed out for them. But they weren't begging now. They seemed to be mocking her, the murder, from just above.

The scents were unmistakable. She was in the darkness of her storage barn. She'd been shot, stabbed in the back, and then, as a final insult, burned on the forehead with a cigarette.

The Mid-Atlantic Fireheads motorcycle gang had left her for dead—and dead she would very soon be, judging by the way she felt and the wide sticky stain beneath her. She realized the chant she had begun when she'd realized they meant to kill her had probably saved her life—or at least, delayed her death.

On the roof, the crows cawed the news of movement within.

Matilda thought of her goats.

The smarmiest and sneakiest of Nico's crew, Pipsqueak, had caught Amos, which meant Argyle would have stuck around until she too was caught.

"Please, Great Pan. No suffering for my babies. *Please!*"

Tears pushed at her eyelids, but there was no time for them. She fought to fold one shaky knee up underneath herself, to gain enough height and leverage to raise her right hand. She could reach across herself, though it was difficult. Her arm seemed to weigh a thousand pounds.

She got her right hand around her neck, spider-walking her fingers till she reached the knife handle. She levered it minutely, weeping from the pain. She worked it back and forth, loosening it, the pain deeper and more intense with each shift—but it was working loose. Within a few excruciating seconds, the knife fell out and off to the side. She gave a weak cry of both jubilation and exquisite suffering, grateful for the spaces between acidic throbs.

She lowered her face to the plywood floor to rest, breathing in the mingled scent of dust and her own blood. Matilda repeated the chant of renewal, then pulled both knees up and rose to a wobbly kneel.

She took a deep breath, though she knew it would hurt her ribs. She underestimated; her entire upper body radiated sharp agony and bolstered the steady throb of her punctured upper back muscle. She felt her life steadily leaking from the bullet wound.

She felt around and found the athame, then crawled to one of the shelving units, using it to climb her way to a stand. Finding and switching on the light at the entryway would be both a great expenditure of precious physical energy and a risk. She knew by the feel of the shelf's contents roughly where she was, and thus determined where she needed to go.

Her feeble knees wobbled when she stumbled to the wall and clambered along it with her hands, till she reached the end and essentially fell to the next one, then the next. After catching her breath, she counted bottles till she reached the one that would accelerate her healing—as long as she took the right amount.

There was little room for error. Matilda always measured the liquid by drops. So, as long as she could keep her hands steady...

Matilda leaned back against the end of the shelving and held the bottle with both hands, whispering the words of revivification. She raised it to her mouth, tilted, and counted out seven drops, each of which assaulted her tongue with a sour putrescence. Fighting her gag reflex, she capped the bottle and dropped to her knees, slapping her hand against her mouth, then clutching her throat to keep the bilious elixir from escaping.

The effort drained her. It would be several more minutes before she could move again.

Vengeance bore her no sympathy.

A difficult trek toward the doors was next, to find the small trunk in which she kept odd tools and implements she occasionally used. Her fingers soon fell upon the trunk's hasp. "Praise ye, Pan..."

Opening it, she chided herself about the squeaky hinges, hoping Nico had not posted one of his soldiers outside. She froze to listen. Hearing nothing, she reached into the trunk and felt around till her fingers met the sturdy pistol grip of a veterinary bonesaw.

With Matilda's more conventional tools in her house, the bonesaw would have to do the work of several. The curvature of its six-inch, kidney shaped sterling steel blade would allow her to cut through the plywood flooring and crawl out at the barn's far corner, unseen.

Then, to cross into the neighboring field beyond the row of scrubby brush that served as a border marker, and there, to begin the work of conjuring.

Knowing she was paying off some of her own dark karma didn't offer comfort. Only vengeance could do that now.

She longed for her grimoire—her life's work. But she could make do without it. The work would be sloppier than she would prefer, less predictable, but she would rejuvenate herself just a little more, and then...

And *then,* by Pan...

Oh, what Dark Doings, what thorny hate and venomous abandon would flourish and fester, to avenge evils still unfolding, this bleak autumn day.

* * * *

Whenever Stuart rode somewhere with DeShaun and Hudson, or in this case Yoshida, it felt like he had a dad, and a brother his age, and they were all doing menfolk stuff, like going to chop down trees, or maybe catch an escaped alligator that was terrorizing the town. Having Bravo around added to the fantasy.

But the needling dread he carried with him as they rode to Jill's only made him feel anxious and helpless and smaller than ever.

Yoshida parked on the street across from the front door and instructed the boys to stay in the department's Durango with Bravo. The Toppers were confused and wary when they answered the door, but quickly warmed to the genial Yoshida and waved to the boys as well.

"Sorry to bother you folks. Just worried about Jill."

"Oh. I thought she was here," said Mrs. Topper.

"Her bike's here," Stuart said through the open window, frowning down at the garage apartment.

"If you don't mind, Mr. Topper, I just want to stick my head in and ask if she's okay," Yoshida told the couple.

The boys knew that just by opening the door, Yoshida would see if lights were left on or off incongruously, listen for suspicious sounds, check for signs of struggle, or smell for decay, heaven forbid. "Stuart, you boys stay in the vehicle."

Yoshi, still being curt with the boys after catching them at the library, told them to roll up the window. Reasonable enough, given Bravo's implacable drive to find Candace.

They did as told, crowding together at the window with their furry friend.

The Toppers handed Yoshida the key, and he made his way down the slope; hand on sidearm.

Bravo whined and scratched at the half-inch opening at the top of the window, his ears pricked up high.

Yoshida knocked and called to Jill.

He unlocked the door and entered with his weapon drawn.

Stuart's eyes took on an intense alertness. "If that guy is in there, and he somehow gets past Yoshi…"

DeShaun's expression went deadly earnest. "…We jump out and nail his ass."

It was a fantasy, and they both knew it. But not at the *front* of their minds, like adults. Very much to the rear, like when they were just a couple of years younger, playing themselves as hardened detectives with black belts in a dozen martial arts, marksmanship world records, and all the right words for women with all the right curves, in the imaginary but dangerous alleys and seedy juke joints of Ember Hollow's quiet suburban neighborhoods.

But this was bigger than that. The boys sensed that Jill's life was on the line.

"I bet Bravo will help too," Stuart said, and the dog gave a low half-bark, as if joining in their pretend scenario. It made the fantasy more comforting than ever.

They watched the open apartment door for a second or so. It seemed so much longer. "Say. Do they keep another piece in here?"

DeShaun leaned up and checked the glovebox. "Nope. But I don't care."

"Me neither."

Stuart's fantasies often included him and DeShaun having to back up Hudson or another of the deputies with a big arrest, working together like Starsky and Hutch—or Jackie Chan and Chris Tucker, if they were feeling snarky.

Right now, he found himself wanting that more than ever; *wanting* the mutton-chopped loudmouth to come running out in an escape attempt, only to be floored by Stuart's magnificent Stan Hansen-style clothesline, followed by a "Macho Man" Randy Savage top rope elbow drop courtesy of DeShaun. Then Bravo would chomp down on his nuts for the *coup de grace*. That would be the *best*.

The Toppers did not seem to share the boys' bravado. They stood on their front stoop in baggy pastel sweat suits, poised to haltingly dash inside at the first sign of trouble.

Yoshida emerged, his gaze narrowed and distant. "She's not here," he called.

The boys hopped out, bringing Bravo by his leash. "What now?" asked Stuart.

Yoshida handed the key back to Mr. Topper and put his hand on Stuart's shoulder. It was more comforting than Stuart would have expected. "Now we find her."

Chapter 20

Within the Darkness

With a burlap sack full of essentials clenched in her teeth, Matilda eased herself feet-first through the triangle she had cut at the corner of the barn's plywood flooring with the bonesaw. She needed a few seconds to let her pain ease, to meditate and renew her precious reserves of energy before she began a crawling trek in the foot or so clearance between the barn floor and the ground.

She had gained a few yards when a scent sent her mind and heart reeling with agony. The bikers were cooking meat.

Her goats.

Matilda trembled with despair, but refused to give it release, letting it feed the flames of her fury. She would need the energy of her grief, if she could contain it long enough, for the ritual ahead. She chanted blessings to Pan, focusing on her love for the goats and projecting it to her patron deity, as much to focus her mind as to maintain her vitality.

* * * *

Well, I'm probably about to get my ass kicked, Stuart thought, as he stood at the front door clenching and unclenching his fists. *But not without leaving my autograph.*

* * * *

Dennis had promised about fifty different people he would not drive while drunk; he would just park somewhere, get his fill and come home when he woke up—or more likely, got dropped off by Hudson, or some other deputy. But the hell with it. What was another broken promise? That's what his whole life was.

Hell, maybe his dad had stayed a little too long under that thresher just to keep from having to see his oldest boy going to hell in a hatbox before his very eyes.

He was running out of parking lots and unused roads where he could park, drink and pass out. When Bert Gilly had started mowing corn early that morning, he must have surely seen the hearse. Out of respect for the deceased elder Barcroft or whatever, he hadn't rousted Dennis and hadn't called the sheriff. Hell, he'd probably even saved the section near where the hearse was parked for last. But Gilly's work had to be done just like every other farmer's, and when he *had* gotten around to harvesting near Dennis's spot, the whiskey buzz had not been quite strong enough to keep him comatose through the noise.

So Dennis had headed home in light traffic, oblivious that the local school system's early dismissal time had come and gone.

Promises broken and snoot quite full, Dennis Barcroft pulled his hearse in at an ugly angle against the curb by his yard and stumbled out, stopping to steady himself when the world spun hard to his left.

He was hopeful that Ma—bless her deluded heart—wasn't home or was busy in the basement with laundry and wouldn't come out to see him fall on his face in the yard, en route to falling on his face inside.

The front door opened. Ma would be in his grill any second, crying her eyes out, making him feel worse than he already did. Good thing he wouldn't remember.

Nah, it was Stuart.

After school already? Well good. He could lean on his little buddy till he got—

Stuart loaded up as he got a running start, landing a solid overhand right hook on Dennis's cheek.

Dennis took a hard step back, all the cool gone from his eyes for once. "Aah...what the *hell?*"

Stuart threw the same punch, landed it again and sent Dennis stumbling back against the hearse. "Stuart? What are you...?"

Stuart went to the well again, lunging to throw the same right. This time Dennis raised both hands and blocked, then shoved Stuart back, making him almost slide into a split in the slick grass. Stuart regained his footing and came at Dennis again, this time firing a left to the gut. Dennis grunted from the impact.

"Jill got *kidnapped*, you *asshole!*" Stuart screamed, throwing haymakers that mostly landed on Dennis's forearms.

"Wh...*Whut?*" Dennis slurred.

Stuart's dad had taught him enough about fighting to know when it was time to switch to straight punches. He popped Dennis with two in a row, right on the mouth—and it felt satisfying as hell.

Then Dennis tackled him to the ground and Stuart knew he was boned, just like every other jackass who had ever pushed Dennis too far.

Dennis pinned Stuart's throat with his left as his right fist rose like a wrecking ball—and froze. "What the hell did you just say?"

"*Jill!*" Stuart began, grateful that he had brought her up before losing his advantage. "She got *taken*, you drunk bastard!"

Blood dripped on Stuart's nose from Dennis's. Through tears, Stuart saw that the tattooed fist remained poised for destruction.

"You remember the chick you swore to protect till the day *you die!*?" Stuart screamed the final words, hoping they could puncture the drunken exterior and find the Dennis he knew.

The fist slowly lowered. The furrows of Dennis's face deepened with regret. "Tell me what happened, Stuart."

"She's missing." Stuart couldn't punch Dennis anymore, but his cracking, accusing voice was as good as a fist. "Somebody got her."

"Tell me *what the hell you're talking about!*?" Dennis was crying just like Stuart. Tears rained on Stuart like the first drops of a catastrophic deluge.

Stuart pushed Dennis's left hand away. "Some hairbag got her because *you weren't there!*"

Dogs barked. Neighbors stepped away from their routines to watch and murmur about the poor drunk punk and all the pain he was causing.

Dennis pushed himself up and pulled Stuart to his feet. "Tell me you're joking."

The despair and guilt in his brother's face broke Stuart. He couldn't stay angry; not any more than he could understand drinking or voting or driving a hundred miles, or hell, even going to bed without the fear of pissing the sheets.

Dennis sank to his knees, just as Ma came to the door. "Boys? What's happening?"

Stuart didn't want her to see Dennis like this. He hugged Dennis and hid him with his little frame. He tried to bring Dennis to a stand, tried with all his might, and just when it seemed he wasn't strong enough, his brother became buoyant in his arms; a helpless soul in need of a stronger one, even if only a *little* bit stronger.

"Boys?" Ma called.

"Come on, Big Bro," Stuart said, leading Dennis toward the door. "Let's fix this goddamn mess."

Chapter 21

The Hatchling

"The parade easily pays three months of my overhead," said Albin Bogan, owner and proprietor of The Gas Giant, a sprawling ten-pump facility just inside the county line that had become a tourist trap in itself, offering costumes, handmade Halloween decorations, baked goods and, for photo ops, two seven-foot resin statues: Universal's Frankenstein Monster and a generic and rather chintzy gorilla for which Albin had nonetheless had a "King Kong" sign professionally carved.

Out-of-towners heading to the parade either knew to stop there or were delighted to find the one stop pre-parade pit stop. It made a killing.

"No parade, I might have to shut down for who knows how long."

The other business owners who crowded the reception area lacked Bogan's influence individually, but more than equaled it as a group—and that group was growing by the day.

"Either way, we need to know now," called Patty Chenoweth of Main Street's Patty Cakes.

"I appreciate your position, folks. We're all feeling the continuing strain from last year's unforeseeable tragedy." Though the crowd, like villagers gathering to hunt down a wayward monster, had been put together on the fly, Mayor Stuyvesant's response was already well-rehearsed. "It's important to use this as an opportunity to strengthen our self-reliance, our sense of community and our commitment to patriotic values. American jobs for American workers has long been my—"

"Can we not go there right now?" Albin Bogan closed his eyes and held up both hands in a defensive posture. "Main thing we wanna know is—is the parade a go, or not?"

"It's too late in the game for waffling, Mayor," said Patty Chenoweth. Mayor Stuyvesant's nervous glance at Hollis had the assistant stepping in front of her like a bodyguard. "Mayor Stuyvesant is stretched to the limit right now trying to salvage the parade. We appreciate everyone coming out but please call and make an appointment if we haven't addressed your specific concerns."

There was more grumbling, even shouting, but the townies shuffled out and dispersed within ten minutes—except for one man.

Guillermo Trujillo, whose landscaping operation serviced many of the frustrated business people now making their way back to their homes and shops, stood outside the reception door, peering in from the side.

Stuyvesant had already retreated to her office, but Hollis saw the greensman and his earnest face and waved him in.

* * * *

Matilda knew her strength, fueled by vengeance, would be a fast and hot fire, and there was still so much work to do. She thanked Pan that it was close to Samhain, the peak of a pagan's power. Her confidence and commitment as a black witch were at peak, free of the regretful misgivings she had borne for decades.

The question of whether this magic—technically baneful—was also beneficent could be argued by her estranged colleagues. As far as she was concerned, ridding the world of Nico's gang would be good for all mankind, even if it was a mere byproduct of her burning vengeance.

As for the ceremony, without her grimoire she would have to fill in some gaps, as with the revivification spell. But that had worked well enough. She had some of the goats' hair scrounged from her sweater and a white gold toe-ring, but these felt like paltry offerings. She would make up the difference with the pure passion of rage.

She stumbled to the massive prize pumpkin she had been growing for Winchell and patted it. Its purpose would have to change.

Unaware of the time—the umber cloud cover gave little clue—Matilda gathered sticks, dried hay and hickory leaves. She took from the burlap bag a small copper cauldron meant as a decoration but perfectly functional in a pinch, and hung it over the kindling.

Allowing herself to feel enough sadness and anger for the loss of her beloved little horned kids to renew her fury, Matilda lit the fire, and began the ritual. She mumbled ancient words she had never spoken before; hoping intention and *blood* would make up for clumsy enunciation.

Smoke rose from bold flames that stabbed at the air. Matilda cast in the offerings.

Blending with the firelight, the setting sun cast the fields and forest—and Matilda's own flesh—in an eldritch hue somehow both gray and luminous.

She created a triangle of sigils in the dirt, then carved these into the pumpkin rind with her athame.

She swiped her hands through the sticky wet patches of her wounds, snarling at the pain, and patted bloody palm-prints on the massive fruit, willing her vengeance into it as she called to The Horned One.

Matilda praised and seduced The Trickster with her words, then begged his consideration. Herb-tinctured sweat stung her wounds, as she spun around and around, whispering all the while.

"Praise ye, beast and god
Blessings and beauty in thy path
Spend thy kindness upon me
Take my blood as wine
Deliver me an agent
A vessel for my wrath."

The candles grew brighter.

She raised her hands as high as pain would allow, as high as hate could force them.

Decades of discipline held drumskin-tight. The chant, the willed vision, the intention rose. When the air was dense with a malignant ether, Matilda drew the athame from her sweater pocket, and released her tears.

She gave voice to the heartache of her loss, the shame of her humiliation. She continued to chant, to desire, to *know* the bloody future without doubt.

Chanting louder and faster, foregoing notions of breathing and comfort, Matilda forced herself to envision what the Fireheads had done to Amos and Argyle, what she knew they had done to others. She spoke aloud these crimes with fury and outrage. She growled and screamed and spun counter clockwise until she felt disembodied.

She fell to the ground and rolled, still to the left. She abandoned the chant for stream-of-consciousness commanding wails. "O Pan! *See* my hatred! Let it be a seed and *grow!* Bring me an avenging demon! An unholy *destroyer!* Great God of Tricks and Terror, please *fill* this gourd with your deviance, and *my* hatred! Let us birth the purest of punishers! The most unforgiving of angels!"

Did the ground rumble? Or was it the sky?

"Choke *closed* the conduits of goodness! Of forgiveness! Of *redemption!*"

She willed herself to a stand, and so mote it be. She coiled her body to draw venom from the earth into her feet, through her guts, and to project it through her fingertips into the great gourd.

Black lightning sizzled, darkening the twilight to full midnight, tracing the pattern she had carved, entering the pumpkin.

"Take whatever piece of me ye wish! Tear it away to create destruction and *destroy* creation! Make them pay! Make the Fireheads suffer, I beg of ye!" Matilda ran at the pumpkin and smashed her body into it, snarling as she bit the rind, rubbing her face along its edges, raping it with pure intention. "I command thee!"

Spent of all her fires of rage and visions of violence, she fell toward oblivion for a third time that day, as her own bitter sobs came to her ears with the vibration of a distant bell's tolling.

Then the pumpkin rumbled, startling her. She scooted back.

The spell fire flared high, billowing like a miniature hydrogen bomb.

The pumpkin rocked and pulsed in time with Matilda's unsteady breath. She wondered if what hatched from the fleshy egg would even be compatible with her worldly senses.

A *crack.*

An inch-wide split appeared in the rind, starting at its sapling-thick stem, plunging to its base.

Brown-orange fluid streamed out, carrying pumpkin seeds in streams of placental goo.

Matilda stood up on her quaking legs and stepped back, terrible expectancy blossoming in her breast. Yet she still mumble-chanted her will toward the thing, conscious enough to target it with her exhilarated fear and fury. Her hand went numb from her death-grip on the athame.

The split widened another few inches, onto utter blackness. The rind shifted and pulsed like maggot-infested corpse flesh.

Something like a hoarse whisper fluttered to Matilda's ears, made them tingle and burn.

More seeds flowed out from the bottom like chunky lava.

Trembling pale fingers emerged to grasp the edge of the broken rind.

Matilda took two steps to help the hatchling and stopped. This wave of energy was more unnerving than even Nico's.

It was all she could do, even exhausted as she was, to keep from breaking into a run, to gain as much distance between herself and—

The other hand appeared on the left side. Blue veins pulsed over spider-leg knuckles, the bones beneath stretching the ghastly skin.

A high-pitched straining sound emerged, and the pumpkin's child peeked an eye through the abyss.

Something familiar.

With another straining effort, the rind cracked and broke with the robust sound of a toppling oak. The pumpkin's huge halves fell to the sides.

A tall, gaunt figure—human, technically—stood naked and glistening in the firelight. He regarded Matilda with an expression of singular joy.

More than ever, Matilda wanted to run. Instead she fell to her knees, beholding the Christ of Killers in worshipful despair.

"Happy Halloween!" croaked the reborn Trick or Treat Terror, Everett Geelens, his gaze brightening as it fell upon the gleaming athame in Matilda's trembling hand.

* * * *

"What do we do if they start slugging?" Yoshida asked Hudson, as Dennis pulled the hearse up outside the Lott house, just behind Hud's battle-scarred Blazer. Pedro walked to meet him there in the street.

"Call the National Guard," Hudson answered, doffing his jacket in preparation of trying to get between two angrier-than-usual punk rockers.

Hopping out of the passenger side, Stuart threw a wary nod at Pedro, and visibly relaxed when it was returned.

Pedro stepped well within Dennis's personal space. Dennis took off his sunglasses and met his bandmate's gaze.

"You sober or what, bro?" asked Pedro.

"Right now," Dennis answered. "Yeah."

"What now?"

"Try to make things right."

"What things d'ya mean, Dennis?"

"Everything I broke." Dennis reached into his jacket pocket for a packet of cigarettes. "All right?"

"You, man," Pedro said, as he grasped the cig pack. "You gotta fix *you*. Right?"

Dennis glared at the cigs they both held in trembling grips.

Yoshida almost took a step toward them, until Hudson mumbled, "Not yet."

Dennis relinquished the smokes to Pedro, who crushed them.

"I guess we're gonna rumble," Dennis said. "With some hairy-ass dirtbags, that is. And get our drummer back."

Pedro smiled. "Damn right."

Dennis did the same, and embraced his friend like they had just finished a brutal set in front of a rowdy sold-out crowd.

"All right," Hudson said, visibly relaxing. "Pillow talk later. Let's all go in and figure this thing out."

Chapter 22

Don't Go in the Woods

Leticia had set out a card table and a couple of folding chairs aligned with the dinner table, at which Hudson took his seat and laced his fingers.

"Gentlemen," he began, "shit just got real."

Deputy Yoshida gave a grim chuckle.

Dennis paced behind him, Hudson's big orange coffee mug in one trembling hand, a filterless cigarette in the other.

Pedro placed right foot on left thigh and tugged at his bootlace.

DeShaun and Stuart sat determined and attentive.

Bravo scratched at the door.

"Yoshida and I could lose our jobs," Hudson began. "But we all have a lot more at stake."

DeShaun, beyond concern for his father and Jill, felt a deep sense of pride. He was the son of a man so determined to save lives he would sacrifice his job and, God forbid, his very *life*.

"The Fireheads have two of our people. We have to get them back. I can't go to the chief or anybody else with some nutbag story about…" There was no need to finish.

Yoshida rubbed his temples, still in disbelief that he had agreed to go along with all this.

"We have nowhere to start. No decent leads," Hudson continued.

DeShaun raised his hands like he was in class, then remembered he wasn't. "We do though, Dad."

"Talk, boy," said Hudson.

"Bravo will take you right to Candace." He pointed at the big mastiff, who took a second from his unending vigil at the door to acknowledge his name. "All you have to do is pay attention. He'll point right toward them." DeShaun went to Bravo and vigorously rubbed the big dog's neck. "Like he is now."

Hudson watched Bravo acknowledge DeShaun with a tail wag before returning to his urgent vigil.

"You guys should try walking him sometime," added Stuart.

"I'd say it's worth a shot," Hudson said.

"So we really do this off the books?" Yoshida asked.

"I'm not ordering or even asking," Hudson said. "I'll go alone if I have to."

Yoshida allowed his head to thump on the table.

"Even with this guy," Pedro quipped, tilting his head at Dennis, "we're a little outnumbered."

"You forget Jill," Dennis said. "When shit hits the fan, she hits back."

"You gonna stay dry?" Hudson asked, not without recrimination.

Tension rose among the men and boys.

Dennis raised his head and met Hudson's stare. "I'm done drinking." He looked at Stuart. "If it kills me."

This was typical alcoholic's bravado. No one thought Dennis was through with drinking. Likewise, no one doubted he would stay sober long enough to rescue Jill.

"Will you be all right with a gun?" Yoshida asked.

Dennis drank several hearty gulps of the steaming coffee. "I don't want one."

"Not sure they'll do much good anyway," said Pedro. "To that thing at the group home, Hud's .44 was like a pellet gun."

"All the same," Yoshida said. "I'll be packing."

Stuart cleared his throat, realizing he'd better say what he'd been withholding. "You guys better get some silver."

Yes, there was a timid tremble in his voice. But there were no gales of laughter in response, only mild incredulity from everybody but DeShaun.

"Bullets?" Yoshida asked. Stuart searched for ridicule in his eyes, but it wasn't there. "You boys know more about this stuff than we do."

"Can you get some?" asked Pedro.

The grownups were taking it seriously. For the first time in a while, Stuart didn't feel like a little kid pretending to be mature.

"They're not exactly standard equip," said Hudson. "Does it have to be bullets?"

"Oh…" Now Stuart felt in over his head. "Well…you can't just flash it at 'em like a cross, I don't think."

"Shotgun shells, maybe," suggested DeShaun. "Replace the pellets with pieces of…forks and spoons, or whatever."

Both Hudson and Dennis winced at the idea of trying to commandeer the good silver from their respective matriarchs. "All right," Hudson said. "Whatever we have to do."

"And something on Bravo's collar too," Stuart insisted.

"Yeah, good thinking," said Yoshida.

"DeShaun. Stuart," Hudson began. "Stay on this town founder thing."

The boys nodded enthusiastically; very much a part of the team that was saving the town.

* * * *

"Miss Stella's car is gone," DeShaun noted as the boys hopped off their bikes and approached the front door of the Riesling house.

"Mr. Riesling's here, though."

"Maybe we can just leave this stuff and come back later to tell her about…" Stuart trailed off.

"We're supposed to keep it on the D.L."

"He's always wrapped up in chemistry stuff," Stuart countered. "Probably won't even care."

Stuart rang the real, year-round doorbell first, then the coffin-shaped Halloween novelty beside it. It emitted a maniacal laugh that sounded like a bad Lugosi impersonation. DeShaun imitated the imitation. "You loook like a good veen-teege, young man!"

Stuart placed his middle fingers against his lips like they were fangs. "And *you* look like you can go f—"

Bernard opened the door. "Boys?" The way he regarded them, one might have thought they were Men in Black. "What's…? Is everything all right?"

"Well sure," DeShaun said. "We just came by to talk to your lovely wife. Is she…?"

Before he could finish, Bernard's face did a dramatic and alarming contortion, going from bewildered to damn near suicidal, his lips quivering.

"Hey, uh…you okay?" Stuart asked.

Bernard slowly moved his head side to the side, like a toddler refusing to go on a merry-go-round.

Both boys cleared their throats. "Um. Should we…?"

"Come in, boys."

"Well we don't really have time for any chemistry experiments…"

"Me neither." Bernard shuffled into the living room, compelling Stuart and DeShaun to follow. He plopped onto the couch, covered his face with both hands and muttered something incoherent that seemed like a question.

"You sure we shouldn't maybe check back later?" asked Deshaun.

Bernard let his hands fall. "Stella left, boys."

"Any idea what time she might—"

"For good," Bernard said, his lips quivering again.

"What, uh…why…would you say that?"

Bernard squeezed his eyes shut tight as fists. "It's a long story. But I guess it was bound to happen." He stood and went to the bay windows, standing where the vertical blinds were open just enough for him to see out. He rubbed the top of his head. "I tell ya. That Reverend McGlazer is one smooth, handsome bastard."

"You think Reverend McGlazer and Mrs.—your wife—are… having an affair?"

"I'm sure of it." His shoulders rose and fell with suppressed sobs.

Stuart regarded the coffee table, the science and engineering journals that lay strewn there the way a cooler guy might toss his fitness and motorcycle and naked girl magazines around at his bachelor pad.

He and DeShaun could only blink at one another helplessly.

Bernard came to the couch to sit between them, taking his eyeglasses from his pocket with a sniffle. "What do you boys have there? Might be a worthwhile distraction."

"Well…" DeShaun gave Stuart a look that meant it was too late.

The boys laid the materials out on the coffee table.

"It's town history stuff," DeShaun explained. "Random notes, sketches. Weirdness."

Bernard raised the polaroid of the mushroom sketch to just inches from his face. "This resembles *Mykespatmosia*."

"You recognize that?"

"Hard to say for sure based on this. Cherokee history talks about a fungus that was brought here by white settlers." He turned the polaroid about thirty degrees, as if its secrets would settle in the corner. "The Indians wanted nothing to do with it. They're believed to have eradicated it."

"What's the big deal?" Stuart asked.

"It's said to have hallucinogenic properties," Bernard answered. "Is this Latin?"

"You read Latin?" DeShaun asked.

"I can ascertain the gist." Bernard stroked his mustache; one side, then the other. "Stella asked you boys to get this stuff? Why?"

"She said she was...worried about..."

Bernard's face crunched up in sadness and regret. "McGlazer. Right?" The boys didn't answer. Bernard clapped his hands over his face again. "Boys," he sobbed through his fingers. "When you get a good girl, you *keep* her! No matter what!"

Stuart and DeShaun patted his shoulders. "Okay, Mr. Riesling."

"I mean it!" There was manic intensity in his face. "Don't take her for granted! Don't brush her off 'cause you're too focused on something else!"

"We really gotta go," explained DeShaun, quickly joined by Stuart. "Yeah! Dinner, homework..." He glanced at his wrist like a watch was ticking furiously at him there.

As they rose and collected materials, Bernard scrutinized the polaroid again. "Are you going to find Stella?"

"Um...Yes sir."

"Well...Will you please tell her I'm sorry? And also, that I miss her, and I need her, and—"

"Sure will, Mr. Riesling." DeShaun popped up a quick wave as he and Stuart backed toward the door. "Gotta go."

* * * *

Wearing her worry like a Dick Smith makeup appliance, Leticia Lott unlocked the china cabinet. She delicately grasped each utensil with a crisp white cloth napkin and set them on yet another pristine white cloth unfolded on the dining room table. It made Hudson think of some ancient samurai pre-combat ritual.

Bravo had left the front door to come to Leticia's side. He sniffed up at the implements, a new sense of optimism in his pricked ears. He *knew* he was going to his little girl.

"You're determined to worry me to death, Hudson," Leticia said. "But if you don't, I am going to personally kill you when you get back, for what you did to our Blazer and what you're doing to my silver."

Seated at the end of the table, Yoshida kept his gaze well clear of any contact with Leticia's as he pried open the end of a shotgun shell with his pocketknife. He was a good cop and a brave man, but he knew his limits.

That wasn't enough. "You can take your little project out to the garage and away from my tablecloth, deputy."

Yoshida quickly complied, leaving Hudson the sole focus of her ire. "You're gonna run for sheriff next election," Leticia began. "You're doing the job cut-rate already."

Hudson didn't say anything as he went to follow Yoshida. She grabbed his big arm in her little hand and made him face her until he said "Okay."

Hudson actually liked the confidence and optimism she expressed in not only his capability but his chances of survival. It was never about browbeating or cynical nagging with her. She loved, respected and *believed* in him. It was only natural she would be, at the very *least*, perturbed by the hardships his job imposed on their family. She *knew* what she had signed up for. But Leticia Lott was no shrinking violet. She was exactly what Hudson had wanted in a woman since he'd been DeShaun's age.

He pulled her in for a tight embrace, smiling when she grunted a little in his powerful squeeze, loving that she squeezed him back equally, despite the eighty pounds he had on her.

* * * *

"So glad we survived back at the library," DeShaun said. "Cause I'd hate to miss out on coming *here* to croak instead."

"Will you please knock that off?" Stuart said.

The boys read the paperboard sign affixed to the closed gate, authoritatively scripted to read:

"Attention Parishioners: St. Saturn will be indefinitely closed for all activities due to renovations. Thanks."

"I'll boost you and you help me down on the other side." They used to alternate when it came to physical teamwork. Neither boy acknowledged that DeShaun did the bulk of the heavy stuff these days.

Once across the fence, the boys faced the church from behind a wide grave marker, as if to shield themselves from the gloomy eldritch feeling it gave off.

They tried the front sanctuary door first, hoping to find Stella inside and avoid McGlazer. It was locked. They decided not to knock, opting to go around and try the rear entrance.

Rounding the corner, both boys stopped upon seeing the old wooden slabs leaned against the wall. They approached the mower shed with caution, like the detectives they'd once pretended they were, exchanging frowns on seeing the rectangular abyss inside.

"There it is," DeShaun said. "The basement."

"Somebody else discovered it before us."

The boys drew closer and peered down.

"Weird," DeShaun crinkled his nose. "I don't like it."

Stuart started down. "You coming?"

DeShaun followed, grumbling about impending demise. At the bottom of the steps, they found themselves eight or so feet below ground level. Stuart examined the doorknob as if it could be booby-trapped. "Let's not make it a big spooky thing." DeShaun grabbed the ancient crusty latch handle, finding it locked.

"I think we should knock," Stuart said. "The sign said renovations, so maybe that's what they're doing. Opening up this basement."

"I hope no termites or, like, millipedes come skittering out." DeShaun gave two quick knocks.

Before he had time to withdraw his hand, robust knocks came in response; shaking dust loose from the edges and casing. They were up the steps before the fourth and final knock.

Backing away from the pit, they grabbed each other's arms. "That was just like at the library!"

"No way we're going in there now," Stuart shook his head violently.

DeShaun cupped his hands around his mouth, even as he continued backing away. "Miss Stella!?"

The sequence of four knocks again, louder than before, echoed like thunder, and vibrated up into their feet, which the boys promptly got moving.

They ran for the fence, until remembering their purpose. They stopped to hold each other again, by the arms, at least, and dare a peek at the shed.

"We gotta find Miss Stella," Stuart said with a wavering voice.

"Yeah." DeShaun's tone sounded more like his old little kid self.

"Back door," Stuart said, and they started walking, staying close to one another, going the long way around rather than having to pass near the basement and its booming door.

Just before rounding that corner, they heard the click of the door and a jangle of keys.

DeShaun yanked Stuart down to the ground in a crouch against the wall—too easily, really—and scrunched against him. The boys peeked around and watched McGlazer, whistling some weird-sounding tune, walk right past his own car and get into Stella's.

The boys furrowed their brows at one another. Realizing McGlazer would see them when he pulled out, they ducked behind the air conditioning unit and crushed together, Stuart having to shrink tightly to accommodate his ever growing friend. "Jeez!" he whispered in annoyance.

"Should we stop him?"

"I don't think so."

McGlazer drove away, and the boys unfolded.

"Let's see if we can get a clue where he's going," DeShaun said.

They stayed close to the wall and watched McGlazer take the big family sedan down to the gates, unlock them, drive past, re-lock and leave.

"What if he spots our bikes?" Stuart fretted.

They waited, tense. McGlazer did not appear to have seen the bikes hidden behind shrubs. Wheeling out onto Main Street, the reverend took the first back road he reached.

"He's trying to be inconspicuous," Stuart noted.

"Now what?"

Stuart put his hands on his hips and huffed at the windows.

"Don't tell me you're gonna do the ninja window gag again," DeShaun said.

"Should we?"

"Did you say 'we?'" DeShaun asked. "This is a good time for me to inform you of your new nickname," DeShaun deadpanned.

"I'll bite," Stuart smirked.

"Yoyo," DeShaun began. "You're on Your Own."

"Sure buddy. Let's go, before he comes back."

Chapter 23

Don't Look in the Basement

A keening whine rising from his throat, Bravo stepped across Pedro and scratched furiously at the rear passenger window.

"Bravo says take the next left, dude," said Pedro as he rubbed the dog's haunches.

Hudson swung the department's Dodge Durango, snuck out for this bit of unofficial business, off the highway and onto Crabtree Road, an artery into the heart of isolation, where moonshine, marijuana and mountain magic had flourished for decades.

The radio, tuned to a just-audible volume, was on WICH. Hudson hoped the station's playlist of spookabilly and horror rock tunes would serve as both a mild distraction and a battle anthem for the quintet.

The department rarely had cause to venture this far, not due to a low crime rate, but because few who lived this far would even *think* to call, unless there was a fire or a corpse. Even then, folks mostly just took care of it themselves. Trust in government tended to dissipate in direct proportion to degree of isolation.

Hudson did a quick and discreet once-over of his troops' faces. Dennis was green around the gills, and a little shell-shocked, but at least he was moving his head with the music. Armed, almost laughably with brass knuckles and a hunting knife, it was doubtful he could be counted on for more than helping to get the hostages to the Durango. With luck, he wouldn't get himself killed.

There was no doubt Pedro would fight and follow orders. The question mark was his focus. His first priority would be protecting Dennis. Hudson didn't have the luxury of trying to keep the punkers uninvolved. If he tried, they would only set out on their own. As long as the musicians carried their own weight, the entire group had a reasonable chance of success.

"Otto here with you—make that "Oddball" through the Halloween season," sang-spoke the radio deejay. "Sure beats what they call me around here when I come in a coupla minutes late! *Sheesh!* You'd think some folks around here were scheduled to change into pumpkins at midnight. Anyhoo, that was Lords of October with "Autumn Fire," finishing up a "howler hour" of seasonal tunes. I'm right back with tonight's "trick or trivia" tune from Haunted Hollow's very own The Chalk Outlines. What ever happened to those kids, I wonder? Last I heard they were on the rise. And then? Nuttin'! Back with that, after these squares pick your pockets."

Hudson discreetly lowered the volume as he cast a glance in the rearview. The boys were facing away from one another, staring out their windows. Feeling Yoshida's nervous glance in his direction he tensed against the weight of sudden silence that made it all the more apparent how desolate their location was, how ruined the road was and what it was doing to the department's SUV.

"*Damn* this crap," Hudson said, loud enough for Dennis and Pedro to hear. He cranked the radio back up. "I guess this is the only way I'll get to hear you dummies doing what you're *supposed* to be doing."

When the song came on—"Freakshow Radio," a club hit that always got the creepy kids grooving—Hudson sang along in his off-key baritone and got everyone laughing. Then Dennis moved his head, and Pedro air-fingered along with his own chords.

* * * *

Before venturing into the black hole again the boys hyped each other like soldiers heading into a suicide mission, reminding one another that lives depended on them.

They descended into the abyss without hesitation and did not knock at the cracked old door this time. DeShaun tugged the old door latch, and when daunted, gave it a good shoulder bash. It gave easily.

DeShaun stumbled several steps into blackness. "Jeez! It's a cracker box, dude."

Stuart expelled a deep breath, his resolve dissipating. "I don't know, man..."

"Come in, already." DeShaun, barely visible in the dense dark, waved him forward.

Stuart felt the beginnings of panic at the prospect of stepping into such unknowable, possibly endless black space. He could not seem to make his feet cross the threshold.

DeShaun huffed his exasperation and moved to take Stuart's wrist. That was when something swept from the murk and covered the bigger boy's face.

Still immobilized, Stuart spasmed and screamed. It was a sound that a girl would make, a girl younger than Stuart, and it was like a rocket booster driving Stuart back and away from the door, which slammed like a coffin lid.

'DeShaun!?" Despair rose, shame close behind.

Finding a quick burst of courage, Stuart lunged for the latch and violently shoved at it. He bashed his shoulder into it as he had seen DeShaun do. But it did not move.

Because you are too small. Weak.

"Shut up!" Stuart told his head, as he bashed again, harder. And failed.

Stuart stepped away and away from the door until his back met the rock wall behind him. "DeShaun!"

All he could hear was the lingering echo of the door slamming—and his own squeal of helpless, childish terror.

Stuart tried the door again and again, squinting his inner eye against the sight of the inhuman appendage—rough and brown—that had emerged from the darkness to cover DeShaun's face.

As small and helpless as he felt, he knew there was no time to shrink into his doubt. His friend was in danger.

* * * *

With Aura pressing a bone-handled butterfly knife against her neck, Jill kept up a constant litany of insults and threats at her captors as they led Candace and her out to the collection of Matilda's belongings piled in the front yard.

Candace cooperated fully. She offered no expression, and only one cryptic sentence. "We should all leave here, before Everett comes."

Nico, now bare-chested to prevent the soon-to-be resurrected Ruth from destroying his vest in nymphomaniacal zeal, greeted the captives with a self-assured tilt of his chin and a puff of cigarette smoke, inspecting them like livestock.

"Light it up, Pips." In minutes the bonfire was well underway, flames eagerly overtaking the furniture, books and knickknacks for which the Fireheads held no regard.

Aura and Pipsqueak roughly shoved Jill against one of a pair of tall planks driven into the ground a few yards from the fire. Pip held her arms behind the board while Aura tied a length of rope around her wrists and waist.

Nico went to Candace, removing his sunglasses for once, to speak to her. "Don't worry little one. You'll bleed to death before you burn," he said. "I ain't *that* cruel."

"When you're dying," Candace began, as if she didn't even hear him, "please remember it's not his fault, what he is."

The bikers all laughed, Nico throwing his head back to cast his humor at the sky, as if defying God, or karma.

"You, though," Nico aimed his cigarette at Jill. "Hell, you're philanthropist of the year! You get to feed us *and* clothe my Ruthie. How's that strike your fancy?"

"Tell your ol' lady congrats," snarled Jill. "This is her only chance at ever being anything more than a psycho skank."

Nico took a quick step toward her, losing only the smallest measure of his icy composure. "I'll mention it, while she's riding me like a rodeo champ," he sneered, "gandering at me with your eyes."

As he ambled away, Jill smiled at Candace to offer some comfort, some love. The little girl bore a serene expression, eyes closed.

"Crack that book," Nico told Pipsqueak. "Let's check our math real quick."

Aura sidled up to Jill and taunted her with the butterfly knife, whipping it open and closed near her face. "I'll make you scream like your boyfriend never could, when I start cutting."

"Oh, you don't know my boyfriend, bitch."

"Please don't hurt my friend," Candace murmured.

Aura peered at the little girl and saw that she was finally streaming tears.

"Hey!" Pipsqueak called, his finger on a passage in Matilda's grimoire. "Maybe we oughta use that little pig sticker the silly bitch tried to gank Jiggy with. It has some kinda ritual relevance."

"Where is it?" Nico asked.

"Still in her, I reckon," said Jiggy.

"Let's go." Nick tossed his cigarette in the fire and headed toward the barn.

Pipsqueak concentrated on the grimoire, referring to the pocket Latin dictionary he had stolen from the library.

Her cocky expression waning, Aura examined the farm, the fire, Candace, and then Pipsqueak. She strode over to Jill and smirked. The petite punker responded by spitting at her. "Oh, you little *bitch,*" growled the Amazonian marauder. "Maybe you should hear what I'm gonna do with your guts."

She strode toward Jill, dodging a flailing kick as she reached to clutch Jill's chin and push her head back against the post. "Listen good!" Then she leaned in, nose to nose with Jill. "The little girl's really messed up, ain't she?"

Jill didn't understand until Aura drew her face back a few inches. There was genuine concern on her face.

"She's been through more hell than either of us," Jill answered through clenched teeth.

"She don't deserve to die like this."

Jill didn't respond. She was far from trusting the towering wolf bitch.

Chapter 24

Hour of the Wolf

There sure is a shortage of so-called capable effing adults around right about now, Stuart thought as he pumped the pedals of his bike, scrolling down an internal list of grown-ups he knew and trusted. It was short.

Panic, helplessness, sadness—Stuart had plenty of experience with these. But not at *this* level. He could almost adjust to seeing his brother slowly self-destruct. He had no precedent for the sudden terrifying loss of his friend.

"Is every town this freakin' scary?" he heard himself ask, as wind stroked his sweaty face.

His thoughts kept returning to Bernard Riesling, who was struggling with some sudden separation anxiety of his own.

Stuart cut through Bill Gault's yard, prepared for the old man's squeaky back door to open just before an earful of profanities. But they never came. It seemed strange that no one sensed the horrors so very near to them all.

He came to the Riesling house and jumped off his bike, alternately jabbing the doorbell and hammering the door itself until Bernard appeared.

"Stuart? Is everything all right?"

"We gotta talk, Mr. Riesling." Stuart was already pointing toward the church. "DeShaun. Your wife..."

"Stella?" Bernard's face grew hopeful, then frightened. He took Stuart by the shoulder and pulled him inside. "What's going on?"

"Something bad!" Stuart said. "The church. DeShaun got *grabbed*!"

"Grabbed by who?"

"I don't *know* man!" Stuart gulped and pointed toward the church again. "We went up there to show her the stuff!" Stuart gulped air to finish. "Listen. We gotta get back there. Save 'em both before it's too late."

"Okay!" Bernard shuffled quickly to the key rack at the door.

"Quick thing," Stuart said. "You know those mushrooms?"

"Yeah?"

"Any ideas on how to fight, um…mushroom *monsters*?"

Bernard slowly lowered the keys into his pockets, maintaining eye contact with Stuart, perhaps awaiting the punchline of one truly epic Halloween prank.

"I promise I'm not goofing around here!" Stuart said. "…Sir!"

Bernard contemplated his wedding ring. "We'll need a few things." He breezed out of the room and returned a minute later stuffing a flashlight into a backpack.

* * * *

Nico tossed the padlock and key from the barn doors off into the weeds. "Hope you ain't too rank yet, ol' biddy!" he called, as he swung the door open.

Jiggy sniffed. "Can't tell, with all the other weird-ass smells in here."

The lights did not come on when Nico elbowed the switch. He and Jiggy both sparked their lighters. Matilda's corpse was not where they had tossed it near the doorway. Bloody spots led several yards into the barn, then stopped.

"She had some gas left in the tank, I guess," noted Jiggy.

Nico smirked. "Check right, I'll take left."

Jiggy raised his lighter as he sidled between a pair of tall steel shelving units filled with jars, pots and boxes. Some of the clear jars reflected his flame in strange ways, as if their contents were phosphorescent. Jiggy picked one up to find dozens of tiny eyes leering out at him. He laughed as he put the jar back. He took two steps and tripped over something.

* * * *

Twilight lingered, yet the canopy of tall trees left the road in full dark.

Piles of leaves filled and obscured the road's ruts and dips. The jarring irregularities of the terrain multiplied the hunting party's stress with every inch.

Bravo remained intent, standing rigid and disciplined between the front seats, his nose and gaze adjusting slightly to the right or left as his senses honed in on Candace. No one in the party harbored any doubts that the dog knew exactly where to go. His focus was unlike anything they had ever seen.

Then he pricked up his ears and growled. Not just a deep warning growl, but an *alarm*. Hudson slowed and unsnapped the holster of his .44.

"Whatcha got, boy?" Pedro whispered, taking up the sawed-off double-barrel he had promised Hudson he would hand over, once the girls were safe.

Dennis slid on his brass knuckles. Engraved with the inscription "PEACE THROUGH PUNK," they were a gift from a fan.

Yoshida switched on the mounted spotlight and shone it forward as Bravo started barking—not at the road—at the upper edge of the windscreen.

"Son of a—" Pedro jammed the shotgun's twin barrels against the roof just before a jolting impact crumpled it down several inches.

Bravo's robust bark was loud, but the screeching, unearthly roar of a much larger canine drowned him out, jangling nerves and reducing seasoned battle reflexes by half.

"Hold on!" Hudson gunned the engine and jerked the wheel to the side. He hoped to use the rutted road to dismount the attacker.

A massive paw, inch-and-a-half talons curving from the fingers, smacked the windshield. Spiderweb cracks spread where the claw tips hooked. The beast on the roof was bracing itself.

"Dammit!" Yoshida raised his personal ten-gauge, which he had often boasted was better than anything in the department's armory.

Hudson whipped the wheel back and forth, braking hard as he crested a hump.

There was a quick sound of metal shearing and surprised shouts from Dennis and Pedro.

Hudson checked the mirror and saw five black claws gouge through the roof. Pedro placed the shotgun barrel in the middle of the claws.

"Don't waste the silver!" Hudson shouted.

Dennis punched at the huge talons with his brass knuckles.

Bravo snarled and roared, dashing from window to window to get at it.

Hudson saw another bump in the road and hurtled toward it.

Just before the tires met it, Hudson caught the shine of feral eyes, ahead just a few yards and closing.

A second wolf.

"Holy hell!" Yoshida shoved the ten-gauge at Hudson. The significance was not lost.

"Everybody *out!*" Yanking up the emergency brake, Hudson opened his door and jumped out, as did Yoshida. Losing their breath to the impact, the men rolled diagonally over sharp rocks and sticks.

"Take the twelve o'clock!" Hudson shouted to Yoshida, pointing to the forward position from which the transformed Hobie was approaching with terrifying speed.

Dennis and Pedro jumped out of the Jeep and spun. "Holy hambones," murmured Dennis, seeing the giant unearthly predator—Rhino—in its fullness for the first time. It set itself to attack but Bravo had something else in mind. Snarling, he made a cat-like scramble onto the open door and then to the roof, attacking without hesitation.

Hudson had a bead drawn, but stopped short, worried he'd hit Bravo. The skinwalker arced its terrible hooks, but Bravo ducked, then sprang for its hairy throat.

Yoshida fired at the incoming second wolf and missed, throwing up leaves and dirt inches from its quick dashing feet. It veered toward Yoshi and pounced, as the deputy pumped his next shell.

The wolf grasped Bravo in its massive claws and chomped into his neck with bear trap power. But instantly, the monster released the unharmed mastiff with a shrieking yelp and pawed at its snout.

The chain of Jerome Barcroft's silver St. Christopher medallion, wrapped around Bravo's collar by Stuart just an hour earlier, burned right through the protective magick of the skinwalker spell, raising smoke from the wolf's maw.

Bravo charged the distracted lycanthrope, knocking it off the roof to crash at Dennis's feet. Pedro rushed to reach them.

The Hobie wolf snarled as it slammed against the passenger door, pinning Yoshida between it and the doorway. His weapon was out of position; useless.

Yoshi could only watch as the first monster hit Bravo with a backhand swipe, sending the dog sailing through the air. Bravo yelped as he smashed ribs-first into a tree.

Dennis stamped four quick rabbit punches onto the Rhino wolf's skull as it tried to stand.

It issued a strange whine and fell again. Dennis raised the knucks. "*Silver plated,* you stinking mongrel."

Pedro aimed his double barrel, but the Rhino wolf, recovering quickly, rolled past the big Mexican. Hobie wolf lunged, knocking Pedro's shotgun flying. The bassist stopped the snarling toothy snout in both hands less than an inch from his face.

Dennis switched the knucks to his left hand as he drew the hunting knife. He hurled it at Rhino, then spun to land a flying punch to Hobie's lupine skull before the wolf man could bite Yoshida's face off.

Rhino was distracted long enough for Pedro to toss him off to the side. As he searched for his double barrel, the monster slapped the knife out of its haunch and lunged again. Its teeth sank into Pedro's calf like a bear trap.

A resounding *boom* rose above Pedro's shriek of agony. The wolf man's ribcage exploded from both sides.

Hudson.

Just a few feet away Dennis raised his arm against the dark wolf's slashes. The swipes tore through his thick leather jacket and thermal shirt, shredding forearm meat like strawberry jelly.

Free of the monster's crushing force, Yoshida stepped out from the passenger door and aimed his shotgun.

The dark wolf lashed out and knocked the weapon away—but not before Yoshida pulled the trigger.

Flesh, fur and red mist erupted from the side of the monster's face as the silver fragments tore through.

The Hobie wolf howled in pain as it flew backwards, landing with an impact that would pulverize any man's bones. The thing popped up and dashed into the woods, beholding its dead partner one last time.

Hudson pumped another shell home and did a quick visual, as the gunshot echoes faded, leaving only the ragged breathing of drained men.

Dennis fell to his butt, then eased himself to his back. He squeezed his bleeding arm, rolled to all fours and vomited like a bursting dam.

Pedro tried to stand but collapsed. "My leg is *wrecked.*" He was just close enough to kick the dead tawny wolf with his good leg. "Rot in hell, ass-wolf."

Bravo rose with a groggy groan.

Dennis laughed with relief. "Bravo. You're the man."

"I'll be damned," Hudson said. "We survived."

"*This* round," said Dennis.

"Should we go after the other one?" asked Yoshida.

"Hell no. It'll come to us, don't you worry."

Yoshida fetched the medical kit. He and Hudson tended to the boys and the dog, as all kept constant watch.

Five minutes later, they were moving again, vehicle and occupants all groaning at their injuries.

* * * *

As he drove to Saint Saturn's, Bernard's hands shook so badly Stuart almost offered to take the wheel, though he'd only had a little driving experience under Dennis's tutelage.

He caught Bernard up on the details: he and DeShaun had found a subterranean level under the church and then something like a mushroom man had abducted DeShaun. Then; what he *believed* to have happened—that McGlazer had *changed* somehow, for the worse, and taken Stella.

Bernard might not have entirely believed there was a fungus creature, but there could be no doubt something seriously strange was afoot.

At the church gates, what should have been a comedy of errors transpired when Bernard climbed the fence. He might have broken his fool neck if not for Stuart helping ease him to the ground, watching out for his gut and crotch as he struggled over like a fat fish trying to flop its way out of a bucket.

Even getting him to a stand became a feat of planning and discussion like the most bloated of military projects. But they succeeded, and then Bernard sat on a tombstone for a minute, blowing out heavy breaths like some sedentary ringsider pulled from the audience to replace a no-show at a boxing card.

"You gonna make it, Mr. Riesling?"

Bernard put a hand on Stuart's shoulder. "I took her for granted," he reiterated, as if on his deathbed. "I didn't take good care of her!"

Stuart had a brief image of being married to Candace, yet still living with Ma, and still watching out for his goddamn drunk-ass brother.

Bernard was ready to tear up again, so Stuart gently tugged his arm and got him standing. "We need to get moving Mr. Riesling."

They made it up the hill, Stuart's patience with Bernard's slow progress drawn taut.

Bernard's expression went from discomfort to dread when Stuart showed him the recessed stone stairway.

"We need to get in there and find out what's going on before Reverend McGlazer comes back," Stuart stressed.

Bernard drew two sturdy flashlights from his backpack. Stuart took one and started down the stone stairs for the second time.

The sun was down. Their descent was into a blackness that could have been an ancient tar pit.

Wheezing, Bernard pointed his flashlight on the old door's rust-covered latch. "Should I call out to her?"

"I'd vote no," said Stuart, electing not to mention the knocking from before.

Bernard took a camping canteen from his backpack and offered it to Stuart before taking a deep gulp himself. He reached for the door latch, finding that it operated like new.

Chapter 25

A Blade in the Dark

Jiggy wasn't generally fazed by corpses. He'd seen plenty. But this one, in its...*condition,* robbed him of composure.

The witch's cadaver lay on the floor in only her underwear. Face up—in a manner of speaking.

The front of her head was gone—*sawed* off, by the messy looks of it. Someone had made themselves an honest-to-God death mask. "God... *daaaaamn,*" Jiggy muttered, drawing his .38.

Footsteps; someone was approaching—and it wasn't Nico.

Jiggy spun with the weapon in time to catch a glimpse; a corner of the figure's flowing clothes whisking around the corner of the shelving behind him.

It had been decades since Jiggy had felt true, pure terror; the kind that left him immobilized and fighting to draw a breath through clenched throat. But here he was, trembling in his size-thirteens, certain he was in the presence of Death itself.

Did he really want to push his luck?

"Pussy-ass!" he grumbled, slapping himself. He extended the .38 and stepped to the corner, where Everett met him with his new toy—a set of hedge clippers.

"*Peek-a...*" came Everett's ragged whisper from behind the flesh and bone of Matilda's face, as he stabbed. "*...Boo!*" as he closed the blades together on Jiggy's guts.

* * * *

Bernard and Stuart cast their beams in. They had to focus their sight beyond the heavy dust languishing in the air to see the puzzle of flat stone blocks that made the floor. Faint footprints, too many, all haphazard, darkened the dusty surface of these stones. "There's been a lot of activity in here lately."

Stuart focused his beam on the blackened lantern sconce near the door, the wraith-like fragments of thick webbing hanging from it, recently torn away. Once more, he chose to stay quiet about it.

The floor was about fifteen-by-fifteen, empty except for clusters of mushrooms, some as big as a foot across. Stuart took a quick step back.

The traveling light beams made the fungus's shadows appear to grow and shrink, lean and sway. "Could the mushroom being you saw be a trick of light?" Bernard asked, waving his beam around to experiment with the effect.

"DeShaun and I didn't have any light, sir."

Stuart inspected the patches of white-specked brown fungi while Bernard moved his beam around the chamber. The beam jumped in time with his cry of fright. There was a black figure standing at the far wall. He and Stuart braced each other, then realized it was a vaguely man-shaped water stain seeping from cracks between stones.

"Crap on a *Chrysler!*" Bernard exclaimed. "I am *not* cut out for this!"

"Mister," Stuart said. "You are in the wrong tow—"

The water stain spread bat wings as it opened sinister solid-white eyes. They screamed and mashed together again as they backed against the door. The shape became a mere water stain again.

"Did...?"

"Yeah." Stuart kept the beam trained on the stain, trying to ignore how shaky his hands made it. "Tr...Trick of the light." He examined it. "But it's *not* what grabbed DeShaun, Mr. Riesling. I swear!"

"Okay!" answered Bernard in a high pitch. "Maybe we should call for them now."

"Wait." Stuart's beam came to an arched door about six feet high, located in the center of the wall to their right. They went to it, walking four or so steps.

"...What the *Sam Hill?*" Bernard said.

They glanced up and *up*. The doorway and ceiling had expanded.

The arching entrance now loomed high and wide before them; at least twelve feet at the top. They peered behind them, toward the door, the ceiling, the water stain. All were as they should be. It made no sense, spatially or otherwise.

They whipped their lights back to the archway again and found it as they had first seen it; around six-and-a-half feet high.

* * * *

"Does this mean Petey and I are gonna turn into goddamn German Shepherds now?" Dennis asked, cradling his bandaged arm.

"You *better* not," Hudson answered. "I doubt either of you is housebroken as *is.*"

Pedro's heavily-bandaged leg lay elevated and straightened between the front seats.

Bravo was as determined as ever, if not as physically insistent. Yoshida had felt around the canine's thick torso and found no broken ribs, but they *had* to be bruised. The dog didn't hold his tail up anymore, but he still gazed ahead in the road, perking his ears at even the slightest sound.

"Definitely something going on up ahead," said Yoshida, peering through the forest ahead at some dim light. "Maybe a mile."

Hudson gunned it, battering the vehicle's undercarriage on the rutted road. No sense in playing pussy-foot now.

* * * *

"Did you say something, Jig?" At the opposite end of the barn, Nico listened, holding the lighter high.

Jiggy didn't answer but there was no cause for worry. He was the most vigilant and observant of the Fireheads.

Nico returned his attention to the chipped old wardrobe he had just discovered, set against the wall. He lifted the padlock that secured the double latch. It was identical to the one from the entrance, though less weathered. "I need that key," he muttered.

"Naaah." He kicked the latches, once, twice, shattering the whole works with the third. Nico opened the wardrobe, startled to find several more animal skins inside, hanging like winter clothes. Bear, coyote, another wolf, and...*something.*

The skin was scaled, not furred, with a thick snake-like tail so long it was coiled up on itself and tied off.

"Komodo dragon!" Nico exclaimed. "That bitch was holding out on us, Jig!"

He pivoted to go find Jiggy, and found his path blocked.

His lighter flame revealed the witch, just three feet away. He had caught her sneaking up on him.

"Oh ho *ho,* shit on *me!*" Nico laughed, shaking away his startled convulsion. "Still kicking are ya, ol' girl?"

It didn't take long for the biker to realize that though the figure wore her dress, hair, even her face, this was *not* Matilda.

"Trick or treat!" The blood-spattered impostor's raspy voice was soaked to the core with madness.

Nico stood still, knowing he had a good chance of out drawing whoever this—

"Oooh!" The eyes behind the witch's sockets widened when their gaze fell upon Nico's tattooed chest, the ragdoll on the cross.

The crazy eyes narrowed, as if remembering something. But after whatever oblivion had held him for the past year, images that once struck him as terrifying were now just "Very very *bad!*"

Nico saw the demon take Matilda's ritual knife from her sweater and knew it was time to draw. He reached behind him.

Fast as he was, Everett was faster with the athame.

In a swift arc, Everett unzipped Nico from groin to gullet.

With a wheeze, Nico dropped his Luger and lighter to catch his falling innards. The lighter's flame blinked out for eternity, just before Nico's own life.

* * * *

"Holy Stromboli," Stuart murmured. "You seeing this, Mr. Riesling?"

The low ceiling of the long-hidden basement had expanded to cathedral proportions, then shrunk again in a blink.

"I'm not sure *what* I'm seeing," Bernard wheezed. His respiratory system had zero sense of rhythm.

He directed his flashlight through the archway into a stone-walled tunnel.

"It's just a few yards to the end." Bernard stepped back, clearly waiting for Stuart to go first.

Stuart gulped as he stepped into a passage with walls of smooth polished stone. Clusters of the weird fungus grew where it met the dirt floor. He took two steps, closing his eyes briefly to focus on shutting out Bernard's Darth Vader-like breathing.

At the end of the tunnel, his beam was halted in the egress by a wall of swirling dust so thick it seemed to blend with the dirt floor. He stepped in—and down, *down...*

He was falling.

He cried out, hearing the emptiness of his own voice echoing in the vast chamber.

Chapter 26

The Last Coffin

Pipsqeak tossed an antique spice cabinet onto the fire, not bothering to dump out the spices, then returned to gazing out towards the barn. "They musta found something good," he said. "Ain't like Nico to waste time."

Aura discreetly offered Jill a puff of her joint. She refused.

"I'll try to get him to let the little one go," Aura whispered. "That's the best I can do."

"And what if he refuses?"

Aura searched for an answer.

"What the hell you gals talking about over here?" Pipsqueak ambled toward them, his right thumb hooked in his pocket, from which the grip of his .25 jutted.

"Let me cut the little girl loose," Aura said.

With a surprised expression, Pipsqueak reared his shoulders back. "You goin' soft, girl?"

"We don't need to kill her."

"Her brother killed the *Chief's woman,*" Pipsqueak reminded. "Blood for blood."

"I'll take responsibility."

Pipsqueak threw his head back but didn't laugh.

"Oh!" Candace exclaimed; the first sound she had made in nearly an hour. "You guys...*you gotta run! Now!*"

Pipsqueak caught movement from the field in his peripheral vision. He took a few steps out from the fire's glare and saw a figure walking toward them with an odd gait.

Nah. One of his brothers, carrying a bag or sack in his right hand, and maybe a rag in the left. Nico or Jiggy was wearing her sweater and dress and—what, her... *hair?* Pipsqueak laughed. "Oh no, you guys *didn't!*"

"*Run!*" Candace squealed.

Aura came to Pipsqueak's side. "I don't think that's Jiggy or Nico."

"Right," Pipsqueak scoffed. "Then who...?"

"Tricks!" Everett raised his left hand. In it were the fresh masks he had made—*taken,* rather—from the bikers.

"What the—"

"Run *nooowww!*" Candace screamed.

"Shoot it," Aura whispered.

Pipsqueak shook his head, trying to comprehend. Aura reached into his pants for his handgun, snapping him out of it. "Hands off, bitch!" He took it from her and aimed. "Stop right there, creep!"

Everett dropped the sack and the faces, his grin growing wider. "Cowboys for Halloween!?" He clasped his hands together. "Yee *haaaw!*"

Everett reached into Matilda's sweater pockets and drew Nico's Luger and Jiggy's .38. He swung them around dramatically like a character from a John Woo film.

Pipsqueak got off one ineffective shot just as Everett fired. Bullets riddled Pipsqueak, knocking him down.

Blood splashed on Aura. She screamed and spun toward the house.

Pipsqueak pressed a hand against the worst of his wounds as he tried to aim his little gun.

Everett was close enough now that Pipsqueak saw the deranged gaze behind the skull-and-flesh mask. His aim went to hell.

Candace was hyperventilating. Aura forgot escape long enough to cut the little girl loose.

Everett stood astraddle Pipsqueak and emptied the guns into his chest. The mortifying death mask was Pipsqueak's last sight—made all the worse in the gunpowder flashes and spatters of blood hitting it.

Aura tried to drag Candace away. "Jill too!" insisted the child.

Aura saw that Jill was at last showing fear. Tears of terror flowed like Pipsqueak's pumping gouts of blood.

Humming, Everett dropped his empty guns and went back to get his sack. Taking the bonesaw from it, he strode back to Pipsqueak's corpse. "*Swappies!*"

"*Hurry!*" Candace shouted,

"Hmm!?" Everett popped his head up. "Canniss?"

Aura sliced through Jill's ropes, gashing her wrist in the process.

The trio dashed into the house. Hands shaking like mad, Aura and Jill worked together to get the deadbolt and chain lock connected. "Run upstairs honey!" ordered Jill.

* * * *

Stuart landed lightly on his feet.

He spun to look above—make that *behind* him, and saw Bernard, at the exit a foot away. "What? You see a spider?"

Stuart aimed his flashlight at his own feet on the new room's earthen floor, about six inches lower than the tunnel he had just exited. "Something's messing with our heads."

He aimed his beam at a cluster of mushrooms growing where the wall met the floor. He touched one with the toe of his shoe, raising a shimmery brown cloud from it.

"Don't breathe it!" Bernard shouted.

Throwing his arm across his mouth, Stuart backed further into the dark chamber, until he stumbled into something solid at hip level.

Stuart spun, training his flashlights on the object—an oblong box.

"Is that a...?" Bernard took a hesitant step into the chamber.

Stuart examined it. The thing lay atop a stone stand that resembled a scaled-down Stonehenge monument. Something like an inverted cone protruded from the top of the box.

"It's a"—given the implications, Stuart chose not to say either of the two-syllable *C* words that came to mind—"box. It's some kind of big box."

Despite Stuart's tact, Bernard rasped with despair.

It was impossible to see what the box was made of through the layers of mushrooms and black moss that covered it. Stuart's impact had raised another puff that swirled in his beam with a subtle glitter.

"Oh god, oh *god!*" Bernard crowded so close to Stuart, the latter could feel him trembling. "Is she...in it? Oh god!"

"Can't be," Stuart said. "It's way too old. Hasn't been open in..." He could not imagine.

Stuart moved the flashlight around the room, finding it to be roughly thirty-by-thirty, housing about a dozen more of the coffin-like structures aligned in three rows, all fitted with open-ended cones.

"They're stone," Bernard whispered, holding an arm across Stuart as if to keep him back. Like that was necessary.

Stuart took a step closer, resisting Bernard's trembling arm, running his light along the room's length. Symbols were painted there. "We saw these weird symbols in some of the historic stuff."

"Up there on the walls too," Bernard said. They held their beams side by side for a broader view. Through the dampness, the runes, painted in some thick dark liquid, were barely visible. Stuart decided to focus on something other than whether the paint was actually *paint*.

But he wouldn't leave here until he found his friends. Not this time.

Hand over mouth, he brought the beam back around, stopping on a casket near the far wall that was separate from the others, clean and white. "There's a newer one."

Bernard's breathing became somehow even more strident, but he said nothing.

Stuart played the beam over the entire chamber, searching for a second newer coffin.

Coming back to the lone pristine box, he swept his beam over its surface, to an inverted funnel that resembled a termite hill. "Maybe this is a breathing spout."

Bernard's wheezy puffs were still strident and urgent, but there was some sense of relief in them. "Can we open it?"

Are you crazy? cried Stuart's brain. But he knew that was what had to be done. He tucked the light under his arm and shoved at the lid to check its heft. It was considerable.

Stuart considered how the labor of removing it would tax Bernard's lungs to the limit. "We have to depend on each other to get this done."

Bernard gulped and took tentative steps toward the container, his light beam dancing before him.

"It's okay, Mr. Riesling," Stuart said, hoping his cracking voice wasn't just making things worse. "We're gonna get your wife and my friend. And we *are* getting the hell outta here."

It took a minute for Bernard's breathing to steady. He held the flashlight between his shoulder and neck, and they set to work.

Bernard began wheezing within seconds, but his engineer's mind rose to the task. He quickly settled into finding the best use of strength and leverage, making adjustments. The lid moved, little by little.

Once a pencil-thin opening appeared at the top edge, Bernard pointed his light into the crack, issuing an ecstatic laugh with a heaving breath. "It's her!"

Stuart was relieved about Stella; more worried than ever about DeShaun.

Bernard went to the foot of the casket and gripped the lid. "Push… it toward…me…"

Stuart did, relieved that he was strong enough to move it. Then he spotted something. "Wait!"

Initially, he was afraid the coffin was booby-trapped. A shining spike jutted downward from where the funnel was, just over the unconscious Stella's pale face. He pushed the light closer, getting a better view of the crystalline lance. It was just shy of touching her. "Should be okay," he said. "Just...go slow."

Stuart kept the light focused on the spike, warning the excitedly puffing Bernard whenever it came too close. After a strange aeon, they had created enough space and leverage to flip the stone lid off. It smashed on the floor with an echoing thunder.

Startled awake, Stella popped up with a croaking scream.

"It's okay, Stella!" Bernard hugged her with a loving ferocity that Stuart remembered from his own parents.

"Bernard?"

"Yes, darling! It's me!"

Stuart wished DeShaun were there to share an eyeroll at Bernard's melodramatic lingo.

While the reunion continued, he checked the inside of the coffin and found clumps of the weird mushrooms, still fresh, along with dried flower petals and—pumpkin seeds.

But there was no time for an investigation. "We need to go."

Stella, still disoriented, moved like an old lady. As they helped her out of the coffin, Stuart felt a sudden strange sense of danger. He panned the flashlight all around and then up, instantly wishing he hadn't.

Crystalline spikes burst from the stone wall and grew down from the ceiling like greedy reaching claws, angling straight for them.

Bernard made a strange squeal as he pushed Stella's head down and covered her.

* * * *

As Candace obeyed, Aura and Jill scrambled to push the remaining furniture—Matilda's old overstuffed chair and a flimsy dining tray table—against the door.

They stood side by side, backs to the door as a minute passed.

Two.

"Why is he not trying to get in?" Aura whispered.

"He is," Jill answered. "You can count on that. And he won't stop till he does."

They went to the window and squeezed their heads together to peek out as Jill eased the curtains apart. The roaring fire's glare ruined visibility past its outer radius of about six feet.

"He went to the back!" Aura whispered.

Jill clapped her hand over Aura's mouth as she saw Everett walk out from the far side of the fire, wearing his new mask.

A mess of twisted bloody flesh, peeling off a cracked skull front, was bound around Everett's head with twine—Pipsqueak's muttonchops were unmistakable.

Everett took a flaming chair leg from the fire and examined the house.

"*Oh my god!*" Jill whispered. "He's gonna burn us out!"

Aura pulled her away from the window and stared intently at her.

"*What?*" asked Jill.

"I can give us a chance."

"How?"

Aura peered back toward the window. "If I can get to one of those skins out there, I can change."

Jill pulled her arm away. "I'm not so sure I bel—"

"We've already *done* it!" Aura insisted. "And *that* is a dead psycho! Do you believe in *that?*"

Jill had no answer.

"If I can get a skin, I'll do the spell and kill him."

Jill wanted to say "Good luck with that" but held her tongue. "Guess I'll have to distract him."

"I can't do both, girlfriend."

"I'm not your girlfriend." Jill took a deep breath. "I can make him chase me I guess."

"What about the little girl? Would he go after his own sister?"

"I'm not gonna put her—"

"We better come up with *something,* goddammit!"

Jill squeezed her eyes shut, dreading to say "I'll run out."

"Get to that barn. Maybe you can hide or hold him off till I finish the spell."

"Doubtful." Jill went to the door. "You just get Candace to Deputy Hudson Lott." She unlocked the deadbolt. "No matter what."

* * * *

Aura nodded. Jill opened the door and dashed out. *"Everett!"*

The madman was closer than she expected, extending the torch toward the dry splintery porch rails. Seeing him so close, Jill was startled. She stumbled down the steps but caught herself with her hands.

Everett dropped the torch—onto the porch's warped floorboards. "The chasing game!"

His takeoff speed was insanely fast. "Catch and cut!"

Before she could go after a skin Aura had to stop and stamp out the fire; a single precious second.

Candace, watching from the room where she and Jill had been held, saw her friend running from her brother. *"No!"*

Aura gathered up the book, the jar of salve and a wolf skin, then bolted back to the house, too afraid to watch and see if Jill would make it to the barn.

She wouldn't. Everett drew the athame from the sweater pocket and sailed it toward Jill in a single, underhand motion.

Jill felt the cold stinging steel invade her lower back, just to the left of her spine. She fell face-forward in the wet grass.

Everett's high-pitched giggle scraped across Jill's brain like a knife on a blackboard, jolting her from her grogginess.

She took a split second to choose between trying to get into the barn or delaying Everett and chose the latter. She pulled the athame from her back and rolled over, hoping Everett would lunge onto her and the knife point.

He didn't. He stopped some eight feet away. Backlit by the dying fire, his form was a twisted parody of a human being. Pipsqueak's muttonchops dripped blood. Matilda's hair trailed in black streams from the scalp crookedly adhered with blood onto the head of the boy-monster. She couldn't see the grin, but her mind's eye knew it was there.

She pointed the knife at him like a warning, though she knew warnings meant nothing to him.

He took several stalking steps toward her—then halted upon hearing the high, stirring note of a wolf's howl.

* * * *

Aura's voice took on a new timbre as she repeated the skinwalk incantation. It was a deep guttural *hungry* sound. The wolfskin shrunk, fitting itself against her. The dead fur rippled with new life and luster. Her eyes, reflecting wild and yellow firelight, fell on Candace. "Go *now.*"

At this crucial stage of transformation, Aura had to focus on the ancient words; on giving herself over to primal ferocity.

Candace ran to the door and burst outside to hit the ground running. "*Everett!*"

An eerie and unnatural howl spread across the night.

Chapter 27

Hellhounds

Stuart hunkered low and yelled, "Not real! Not *real!*" With an angry cry, he swatted overhand at the nearest one.

The stalactite dissolved to nothing, followed by the others.

"Move!" Stuart ordered, placing Stella's arm over his shoulders.

They went as fast as they could through the aisle between coffins. In the lead, Stuart lurched to halt when he heard the coffin lids *shifting.*

Disturbed dust puffed out and swirled in their beam.

"Is that real?" Bernard cried.

"Just *come on!"*

Stuart blasted past the rumbling coffins, summoning lyrics to "13 Unseen," the song he had written with his brother, to drown out the sound of stone scraping on stone. Imagining the feel of scrabbling fingers brushing his hips, he ran faster.

He braked hard when he saw the archway. It had *shrunk.*

The exit was barely large enough for his frame—certainly too tight for Bernard or Stella. Stuart made a quick check to see if he had somehow gone the wrong way. The tiny port was the only way out.

His flashlight revealed an uncertain terror on the face of the couple behind, counting on him to vanquish it.

"What do you guys see?" he asked them.

"It must be the wrong door!" Bernard said, repeating the futile exercise of panning along the wall.

"We…can't fit…" Stella lamented with groggy despair.

Stuart heard stone shifting, saw shadows rising and writhing behind them.

He focused hard on the archway, fighting like mad to dispel what had to be an illusion. A touch of the cold stone was no less convincing than his murky vision.

"Oh god!" panted Bernard. "We're gonna die!"

With the sound of sliding stone and moist, malicious movement growing in the dark behind them, Stuart knew there was no time to waffle.

* * * *

"Getting close, boys."

The tree cover above the pitted road thinned, a sign they were approaching the fields and yard around Matilda's property.

Tensions rose like steam.

"You're grounded, Petey," said Hudson. "You sit right there till this is finished."

"Huh!? You guys *need* me, dammit!"

"We need to make the most efficient *use* of you. Sit right there and snipe."

Yoshida was already handing him the scoped rifle. "Give that hog leg to Dennis."

Dennis accepted the double barrel without argument.

"Son, don't you dare pick tonight to put that to your head," Hudson gruffed.

"Who's got time?" Dennis said, loading the chambers with Yoshida's special shells.

Bravo went crazy, barking and scratching glass.

* * * *

Despite the darkness, Yoshida's trained eye caught peripheral movement. "Watch *out!*"

With a resounding crack, a foot-thick locust trunk fell toward them. It smashed into the vehicle at an angle, further crumpling the roof. The windshield gave way entirely, a sudden waterfall.

"Everybody okay!?" Hudson asked, trying to twist his body around in the shrunken cab.

"Still alive!" Dennis and Pedro were hunkered low in their seat, hands pressed against the sunken roof by reflex, as if they could keep it from sinking farther.

Yoshida fought with his mangled door. "We're *trapped.*" Bravo clambered over him, furiously searching for a way out.

The dark wolf, Hobie, thrust its huge bloody snout in through Dennis's window and snapped at the shocked singer's face. Dishearteningly, it was already half-healed.

Hudson grabbed Bravo's collar before the dog could counterattack.

Yanked away by Pedro, Dennis had room for a short uppercut with the brass knucks. Hobie withdrew with a piercing yelp,

"This thing is *useless!*" Pedro said, regarding the scoped rifle.

Bravo barked and growled furiously.

"Dammit!" Hudson battered the door with his shoulder. "Cover me, if I ever get out—"

Hobie's black claw arced in from above, slashing across Hudson's forehead.

"The roof again!" shouted Pedro, fruitlessly trying to angle the rifle pointed up.

"Where's that goddamn double barrel!" Yoshida shouted, pressing his hand to the dazed Hudson's head wound.

The shotgun had fallen to the floorboard during the crash. "I'm working on it!" Dennis contorted like an octopus trying to reach it.

Hudson recovered his senses and pushed Yoshida's hand away. "Get that chaser, Pedro!"

Pedro wrangled the gun toward the window, cursing.

"One hog leg coming up!" Dennis called. Now he just had to get back in position.

The beast on the roof roared as it tore four long rows across it. The wolf peered through with one huge feral eye—the one it still had.

Yoshida aimed his service revolver at the roof. "Duck *lower,* Pedro!"

Pedro frantically worked to position the cumbersome rifle through his window. "Just *shoot,* man!"

"Nevermind!" Dennis shouted. He had just enough room to thrust the double barrel up through the claw canals. Before he could fire, the beast snatched the barrel to wrest it away.

Pedro sucked in a huge breath and placed his palms on the roof, rising up in his seat to put his massive traps against the depression as well. With a powerlifter's shouting grunt, he exerted, pushed, straightened himself.

The weight of roof, tree and werewolf rose like a swimming pool float.

Dennis, thinking quickly, kicked at his door. Without the weight of the tree, it gave way easily. Bravo dashed out, ignoring the monster above, bolting toward the clearing ahead.

Dennis rolled out and aimed the sawed-off toward the roof.

The beast slapped the gun just as Dennis fired. Silver fragments tore through the back tire.

Trying to crawl out, Pedro could not defend against the wolf's arcing kick that left him dazed.

Yoshida fired his handgun over his seat, putting two bullets in Hobie's neck; a mere annoyance. But it bought Hudson time to aim the shotgun.

The wolf rolled past Dennis and hoisted him up as shield.

The chief deputy stopped himself from pulling the trigger by a microsecond. *"Damn!"*

Held aloft, Dennis rained down a series of rights onto the beast's raw eye socket with the brass knuckles. The cracking of Hobie's skull and the sight of blood spurting from his eye were as satisfying as a gulp of Diamante's.

Hobie's rage only grew with the assault. He dropped Dennis to his feet and clamped his head in his huge hairy hands, sinking his talons into the punker's skull, crushing.

Through blurring vision, Dennis saw the double barrel driven like a wedge into Hobie's toothy maw. The bestial biker's head exploded in a spray of blood, bone, brains, and Leticia Lott's finest heirloom Sunday silver, courtesy of Pedro.

Propelled to the ground, Dennis was knocked breathless for the second time.

* * * *

Everett stopped laughing and chasing to listen for the eerie howl, cocking his head like a curious bulldog. It sounded again. Everett answered, throwing his arms and head back to bellow the "O" sound with all his might.

Jill had a chance, slim as a knife's edge, of getting away. Better still, she had no doubt that the howl meant Aura had made the change.

She hoped to spy something useful in the open barn, but had to fight not to puke.

Jiggy, cut mostly in half. The handles of a set of hedge clippers stood up from a mess of bloody intestines that lay strewn about like New Years' Eve party streamers.

Jill jerked her head away from the sickening sight, and saw Everett staring toward the house, awaiting an answer to his howl. His attention span was short. Especially when there was killing to do.

Jill eased herself to a stand, fighting like hell not to cry out at the pain of her wound. Could she sneak up and stab him? Hell no. The barn was her best choice.

Soon he would remember her. With luck, she could keep him busy until Aura...*changes into a goddamned werewolf—am I really counting on that?* she thought.

She rose, eyes locked on Everett. She *willed* him to stay distracted.

He remembered her, just as she made it into the barn. His laughter shish-kebabed her spine.

She swung the barn doors shut and hit the light switch. Cursing its failure, she searched for something to use as a blockade.

The stench of Jiggy's innards punched her in the nose. But she held her breath and dragged his lower half to the door; grateful that the darkness at least spared her from the sight of still-attached guts unraveling and stretching, fluids sloshing out onto her boots.

She scuttled toward of the barn's far corner, hoping to find a place to hide or a decent weapon amid the dark clutter.

The bulky silhouette of an antique wardrobe stood against the wall just a few feet away. She felt her way along the shelving to get to it.

Everett opened the barn doors with a triumphant cackle, only briefly distracted by Jiggy's legs in his path.

Jill lunged to get to the wardrobe, stunned when she stepped deep into a slippery, goopy mess. Nico's legs and arms. She was standing in the middle of him.

Her gorge sped to rise yet again. Only the prospect of Everett catching her or Candace gave her the willpower to keep it down.

Shutting her eyes tight as a bank vault, she made herself pat down the gang leader's blood-soaked corpse for a weapon; maybe a gun in his boot.

She heard Everett's uneven shuffle, surely no less than—

The Trick or Treat Terror snatched her by the hair and forced her nose-to-nose with his—or rather, *Pipsqueak's*—face.

The smarmy biker's countenance bore a slack sadness that belied the screeching laughter emerging from behind it. Scents of blood and pumpkin washed over her.

"Pretty!" He raised the athame and poked her face with it. "For Canniss!"

Beyond her fear of dying at this twisted devil's hands, Jill thought of poor Candace being forced to wear the flesh and bone from one of her only true friends. She reached out to the shelf at her side and found a jar, even as the reborn killer hurried toward the door, dragging her head forward with too much momentum for her to gain any footing.

Chapter 28

Attack of the Mushroom People

McGlazer might as well have been shaken from his stupor and slapped.

On the foggy screen of his office wall consciousness played the image of Stella Riesling—his assistant, confidant, friend.

She, along with the Lott and Barcroft boys and her husband Bernard, were down here in the subterranean sub-level of the church that his possessor had re-opened using McGlazer's body.

But he already knew that.

"Leave them alone!" his mind bellowed.

Then he was underneath Ragdoll Ruth again. With righteous rage, she pummeled him with the shiny pistol. He saw only stars, heard only shrill, jagged shards of madness and hatred between.

Stuart dropped his light just past the narrow threshold of the shrunken archway and thrust his head in. The opening shrunk fast and clamped on his head.

Terror filled him; a need to be free so intense it robbed him of breath.

Mockingly, the tunnel ahead yawned wide and high, like a castle keep.

His cries of suffocation and despair had triggered the same in Bernard, and in the still-recovering Stella. He could hear them.

He was certain his head would be slowly crushed. He just hoped he would black out before the pain.

Then, muffled by either stone or mere perception, Bernard shouted, "Stuart, you know it's not real!" He felt the engineer shoving at his butt. "Just keep *going!*"

With a roar, Stuart crawled, exerting all his strength. He was propelled forward like a torpedo.

He grabbed the flashlight and spun around to see its beam dance across the terrified faces of the two grown-ups, framed within the comfortably wide archway. "Come on, losers!"

Bernard pulled Stella behind him.

Once they were all past the mercurial archway, Stuart got moving again, his beam and gaze fixed on the doorway at the other end. "Don't pull anything crazy!" he commanded it.

He stopped to help Bernard and Stella get through, then checked behind him to the coffin chamber entrance. It was sealed; solid obsidian.

Stuart wondered if he had left DeShaun behind in that dank deadly room, stuffed in one of those coffins.

Bernard grabbed his shoulder and pulled him through, into the first room. "Real or not, we need to get out of here!"

Stuart, scared and exhausted, said "I can't."

"*What?*"

"I can't leave DeShaun." He willed tears back into their ducts. "You guys go."

"I don't think we can," Stella whispered.

Limned by weak moonlight, a man's silhouette filled the open doorway of the outside stairway.

Their flashlight beams revealed McGlazer.

"The veil is thinning," said a strange man through McGlazer's mouth. He held the oil lamp from the door-side sconce. "We are coming through."

The room seemed far different in the glow, but no less oppressive. He went to place the lamp back on the sconce, revealing a figure behind him.

"DeShaun!" cried Stuart, stopped from going to him by Bernard.

The other boy seemed like death warmed over, his unfocused eyes glazed nearly solid white, his posture slack.

"Another guardian." McGlazer guided DeShaun to his side. "For our children," he told Stella.

"No..." She was back to her senses.

"What are you—?" Bernard quieted when Stella put her hand on his arm. "Abe is not in control. He's possessed. Isn't that right, Mr. Bennington?"

* * * *

Feeling a cold rush of menace behind him, Stuart spun with the flashlight. Figures wriggled in the arched corridor. Things from the coffins, shambling toward him.

He cried out, causing Stella to do the same. Bernard followed Stuart's light with his own.

The approaching figures were monstrous mushroom men.

White-speckled brown caps grown together and walking on two legs.

McGlazer extended a commanding hand that froze the fungus demons. "Mykespatmosia." The voice was booming, ethereal. "From the caves of the Greek island Patmos."

"Saint John..." whispered Stella.

"His doorway to revelation."

DeShaun's mouth fell slack, and several fungus caps fell out. Stuart's heart ached for his friend.

McGlazer knelt to scoop up the caps, grandly gesturing. "It has the power to awaken souls"—now he motioned to DeShaun—"to join them together"—he closed his hand over them—"and much more."

Stuart had a revelation. "You're not Wilcott Bennington."

"What?" Stella asked.

"He's possessed all right. By a real assclown named Conal O'Herlihy. *Not* Wilcott Bennington." Thinking of what O'Herlihy had said about DeShaun being a guardian, Stuart wondered whether the things had a crude sentience or were just glorified scarecrows.

"I brought the excrescence here, for my people," O'Herlihy said. "To create a new world, a new Man. To conquer first fear, and then death."

"Why do you need Abe?" Stella asked. "Or me?"

"Vessels. That my faithful followers may be reborn." He cocked his head toward the tunnel and the chamber beyond. "The two of us will spawn them." He gave her a wink. "The *three* of us, if you prefer to view it so."

Bernard found a reserve of indignation. "Now just a minute!"

O'Herlihy cast a domineering finger at him. "Hold your tongue, *cuckold.*"

Stuart, watching the mushroom men, saw that they almost emulated McGlazer's gestures, as if vaguely connected to the man.

"You'll all serve a noble purpose."

"There's no noble purpose in controlling a man when he's weak," Stella said. "Or imprisoning children."

O'Herlihy stalked toward them, pointing to the floor. "Man and boy. You will kneel."

Stuart glanced at Bernard and thought the engineer's face must have been tired from holding the same expression of extreme terror for so long.

He looked at the silhouetted DeShaun, slumped like a rejected mannequin, then back at the man before him, who was both friend and enemy. "Go to hell, you dillhole."

"*Die!*" McGlazer's hand and O'Herlihy's will waved the fungus demons forward. They marched into the room with unexpected quickness.

DeShaun shuffled toward them as well, his blank eyes seeming to glow. The frightened trio clambered to the far corner,

"Okay, *okay!*" Bernard knelt, pulling Stuart down with him.

Stella stood in front of them. "If you want them, you'll have to kill me!" she cried. "And you *need* me!"

With a gesture, the town founder halted his slaves just a few feet from the trio. Stuart saw that the nearest of them was not yet entirely covered in the ugly growth. His dark brown pants were those of the county sheriff's department. It was Deputy Shavers. And they would soon share his fate.

"On the contrary," O'Herlihy said. "You're quite replaceable, woman."

He cast mushroom caps at Bernard and Stuart. "Take. Eat this, the Flesh of The Saviour."

* * * *

Jill could not get her feet beneath her. With freakish and fearsome strength, Everett dragged her along like a ragdoll toward the house. Then his laughter stopped. He let her fall.

Jill raised her dizzy head to see Aura in full wolf form.

The transformed biker stood poised on all fours in front of the little girl, glowing amber eyes laser-focused on Everett. Wolf and child were less than twelve feet away.

Aura growled a warning. Everett only giggled more enthusiastically, overjoyed at all the fun Halloween games. He threw his head back and issued his attempt at a werewolf's howl.

"Come on, Jill!" Candace called, reminding Everett of his new mask source. He grabbed Jill's jacket as she rose to run, yanking her back toward him with a nauseating snap. She felt her breath flee with the impact, saw with dazed eyes and mind the monster Everett looming over her a hundred feet high.

Laughing like mad, he raised the athame.

Then Aura crashed into him. The jumble of fur and pale flesh fell into the high weeds and out of sight.

Jill opened her mouth wide to welcome any kind patch of air, as Aura roared and snarled and ripped—and Everett laughed and laughed, ecstatic in both destroying and being destroyed.

The Aura wolf yelped horrifically as she rose to her hind feet then fell again, rolling side to side, rhythmic gouts of blood spouting from her throat.

Witches' blades are silver, Jill realized.

Jill stood, but couldn't maintain it; she was too dazed. She dropped to one knee, stars and fireflies clouding her vision and mind.

Candace was coming toward her, but the little girl stopped to scream. A screen of blackness fell over all of this, cancelling all but the least shred of awareness.

Chapter 29

Versus

"*Pretend you are doing what he says,*" Bernard whispered. "*I just need a sec.*"

Stuart, seeing Bernard discreetly fumble with a lighter, reached for the mushrooms, dragging out the act like he was fighting to resist O'Herlihy's command.

The lighter sparked. "Move aside!" Bernard shouted.

Stuart did, dragging Stella with him. In an instant, the room lit up like a football stadium, reducing suffocating darkness to stark shadows that bent and swayed in all directions. The nearest mushroom men instantly began to smoke. Their brethren behind instinctively retreated toward the darkness of the tunnel.

Bernard held up two burning strips of magnesium—miniature suns.

With a cry of shock, O'Herlihy covered his eyes.

"*Here!*" He thrust one out to Stuart, who shielded his eyes as he accepted it.

Bernard drew another strip from his pocket and lit it from the first, then tossed it toward the mushroom men. Eerily silent in their death throes, they collapsed, shriveled and smoked. Oily ichor puddled out from them onto the dusty floor.

"Let's get out of here!" Bernard shouted as he went to McGlazer. He tossed the strip down and grabbed the possessed minister by the arm to haul him out. Stunned but not defeated, O'Herlihy slugged Bernard, sending him crashing toward the writhing mushroom men.

Stuart shoved Stella and the torpid form of DeShaun toward the exit door, but Stella resisted. "Get DeShaun up top!"

Stuart eyed her doubtfully. "What about you?"

"DeShaun needs you. My husband and my friend need me."

Stuart grabbed DeShaun's arm and yanked him through the old door, telling him, "You're gonna owe me a million ZingGo bars, butthole!"

O'Herlihy dropped his knee into Bernard's stomach, forcing out an agonized retching.

"*You* shall become a vessel then, cuckold!" O'Herlihy forced Bernard's mouth open, as he dug into one of the dying, melting mushroom men, ripping away its "flesh."

Bernard tried moving his head away, but O'Herlihy was far too strong. He clamped down on Bernard's throat, forcing him still.

"Abe," Stella said; almost a whisper.

O'Herlihy grimaced at the woman kneeling there beside him, humble and fearless.

"Still your tongue!"

She shushed him like he was a toddler. "I'm not talking to you." She raised her hand in a simple summoning gesture. "Come on out of there, Abe. You know what's real."

* * * *

Stella's voice carried something to the minister's shrunken psyche, an importance and a Truth. It was far greater than the promise of alcoholic oblivion, or the threat of endless bludgeoning.

"*Blasphemer!*" rasped O'Herlihy—louder, stronger and *much* nearer than the weakened Stella. "*Deny* her, or you will witness her damnation alongside your own!" O'Herlihy's voice was everywhere.

Stella's voice was only in his mind, just beyond his ears. "Come out, Abe."

He took a step toward the door.

O'Herlihy's furious bellow, just outside now, froze him, blasted into his skull, shook his bones. "I will *rip* you apart and sew you back together with *burning needles*—a thousand times a thousand!"

His desk lamp sparked and popped, casting quick shadow puppets of mutant ragdoll ghosts upon the door, a terrible promise of what waited beyond.

A knock vibrated the office door; three resounding thunder crashes. The office quaked, throwing McGlazer's plaques and photos to the floor, where they shattered and vanished.

"Just step on out, old friend." Stella calmly encouraged.

Cracks opened in the wall around the door frame, releasing blistering sprays of steam that drove McGlazer backwards.

"Yesss!" O'Herlihy taunted. "Come open this door, dearest *Reverend*! Why not begin your unending suffering *now!?*" From the cracks, a high-pressure burst of steam hit McGlazer square in the face. He realized it was moonshine. "You send her *away,* you little drunk failure!" commanded Ruth.

There was a nauseating gravity shift—the whole room tilted roughly forty-five degrees, the rear wall behind his desk dipping backwards. McGlazer pinwheeled his arms as he fell into the edge of his desk, slamming his lower back.

As he rolled off to all fours, his hands splashed into liquid pooling in the triangular tilt of floor and wall.

He wiped stinging moisture out of his eyes and saw that he was in bubbling moonshine—elbow-high and rising fast.

"Forty days and *forty nights!*" cackled O'Herlihy.

"You're needed out here," murmured Stella.

"DRINK your *FILL!*" screamed O'Herlihy.

McGlazer gazed toward the door at the end of the ramp that his shine-soaked floor had become. He pushed himself off the desk and lunged for the knob. The liquid stunted his progress.

"Here," Stella said. "Take my hand."

...How, dammit!?

"It's here. It always will be, Abe."

McGlazer stood on his feet, defying the pull of gravity. He spat out the bitter burning liquid in his mouth, and walked to the door, just like he was going to step out for some fresh air.

O'Herlihy had gone silent. He would not be behind the door because he *couldn't* be. He was dead and powerless.

Stella, the source of the voice, and so often the source of his day's ration of strength, was alive, and so much more.

She was an *anti*-hate—and a hyper-love. A force that would not deny healing; would, in fact, insist on it. Stella Riesling was a reality that reduced doubt and hate to mere quick-dying sparks buffeted by monsoon winds.

McGlazer opened his office door and found himself in some strange cave, pinning poor terrified Bernard with a knee on his chest. Stella was kneeling there before them. Near her side was a flame, something burning so intensely it hurt his eyes.

* * * *

Once they got up the stairs, Stuart eased DeShaun onto his back on the grass. In the quiet night he listened to DeShaun's breathing. It was shallow and ragged.

With the flashlight, he checked DeShaun's airway. Just within sight was a slimy blackness.

Pieces of mushroom. He rolled DeShaun over and got his arms around the bigger boy's upper abdomen to administer the Heimlich maneuver, as the boys had learned together in gym class. *Good thing we decided not to goof off and actually learned something that day* he thought.

He could hear the hitching sound of DeShaun's breath pushing at an obstruction. The problem was, the fungus wasn't a full blockage; air could pass *around* it just fine.

"Jeez, you weigh a *ton,* dude!" Stuart complained, as he rolled DeShaun over again to his back. He stood and wracked his brain, trying not to think about what might be happening to the Rieslings.

Right now, he had to make DeShaun puke.

The boys had a game they played: they would take turns assailing each other with descriptions of gross and gory things. A couple of times he had succeeded in making DeShaun almost lose his lunch. But alas, that required consciousness.

Still, perhaps to comfort himself, Stuart began reciting such a litany, and visualizing the boy projectile vomiting like Regan in *The Exorcist,* or...

Joan Crawford.

Not the soul-withering old bat from the only horror movie his ma had ever watched—*Whatever Happened to Baby Jane*—but Pedro's fat-ass Siamese housecat.

On the rare occasions when she broke jail, as Petey called it, she invariably found a patch of grass, ate her fill, then waited till she was caught and thoroughly chastised before unloading the green slop on the carpet, robbing Pedro of any hope he would ever again see his security deposit.

"Big, fat roaches from the cafeteria floor after last lunch," Stuart said, as he dropped to his knees and started ripping up grass, "all full of whatever that Tuesday pudding stuff is..."

He stuffed the grass in DeShaun's mouth and pushed some down his throat, where it would tickle him, and with any luck...

Stuart had gotten about four big wads of the dying lawn in when DeShaun bolted up and heaved a painful-sounding retch. Stuart smacked him on the back, harder still when the second heave failed to expel anything.

Stuart stood and battered DeShaun's back with both open hands, like he remembered seeing Gordon Liu do while training "iron palm style" in some Shaolin kung fu flick.

DeShaun awkwardly worked himself to all fours and blasted out a massive wad of vegetation, mucus, fungus and what must have been the pizza they had shared earlier that day.

Stuart continued to pound. "Veiny eyeballs, served in a room-temp soup of bull urine, lard, and French dress—"

"Dude, *okay!*" DeShaun croaked as he collapsed to his side in a coughing fit. Stuart went to the garden hose rolled up beside the lawn shed, opened the flow, and dragged it to his friend. DeShaun drank gingerly between coughs.

* * * *

A sensation of movement and pain; her hair being yanked again. Jill's vision returned, revealing the ground racing under her torso and legs. Mad laughter stabbed into her ears, joining Candace's ever hoarser scream.

"Mask for Canniss!" said Everett.

"Please, *no* Everett!" Candace wouldn't run away; wouldn't abandon her friend. "I like her!"

"No, Candace… Guh…" Jill hadn't even the strength to finish. "*Go, Can…*"

A rapid-fire, rhythmic thumping drummed the ground, and Everett's hand was ripped from her hair. A cry of surprise escaped him as he was driven back.

"*Get him,* Bravo!" Candace shouted.

Jill raised her head and saw the dog, the very very *good* dog, mauling Everett, snapping, biting, shaking, barking, growling with ferocity to equal the skinwalkers—and not particularly fazed, not yet, by the silver blade that Everett plunged into his shoulder hock.

Bravo only grew more ferocious, tearing off the face and skull Everett wore, then snapping into Everett's real face, tearing open his cheeks.

Everett stopped laughing. Instead he cried in terror and confusion. "No!" he said. "*Bad doggie!*"

He scrambled for the knife handle in Bravo's shoulder, found it, yanked it free.

"Everett, *Stop!*" Candace cried. "Get away *now,* Bravo!"

Jill was shocked back to her senses by the dog's yelping. Everett stabbed him again. Where, she could not see.

She remembered the jar she had grabbed in the barn, ran to it, picked it up. In her fatigued arms, it weighed a hundred pounds.

She stumbled toward the melee, grateful that Everett's back was to her. She raised the jar in both hands.

Everett sensed her and swiveled to thrust the knife into her for the second time, piercing her stomach.

Jill brought the jar down on the walking horror show with all she had left, falling into the attack.

The shattering sound gave way to a great whooshing shockwave. It blew Jill's hair back like a jet turbine.

Everett could no longer laugh, for he had to shriek, as the contents of the jar, some kind of powder or grain, spread down his body from top to bottom, adhering like paint from a can dropped from stage rafters.

The substance smoked and sparked like a fuse, instantly erasing all it touched.

Jill crawled backwards. She had barely enough strength to hold her face up, to watch the jar's malignant contents fulfill its purpose.

Even with his head gone, the rest of the maniac danced and spun in confusion, batting at the material with fast-vanishing hands and arms, until the substance burned its way down to his bare feet and disintegrated them as well, along with the weeds beneath him and a good layer of soil beneath that.

Then it simply winked out.

From his head to his toes, Everett Geelens had smoked away to nothing.

Something large loped off into the dark woods. Aura was nowhere to be seen.

Jill checked on Candace and found her on her knees with her hands over her face, once again crying for her brother.

Chapter 30

The Evil Within

O'Herlihy grunted with fury, closing his choking grip on Bernard's esophagus.

"It's *your* body, not his, Abe. Let Bernard up now." It sounded like simple mild admonishment; good advice.

O'Herlihy tried to stuff the mushrooms into Bernard's mouth, but could not open his—make that *McGlazer's*—fingers.

"That's right, good. Now, just let him up before you hurt him," she said this as she casually leaned to her side to pick up one of the burning magnesium ribbons. "Here, focus on this."

O'Herlihy covered his eyes with his hands, emitting a cry of helpless anguish. Bernard rolled away, sputtering and coughing.

"Abe. Put your hands down. You need to see this."

Trembling, McGlazer's hands came away from his face, revealing rapidly blinking, bleary brown eyes.

"Look!" Stella demanded.

McGlazer brought his thumb and forefingers to his eyelids and held them open.

O'Herlihy's enraged scream became McGlazer's cry of effort, louder and louder, echoing and amplified in the chamber.

As the grunt faded, so did O'Herlihy.

Reverend McGlazer collapsed onto his face. Stella stood and pulled Bernard to his feet. "Help me with Abe!"

She wrangled her two burly menfolk to the top of the stone steps, where she was relieved to see Stuart tending DeShaun, now upright and lucid. "Whatever you did for him, you need to do it again."

* * * *

"County sheriff!" called Hudson. "Anyone hurt?"

"We're okay," Jill responded. "Sort of."

Bravo broke from the embrace he shared with her and Candace to meet the rescue party, barking assurances.

Hudson appeared, aimed his .44 from left to right, and holstered it. Behind him was Yoshida, essaying a weary wave as he slumped in exhaustion.

Then Dennis, the double barrel over his shoulder, his blood-spattered face going from worry to relief as he went to the girls. "Here to save the day."

Jill wasn't sure what to do—but Candace led the way. The little girl ran to meet Dennis, hugging him hard.

Jill joined them.

* * * *

The quintet limped their way to the church sanctuary. Once the lights were on, DeShaun and McGlazer were made to lie on pews, their heads elevated on hymnals. They were given cup after cup of water to clear the spores from their systems and restore their strength. Stella prayed over them, and Bernard even bowed his head, if only to be doing something for—and *with*—his beloved wife.

It was nearly twenty minutes before either of them could reasonably speak. DeShaun smiled at his friend and clasped his hand. "Man, you pulled me right outta the deep fryer."

"Blood brothers," said Stuart.

McGlazer sat up, his hair a comical mess. "I don't know whether I want to believe I just came off a bender or did internal battle with one of our town founders."

"The latter," said Stella. "You're still a good many years sober."

"There sure was some corny stuff coming out of your mouth," Stuart said.

"Glad you're back, Reverend," Bernard said, and shook McGlazer's hand.

The reverend drank another cup of water and eased back on the pew with a groan, grateful to be back in his own world of substance and sobriety.

Bernard took both Stella's hands in his, wearing an expression so earnest it reminded the boys of Bill Paxton.

"Stella, my love," he began. "I am so, so sorry for being a bug butt."

DeShaun's mouth squinched up as he stifled a laugh. Stuart put his hand over his friend's mouth to help.

"I treated you like garbage. I got so caught up in this tainted candy mystery...I guess I thought it would make me a big famous hero. Like Thomas Rutherford or Arnold Orville Beckman."

Stella furrowed her brow.

"I've taken you for granted for too long, my bride!" Bernard continued. "I don't ever want to lose you. I can't! I want us to have a family. I want to adopt Candace."

All sat stunned.

The big room was so silent that the girl's name echoed in Stuart's head like the sweetest-sounding bell.

"Who's corny now?" McGlazer whispered.

Stella stood. "Bernard? Do you...?"

Bernard rose too. "Yes! As soon as we can!"

"You think she's okay?" Stuart asked DeShaun. "Candace?"

"Never bet against my dad, dude," DeShaun assured him. "*Or* your brother."

Epilogue

HALLOWEEN NIGHT

Gathered just inside the gates to Saint Saturn Unitarian, the survivors of Ember Hollow's latest Halloween horrors—most of them bandaged or on crutches—gazed upon Main Street, where the town residents, many in their Sunday best, stood still and solemn on the sidewalks.

Some had painted their faces in exaggerated sad or happy expressions, others in skulls or caricatures of their deceased.

Candace, with the heavily bandaged but smiling Bravo at her side, took Stella's hand on one side, Stuart's on the other.

A little hand extended down toward her. Emera, Candace's sister-to-be, perched on Stella's hip, smiling and at ease. Bernard stood behind them, one hand on Stella's shoulder, the other on the shoulder of his friend Abe McGlazer.

Dennis, having rediscovered his inner wiseguy, sat on the lap of his wheelchair-bound best friend Pedro. He and Jill weren't holding hands again, not yet, but she stood close, and glowed like a moonbeam.

DeShaun proudly and gratefully stood tall beside his father.

At the church and on the street the spectators watched the corner where Shadwell Jeweler sat, just a few buildings down from The Grand Illusion Cinemas. In past years it would have been the towering orange-and-black-striped Uncle Sam dubbed The Night Mayor they were watching for. But not this year.

A whining buzz rose, a sound they had all heard throughout the days of every summer, when Guillermo Trujillo had more business than he could handle working his trade for various clients astride his triple bladed V-Ride mower.

De-bladed for safety, the mower moved at barely a crawl. His two little skull-faced girls stood on the garlanded platform Guillermo had made for them and gave out bread loaves and flowers to the bystanders.

Behind him came a flatbed truck from which a quartet of amateur mariachi performers serenaded one and all with the mournful yet lively strains of a song older than anyone there.

Then six smiling women in colorful dresses, swirling their skirts and waving to children.

Under Guillermo's leadership, Ember Hollow's Hispanic community had come forward with a solution to the parade issue. In lieu of the usual outrageous cavalcade of cartoonish creepiness, the parade was a Dia De Los Muertos-themed celebration.

Family and friends mourned and celebrated their loved ones in funeral dress or costume. Anyone could join or exit as they pleased. Memorial placards, photos, papier mache sculptures and favored belongings of the departed were held high.

Mayor Doris Stuyvesant, holding a feathered Mardi Gras-style mask, waved and smiled, mostly with relief, from the sunroof of her limo, driven by top-hatted vampire Hollis.

It was a beautiful understated compromise between the Day of the Dead celebration of the Mexican locals and the Annual Pumpkin Parade. The Bruner folks had picked up the tab for this improvisation. The community and the parade would survive.

The paraders, followed by the crowd, strode past Stella and company, through the gates and into the cemetery to place food, flowers, cards and art on graves celebrating their one-year birthday.

As the line wound its way up the hill and dispersed to various graves, the death of October approached too, and with it, the renewal and strengthening of family bonds.

Acknowledgment

Les Dutcher, in his endless devotion to helping others, has learned a thing or two about the adoption system. He shared his experience and knowledge to give this story veracity. Likewise, his brother Randy, a lifetime law enforcement officer, was happy to answer legal questions.

My wife, Jennifer, is my Mr. Spock, only she should get top billing. Actually, my job is more like Mr. Scott, or someone who works under him, I guess.

Horror punk bands are the friendliest and most outgoing in music. I've been lucky to strike up social media friendships with several. The Karnsteins and Lords of October and great people and great bands. Their music helped set the tone for much of this story.

The people at Lyrical are the best ever. Many thanks to Michaela, James and Lauren!

Sneak Peek

Don't miss the next scarifying chiller in the
Haunted Hollow Chronicles by Patrick C. Greene

DARK HARVEST

Coming soon from Kensington Publishing Corp!

About the Author

Photo by Scott Treadway

Patrick C. Greene is a lifelong horror fan who lives in the mountains of western North Carolina. He is the author of the novels *Progeny* and *The Crimson Calling*, as well as numerous short stories featured in collections and anthologies.

Visit him at www.fearwriter.wordpress.com.

Printed in the United States
by Baker & Taylor Publisher Services